WANT A BONUS SCENE FROM TRUST ME?

Make sure you sign up for The List at the end of this book, and we'll send it to you. Not only will you get your scene, but also access to our no-spam newsletter including exclusive news and updates, sneak peaks at the latest book, and giveaways just for The List.

TRUST ME

GRAHAME CLAIRE

Editing And Proofreading:

Marion Archer, Marion Making Manuscripts

Karen Lawson and Janet Hitchcock, The Proof is in the Reading

Cover Design:

Hang Le, By Hang Le

ISBN: 978-1-951878-06-1

For those who have the urge to run.

CHAPTER ONE

BAKER

"DAMN IT, Baker. If you don't hurry up, I'm getting in that shower with you."

The warning came from the other side of the bathroom door, low and feral.

"Door's locked. And the more you distract me, the longer I'll be." I smiled to myself, leisurely rinsing the conditioner out of my hair.

"I can't be late again or I'll be fired."

"What do you need a shower for anyway? Three minutes after you get there, you'll stink like motor oil." Somebody should bottle that stuff. Or maybe it was just the combination of Holt and grease that had me in knots.

"Three . . ."

"Five more minutes. That's all I need." I bit my lip to stifle my laugh.

"*Woman.*"

Scratch that. Ten more minutes. To get myself off and bask in the aftermath.

"Grease Monkey," I called back. My face hurt from the smile splitting it in two.

Over the noise of the shower, the door knob rattled a few times.

He wasn't coming in. Holt was too much of gentleman for that. I'd blatantly strolled into the kitchen a few times in only a towel, just to see if I could rile him. Every damn time, he looked everywhere but at me and scampered like his ass was on fire.

Crack. Split. Wham.

I jumped at the sound of destruction. Through the steam of the glass shower, a shadow stalked toward me.

Holt yanked open the door, threw me over his shoulder, soap suds and all, and hauled me into the bedroom.

"You jackass. I'm soapy."

He tossed me onto the center of the bed. I bounced twice, opened my mouth, then snapped it shut at the heat in his eyes as they roved down my naked body.

"I warned you." He spun and disappeared into the bathroom, slamming the door shut behind him. It boomeranged off the broken frame and opened wide.

I stared at the space in stunned disbelief. Had he really just taken me from the shower? Anger spiked, sharp and deep, propelling me off the bed.

I stomped into the bathroom and threw open the shower door. "Oh, hell no."

I grabbed his wrist and tugged. He stumbled, caught off guard, and steadied himself on the wall behind me. Pinned between the tile and his solid body, I stopped breathing. Fury blazed at me while I tried to pretend like I hadn't just seen the most perfect ass God ever sculpted.

"I wasn't finished," I snapped once I figured out how to breathe again.

"Then you should have been more considerate." His breath was hot as he spit the words at me.

"You can't go breaking down doors and dictating how long I shower."

"I wouldn't have to if you didn't take all damn day." His shoulders rose and fell in fractured movements.

I pushed at this chest. "It's still my turn."

"The hell it is." He didn't budge, leaving his hand braced above my head.

I hadn't let go of his wrist like I was welded to him. At the realization, I released him and immediately felt the loss.

He inched his face closer to mine. My lips tingled, swelled in anticipation for him to touch me. Thunder ricocheted inside my chest.

Kiss me.

Kiss me.

Kiss me.

Horror filled me at the thought, my eyes growing wide.

Don't kiss me.

Don't kiss me.

Don't kiss me.

I panicked. He was my roommate. We'd both already crossed a line this morning. I'd been too blinded with rage to realize it until now . . . when I was breathing in his air with his body pressed against mine. *And we're both completely naked.* Shit.

"You don't seem like you're in a hurry now." I'd meant it to come out as an insult. Instead, I might as well have asked him to come back to bed with me.

Eyes locked.

Chests heaved.

Something thick and potent swirled between us, so strong it was suffocating.

My head fell back against the tile. The irritation disintegrated to a near non-existent level. What was left of me felt exhausted and weak.

He eased closer until our lips were mere millimeters apart. "Tomorrow and the next day and the day after that. Every day from here on out. I go first. You feel me, Easy?"

"Easy?" I shoved at him with all my strength, but it was useless. "How dare you say such a thing to me? You don't know if I'm easy or not." Just like that, the anger was back, exploding from my pores.

He grinned and lowered his arm to keep me caged as I tried to duck underneath. "Easy On The Eyes."

The first time he'd called me that I'd wanted to crawl in his lap and beg him to do again. Something about the way he said it made me want to purr and rub up against him, and I freaking hated cats.

"I'm going to be late for work," I huffed. I had no idea what time it was and, at this point, wasn't sure I really cared.

"Totally your fault." He planted his hands on my hips, and I jolted from the fire that shot through me.

With ease, he lifted me and set me outside the shower on the plush bath mat. He shut the glass door, and I stood there dripping wet and staring.

"I need some privacy," he called, drawing GO AWAY with his finger in the steam. "And you left me no hot water."

I let out a scream of frustration and got right back into the shower with him. I plowed around him, careful not to touch his wet skin as I muscled my way under the water to wash off what was left of the soap clinging to me.

He slipped around me until he monopolized the stream of now lukewarm water. It cascaded down his body. I was rapt as he slicked his hair back with both hands, this my own personal men's body wash commercial. Except live and in the flesh was so much better.

How many times was he going to stop me in my tracks in one morning?

I fought the urge to open my dry mouth and gulp down gallons of water. I couldn't move anyway. Holt reached around me and grabbed the soap, running it over every plane of his body as my eyes followed along. Forget my own honey body wash. I was so using his soap tomorrow.

"Thought you were gonna be late?" he drawled, rinsing the lucky suds off.

One found resistance as it slid down his pec to his nipple. How had I missed how tan he was? No farmer tan, either. Did park rangers chop wood without their shirts? In the fantasy that had popped into my mind they did. It was easy to picture his sweat-slicked body when he was soaking wet right in front of me.

That's how he got those thick biceps. Hard labor. Or rock climbing. Definitely rock climbing. Not the gym.

I hummed my approval as my gaze drifted down cut abs to the defined V—my field of view blurred until blue eyes met mine.

Holt kept a firm grip of my chin. "*I said* I thought you were going to be late."

I shrugged one shoulder, darting a quick glance between us. Couldn't see a darn thing past his chest. And I'd almost gotten to the good part.

"Get enough of a look?"

Heat flooded me. This morning had not gone to plan at all. Not that I'd had one, but if I had, it wouldn't have been this.

"Might want to see about getting that door fixed." His eyes flared a fraction before he strode out of the shower.

"I thought you were the handyman," I called after him. Apparently, my voice did still work.

"I'm expensive." He sounded farther away.

"Don't you dare come in on me in the shower again." Oh, *now* I was bold?

"It's seven forty-five," he yelled.

"Crap."

Now I actually would be late, because of that jerk.

Who had his hands on my naked body.

Twice.

What the hell just happened?

CHAPTER TWO

HOLT

I'D LOST MY MIND.

That was the only viable explanation I'd come up with after eight hours under the hood of one car or another. What kind of asshole walked in uninvited on a woman in the shower? One that had up until a few months ago lived in an abused women's shelter for reasons unknown.

I dropped the wrench in my hand. It fell to the concrete floor with a satisfying clatter and I rolled out from underneath the 70s model Ford truck.

"Good as new." I sprang to my feet and wiped my hands down my coveralls.

"Um, excuse me." A lady peered into the garage area through the doorway from the waiting lobby. Her eyes darted around. She clutched the door handle like it was her life line.

"Hi." I smiled and strolled around the truck I'd been working on. "Can I help you?"

"My-my brakes are smoking." She hadn't released the door handle yet.

"You parked in the drive?" I lifted my chin in that direction. She nodded. "Let's go take a look."

Once we were outside, sure enough her right front brake was smoking. I squatted down by her tire and inspected it. "Any grinding?" I asked.

"No. Just this."

"Pretty sure your calipers are locking. We replace that and she should be good as new." I patted the tire before I straightened.

"You mean I don't need a new set of brakes and rotors?" Now she had her purse strap in her fist. I hated how uncomfortable she seemed.

"From what I see, nope. We can replace just the one, but it would be better to take care of both."

"How much is a caliper?"

"Rough guess? About two hundred bucks."

Her eyes bugged out. "They were going to charge me over eight hundred down the street."

No wonder the woman was nervous. Most people didn't know what was what when it came to their cars, but it was wrong to take advantage of them.

"Why don't we go inside? I'll work up a quote and see how quickly we can get the parts."

THE BELL above the door jangled when I opened it. I held it for her. She stared at me like I was the most bizarre thing she'd ever seen. She shook her head again. Weird.

I gestured for her to step in.

Ed was behind the window.

"The lady needs a caliper on a 2014 Explorer," I said.

She lifted a brow in surprise.

I pointed toward the window. "Ed here will help you. I'm going to take a look at that other side and see if it's okay. Locking calipers normally puts stress on the braking system but can also strain the transmission. And then things can get expensive."

Ed was generally a grumpy man, but he had his version of a

pleased expression on his face. "Get that VIN number, Dixon," he said as I went back through the door.

"BE HERE BY SEVEN TOMORROW," Ed grunted once the woman left. I'd already gotten a lecture from my boss this morning, before lunch, and during my afternoon water break.

"No problem."

"If you're late again, we'll have to rethink this."

If I had my own garage, I could set my own hours.

I'd been working at his shop since I'd decided to stay in New York. He was a friend of my dad's, but I was the best he had. Ed wasn't rethinking anything.

"No problem," I repeated. "See you in the morning."

I STRAIGHTENED up the scattered tools around my station, the only one besides Ed left at the garage. I checked my phone. It was after seven. All I wanted to do was go home, take a long hot shower, and imagine a replay of this morning with a different ending.

But I couldn't go home. Not with her there. I wasn't ready to face Easy even if it made me a coward. All I could think about was her naked, wet body. Those perfect breasts. That round ass.

My dick grew painfully hard just like it had every time I'd let my mind wander today. It was a wonder I hadn't poked somebody's eye out with the thing.

Nope. Most definitely couldn't go home. I'd embarrass the shit out of myself.

My finger hovered over my brother's number. I hesitated. He had a new family. A baby. I couldn't call him.

I scrolled to my sister. She was a single mom. Had her own child to take care of. She didn't have time to go out drinking with me.

There was only one person left.

"Hey, Dad," I said when he answered the phone.

"Hey, son."

I instantly relaxed at the familiar sound of his voice. "You busy?"

"I'm warming up dinner."

"You eat late for an old man," I teased.

"I was about to invite you over, but I don't believe I will."

"Are you by yourself?"

A long sigh filled my ear. "Yeah."

"I'll be there in twenty."

"YOU DIDN'T COOK THIS?" I pointed at the steak Diane with my fork.

"Nope. Trish does it better than I do, so I picked it up from the truck." He wiped his mouth with his napkin. "Why are you avoiding going home?"

I choked on the swallow of beer I'd just taken, though I wasn't sure why I was so surprised. My old man knew his children better than we knew ourselves.

"I thought the new roommate was working out." He looked at me expectantly, and I took another sip of beer.

"Yeah. It's fine."

"Fine, huh?"

"Fine."

"How's work?"

I paused mid-bite and stared at him. He'd let that line of questioning go way too easily. But I'd take it. Just because I couldn't stop thinking about Baker didn't mean I wanted to talk about her.

"Good. I was a little late this morning. Pissed Ed off, but I stayed late."

Dad frowned. "That's not like you."

At least he wasn't going to lecture me too. I already knew I was a reflection of him.

"It won't happen again." He gave a satisfied nod and returned his attention to his plate. "How's Mrs. Quinn?" I asked.

Something resembling a snarl turned his mouth down. "I wouldn't know."

What? The last I'd seen them, they were happy.

"Why wouldn't you?" I asked carefully.

"I broke it off with her." He shoveled a piece of broccoli in his mouth a little too aggressively.

I stared at him incredulously. "You what?"

He set his fork down on his plate and leaned back in his chair. "It's not fair to her. She shouldn't have to accept that I don't think I can go through a relationship again."

I put my own fork down with a clatter and pointed at him. "Does this have to do with Mom?"

He banged his fist on the table in an uncharacteristic display. "No. And I don't want to talk about *her*."

Whoa. Seemed like I was getting warmer to the root of what was going on.

"I'm just trying to figure you out. I thought you and Mrs. Quinn were on fire."

He shot a *shut it* look in my direction. "On fire?"

"Yeah. Hot for each other." I leaned back in my chair and polished off my beer, relieved the conversation was less intense.

"You aren't trying to do anything but avoid telling me why you won't go home. I'm thrilled to have you here any way I can get you, but if you want to get real, let's get real. Why are you calling your old man after work instead of that beautiful roommate of yours? Or hell, even your brother or sister?" He pushed his mostly empty plate away from him and folded his hands on the table.

My dad avoided some things like it was his job. Mainly anything to do with my mother. But he didn't shy away from the hard stuff. He always knew when to push and when to leave things alone.

"Andrew and Marlow are probably in bed." I picked at the edge of the label on my bottle, avoiding his eyes.

"Not with my two grandkids." He winked.

"What kind of trouble did they get into today?" I loved my nephew and niece. Well, technically she wasn't my niece yet, but I was never one to get bogged down with technicalities.

"We're back to avoiding the subject at hand?" Dad tilted his beer back. "Suits me."

"I just needed some space." I worked harder at peeling the label off in one piece. It began to rip when I had a quarter of it off.

"Living with her isn't what you thought?"

I concentrated on the label, slowly pulling on the edge to stop the split. "No. It's pretty much exactly what I thought." Aside from not being able to control this need to touch her. If anything, it was getting worse. "Can we not talk about Baker?"

A smirk toyed on my father's lips. "You pushed about Audrey and Ivette."

"Fine. Let's just forget about women for now." I held up my bottle. "Want another?"

"Please." He handed me his empty.

I paused in the doorway to the kitchen. "You aren't the same without Mrs. Quinn." Now that he'd confessed he'd let her go, it was painfully obvious he was struggling.

Plates clattered from the dining room as I disposed of our bottles in the recycling bin. I opened the fridge and pulled out two more. Dad dropped our dishes in the sink.

"No, I'm not," he admitted through a stiff jaw. "But I've made my bed."

"Just want you to be happy, Dad." I held the fresh beer bottle in front of him.

He took it greedily from my hands. "Why do all my children keep saying that to me?"

"Because it's the truth."

"If all of you are happy, then so am I." He meant it. I knew that with everything I was. But there was a halo of loneliness around him that burned brighter than it had before I'd left for Wyoming.

"Call her." I couldn't keep my mouth shut when I knew he was being a fool not to try with Mrs. Quinn.

He hooked an arm around my neck and pulled me in. "Have I told you how glad I am to have you home?"

"Once or twice." I hugged him back. The man told me every single day in some way, shape, or form. I was glad to be back too. "Mind if I crash here tonight?"

"You never have to ask."

His phone vibrated in his pocket. He checked the caller ID and shoved it back where it came from.

"More lady friends?" I teased.

His eyes looked haunted. "No. Your mother."

"What does she want?" I couldn't hide my disbelief. The little boy in me clapped with hope that they might get back together. But the man in me was worried for my father.

"I can't imagine after nearly forty years." He leaned against the counter for support. "But she's reminded me why I can't be with Audrey. I can't go through that hurt again."

"Dad."

Wariness was in his eyes. "Your mother surfacing has brought it all back up again. I—I just can't."

I hated the pain radiating from him. His struggle was palpable, and I wanted to take it away, but didn't know how. My mother had dredged up things that were better left alone, even if it was hard.

"Why did she leave right after I was born? Is it because she didn't want more kids?"

He slammed his beer down and took me by the shoulders, shaking. "She left because of me, son. Don't you ever think otherwise. Ever."

I was taken aback by his adamancy. I'd thought the questions a million times in my life, but never voiced them aloud to my father. There just seemed to be too much of a coincidence that I was born and she took off right after to not have a connection.

"Are you sure? Because—"

"I'm sure." He cut me off, shaking my shoulders again. "It's my fault. Not yours. Do you hear me?"

I nodded automatically, though I wasn't convinced. I'd wanted to ask this question for so long, and part of me couldn't be satisfied. *It's my fault. Not yours.* How could I reconcile that with the guilt and pain, believing for over thirty years I was responsible for all the hurt my family had endured. I *wanted* to believe him. *But was he still trying to protect me?*

"It wasn't your fault, either," I said quietly. She'd left all of us for another man. Another life. And she'd never looked back. Not until lately.

I'd reached out to her. If it weren't for me, she probably wouldn't be dragging Dad back through this confusion and hell. She'd have left well enough alone if I had too.

His eyelids shuddered. "We have to live with the choices we make."

A rope knotted around my gut. "I know. But we have to live with the choices other people make too."

A shrill ring cut through the room. This time my own phone rang.

"Don't answer that," Dad said severely when he saw the caller ID. He covered my hand with his.

The number was one I didn't recognize. "It could be work."

"It's her."

Her? "Mom?"

He nodded, his grip on my hand pleading. I stared at him, one part of me insanely curious to find out what she wanted, the other terrified to hear what she'd have to say.

Frozen, the phone seemed to ring forever until it stopped. Silence enveloped us, thick and heavy.

"Why is she calling me?" I whispered. I'd wanted that for as long as I could remember. For my entire life. I just wanted my mother to want me, no matter the reason.

"I don't know." His voice cracked. "I can't tell you not to speak to her. I want to, but I can't."

"I don't want to betray you." There was longing in what I hadn't said. That I wanted to at least have a chance with her, even if I was a grown man.

"You couldn't. Don't let my feelings shape yours." The sound was rough, pained, but selfless.

"I need to talk to her. To know the truth," I said honestly.

His face dropped, but he nodded once. "I understand you want to know her side, but that doesn't make it the truth. Be careful, son."

CHAPTER THREE

BAKER

HE HADN'T COME HOME.

If I said I hadn't waited up, I'd have been lying. Because I had until I couldn't keep my eyes open any longer. And after I'd gone to bed, nightmares plagued me and every noise had me on alert. But I'd known he wasn't here. Felt his absence.

As I turned my key in the lock after a long day at work, I half expected his things to be gone.

I pushed open the door. Quickly peering around the open space, everything seemed the same. His books littered the coffee table. The mug he'd left on the kitchen counter three days ago was still there. A T-shirt draped the back of a barstool. The apartment was still, lacking the energy that hummed through it when Holt was home.

Home.

What a joke. I'd jumped at the opportunity to get out of the shelter. To leave behind the first place that had been a real home to me in a long time. Because I wanted it all. The place to come back to that had nothing to do with the surroundings but who was in it.

Foolishness.

That desire for things that didn't exist was what had gotten me into trouble in the first place.

Illusions.

I still had a hard time distinguishing what was real and what wasn't. This was something I'd worked on with my therapist, but I'd taught myself to put up a good front. Deep down, I hadn't learned who was to be trusted and who wasn't. Like an innocent little girl, I let my heart do the picking.

That was why Trish was my best friend. Why I loved her baby like she was my own. Why I was living with a man I had no business being around.

He could hurt me. I doubted the way I had been in the past, but he had the power nonetheless. And he shouldn't.

I didn't even know him.

But the fact he hadn't come home after the morning we had stung me something deep and fierce. And I wasn't brave enough to wonder if that was because he could have hooked up with someone last night. I'd even stayed late at work and contemplated asking Trish if I could sleep over with her just to give Holt a taste of his own medicine.

In the end, the pull toward home had been strong. I couldn't stay away. Needed to know if he would come back. I had my answer.

No.

And that stung.

I dropped my bag on the counter and went straight for the wine. Some of my co-workers had asked me to go out tonight, but I'd declined. Now that I'd come home to an empty place on a Friday night, I reconsidered.

Phone and wine in hand, I leaned against the counter and took a long, satisfying swallow. Immediately, some of my muscles loosened. I thumbed through my contacts about to press Call for one of my colleagues when the front door opened.

Holt's coveralls were filthy. He had a smudge of grease on his cheek. His hair was a wreck, strands of it haphazard in opposing directions.

Relief rushed through me even as I stood a little straighter.

"You should lock the door." He kicked it shut and shucked off his leather jacket, tossing it on the back of the sofa.

My pulse thrummed a rapid beat with every step he took toward the kitchen. His eyes were locked on mine, but I couldn't read anything but the heat in them. Fury or desire, I didn't know. He looked exhausted, that much I could tell.

He swiped the glass from my hand and drained half, making a disgusted face when he handed it back to me. "How do you drink that stuff?" He grimaced and went to the fridge, grabbing a beer and twisting the top off.

"Like this." I made a show of putting the glass to my lips, slowly tipping it back until the dark liquid flowed into my mouth. "Delicious," I said once I'd swallowed.

His throat bobbed as he watched me. His eyes slid down my body when I lowered the glass to the counter.

"Nice dress." His gaze lingered at the V where just a hint of cleavage peeked out.

I'd worn the red A-line dress for him. To get his attention. Pathetic.

"That what people who work at a magazine wear?" He pointed his beer toward me, heat burning a trail where his eyes wandered down my body all the way to my heels.

"Only the easy ones."

"I already explained that," he said with a hint of impatience.

"I *know* what easy means." He had explained and I loved his nickname, but I was still pissy after he hadn't come home last night. "Apparently you're well acquainted with the definition."

He wiped the back of his mouth with his hand. "What the hell is that supposed to mean?"

I lifted one shoulder to my ear. "Nothing."

He set his bottle down and closed the distance between us, though he was careful not to touch his clothes to my dress.

"You'd better clarify, Easy. This grease monkey isn't following."

I barely heard what he said, blindsided when the scent of motor oil wafted into my nostrils. I gripped the rounded edge of the counter and pressed my lower back into it to get away. It was useless. I was dizzy with the combination of sweat, garage, and Holt.

"I said nothing." I lifted my chin, as I pretended not to be affected. There was no way I was *asking* if he'd been with someone the night before. "And stay out of my room."

"That's where the only working bathroom is. You knew that when we moved in."

"Sounds like you've got a problem then." I shrugged, and he scowled.

"No problem." His voice held dark promise and unspoken desire.

Every inch of me ached for him to touch me, his breath ghosting across my face not anywhere near enough. I clenched my thighs together. That did nothing to stop the throb of heat in my core.

"You stink." I wrinkled my nose and prayed he believed the lie.

"Then why'd you just inch closer, Easy?"

"I didn't," I said indignantly. "Can you back up, please? I have plans."

He flattened his palms on the stone surface on either side of me. "We have plans."

I held my breath to keep from taking any more of that intoxicating scent in, but I had to let it go so I could speak. "We do not."

Holt winked at me, a signature move of the Dixon men. I should have been immune, but I melted. "Sure we do. It's in our roommate agreement. Friday nights, we hang out."

I shoved at his shoulders. "What are you talking about?" My voice was shaky, far too affected for my liking. "We don't have a roommate agreement."

"Sure, we do," he said easily. "Did we or did we not agree to be roommates?"

I stared at him a moment. This was a trick question. It was too easy not to be. "Um . . . yes?"

He tapped the tip of my nose and grinned. "Exactly. And since we agreed to be roommates, we agreed to Friday nights. I'm picking this week. Pizza. Beer. And The Walking Dead."

"Did you get hit on the head at work today?"

"Not that I remember," he said cheekily.

I quirked my mouth to one side. "Inhale toxic fumes?"

"Probably." He flashed his perfect white teeth at me.

My gaze dropped to his mouth, and I had to fight desperately to keep from doing something really stupid. Like kiss him the way my lips burned to.

"I have plans," I said weakly.

"I know. We just went over them. Pizza. Beer—"

I held up my hand. "I got it. I got it."

"Good." He dipped his head closer to mine, our eyes locked. His were full of the kind of mischief I definitely wanted a part of.

He rapped his knuckles on the counter twice, and I jumped, narrowly avoiding head butting him. That grin turned knowing before he backed out of my space.

"Wait to change until I'm out of the shower. I need my privacy," he said over his shoulder as he sauntered toward the bedroom.

I sagged against the counter when he disappeared, blindly feeling around for my wine glass. Once in hand, I downed the rest in one long swallow. Sweet Jesus that man put me in a tailspin.

He couldn't get that close again. I'd never survive however long we lived together.

I marched down the hall with determined steps.

"We need to establish . . ." I lost my train of thought at the sight of him bare-chested, coveralls hanging off his hips. We had to get that bathroom fixed. Stat.

"Establish?" He twirled his hand in front of him in a *finish that thought* gesture.

I cleared my throat and dragged my eyes away from those cut abs up to his face. So that wasn't really a hardship. "Boundaries. We need to establish boundaries."

He shook his index finger at me. "Yes. I told you I needed some privacy, yet you tear in here like the house is on fire."

"You can't get in my personal space again."

Holt shoved his coveralls off his hips, leaving him only in charcoal gray boxer briefs. "Easy, we live together. You can't get any more up in each other's personal space than that."

I cinched a hand on my waist. "This what I'm talking about. You can't walk around in your underwear. Or drink my wine without asking. Or—"

He stepped closer, a distinct ridge evident against the cotton of his underwear. I stepped back.

"*That's* what this is about. I drank your wine." His smile was conciliatory. "We've got nothing to worry about. That sure as hell won't happen again."

Holt moved toward my bathroom, pausing when he got to the splintered doorframe. "Since this is broken," he motioned to the door, "can you give me a minute? I won't be long. I need my *privacy*."

The bastard didn't wait for a reply, dropping his underwear to the floor, so that all I was left with was an unobstructed view of his perfect ass.

Taut muscles defined the planes of his back, which gave way to his solid behind. And damn his legs. Long, thick with muscle I imagined came from hiking or mountain climbing. He was the picture of strength, and my second time looking at his naked form was no less awe-inspiring than the first.

My nipples pebbled into hard buds that stabbed through the thin lace of my bra. The silk fabric of my dress did nothing to disguise my physical reaction to him. I couldn't make myself move, not even when the water turned on.

Holt's face appeared in the doorway. I ignored the disappointment that I couldn't see any more of him.

"You still standing there?" He knew damn well I hadn't moved if that smirk was any indication. "I'm sorry. Guess I should've extended an invitation. But you wanted your boundaries, right?"

"You apparently don't know what that word means. Enjoy your shower." I lifted my chin and strutted from the room with an extra sway to my hips. Tit for tat and all.

Once I couldn't feel his eyes on me any longer, I picked up my pace. I breezed through the kitchen, picked up my purse, keys, and phone. No way in hell was I doing roommate night or whatever he called it. Not when all I'd be able to think about was him . . . naked . . . and wet.

I leaned against the wall as I waited for the elevator. Wasn't he the one who was supposed to be having illicit thoughts? Instead, it was me who had soaked panties and heart palpitations.

Nope. I was going out. And if all went to plan, I wasn't coming back home to face more of this tension. How had this suddenly gotten so complicated?

CHAPTER FOUR

HOLT

"EASY?"

The apartment was quiet. Too still.

I readjusted the towel around my hips and went in search of her in the kitchen. No luck. If her missing purse was any indication, she'd bolted.

Had I scared her? In a creepy, pervert kind of way?

I'd meant to keep my clothes on, but that red dress had me going straight out of my mind. I was torn between wanting to leave it and those sex-kitten shoes she was wearing on and getting her naked as fast as possible. For the first time in my life, it was well and truly a toss-up.

Fuck me, I was hard again just thinking about those pouty lips and what they'd feel like on me. Anywhere. I'd take anywhere.

I grabbed a beer out of the fridge. If I was a pervert, I'd still turned her on. Those crimson stained cheeks and dilated pupils didn't lie.

Damn it all to hell. She made it easy to forget she'd been abused. In what way and by who, I didn't know, though I was determined to find out.

That right there—my inability to keep my clothes on around her—was exactly why I hadn't come home last night. Look where it had gotten me. Alone. No Baker anywhere to be found. And wasn't that why I'd moved in with her in the first place? To make it impossible for her to avoid me.

Clearly, I didn't think this through.

I tossed my towel on the bed and shoved one leg into my jeans. What did I want from her? A relationship? I laughed, a mirthless sound. God, no. Sex? God, yes. But it was more than that. I didn't know for sure, just that I *wanted*. And whatever that something was, I wanted it from her. Only her.

Three months in and I'd already screwed up. Hence, I was here by myself wondering where she took off to.

I yanked a gray Henley out of the clean clothes hamper I'd yet to fold and pulled it over my head.

My brother was going to kill me, but I had to call in a favor. I hoped Trish was on board to help me out.

———

THIS WASN'T her kind of place.

The thought was rich, considering I didn't really know her at all. But the thumping bass and throngs of bodies mashed together weren't Easy. She'd like a dim bar with a softer music so she could actually have a conversation.

I scanned through the backlit club. This wasn't my kind of place, either. Leather and lace abounded on men and women who hopped around like the music pumped straight into their veins.

Suddenly, I felt like an old man. There was a time when I would have eaten this scene up, been right in the thick of it with all these people. Now, I just wanted to find Baker and go home with her.

This was like finding a needle in a haystack. Thank goodness I was a patient man.

I circled the perimeter, checking the few tables and the parts of the dance floor I could see. She was nowhere to be found.

I scaled a set of stairs and pushed my way to the railing of a balcony.

Like a beacon, my eyes landed on her in the center of everything. Her hands lifted above her head and she moved with a sensuality that had me leaning closer. I couldn't take my gaze from her. That red dress glowed under the lights. She tossed her head back as if drinking in the scene. Gathering strength or peace or maybe a little bit of both.

Guess I was wrong. This was definitely her kind of place.

My feet were moving before I realized it. Back on the main level, I snaked my way to the middle of the dance floor until Baker was in my sights. Her smile lit me up, but as I caressed down her body with my eyes, I had to get my temper in check. Hands that most definitely didn't belong to her gripped her hips.

I closed the distance between us. Her eyes rounded when they found me before they dared me to take what I wanted.

"Easy On The Eyes," I murmured in her ear as I slid a hand between her back and her dance partner.

I gently pried her away from him, pulling her body flush with mine. Heat streaked through me, possession hot on its heels.

A glare came at me from over her shoulder, but I had zero regrets when she relaxed in my hold. I fired a look back that left no room to doubt she was mine. The guy shrugged and started dancing with another woman nearby.

Baker's arms hung loosely at her sides. I took her hands and twined them behind my neck. Her touch against my skin was like wildfire. I replaced my hands on her back and circled my hips, taking her with me.

"If this was what you wanted to do for roommate night, you should have said something," I rasped, my lips ghosting the shell of her ear.

"We're not having roommate night." Her words came out firm, yet she yielded, her body following my lead.

"You want more than one?" I gave her a curious look and finally shrugged a shoulder. "I guess we can do that."

She dug her nails into the back of my neck, and I hissed.

"None. I want none."

Her chest pressed against mine, breath short and fast. I didn't think it had a damn thing to do with the dancing.

"Aww, Easy. Don't be that way." She stared straight at my chest. I slid my hand up her spine until I cupped the back of her head. Livid eyes met mine. "If I didn't know better, I'd say you're acting like you want me to ignore you."

Indecision flickered on her face. That stung, but I got it. I'd spent the better part of two days in the push and pull of needing to get away from her and be close to her.

Our hips clashed as we moved to the beat. "That what you want, Baker? Radio silence?"

I held her so she could *feel* me. How much I wanted her. She gasped, a sweet, sharp sound that I heard clearly over the house music.

I leaned in and got lost for a moment as I breathed her in. She smelled delicious. Like honey. "I didn't hear you."

She shivered at my breath on her ear and dug her fingernails farther into the back of my neck, struggling to hang on to her sanity. Just like I was doing to mine. The woman made me crazy.

"No." The word was a whisper, but it went straight to places I didn't allow anyone.

"No what?" I asked huskily.

"No, I don't want radio silence."

I grinned, and her eyes went wary. "Good." I ran my nose along her jaw until my lips were against her ear. "Because I couldn't give it to you anyway."

A little growl escaped her. I wanted to hear that again and soon. Preferably with my name attached.

I turned her so her back was to my front. Immediately, she stretched until her hands were latched around my neck. My fingers trailed down her sides, memorizing the feel of her lean body. She ground that perfect ass against me.

"You drive me crazy."

"In a good way?" she asked saucily, pressing back into my erection.

"In every way."

My hands had a mind of their own, not content to stay glued to her hips. They wandered across her flat stomach, over her ribcage, and back down her sides. Her silk dress was hardly a barrier between us, yet it might as well have been a concrete wall. I knew just how soft her skin was and burned to touch her again.

She rested her temple against my jaw. "You mean you don't go throwing all of your roommates out of the shower?"

I wrapped my arms around her at the tease in her voice. My body relaxed into her even as she wound it up tight.

"Nope. That's all you, Easy."

"This would be the moment when you say you're sorry." She smiled against my cheek.

"Can't do that." I nibbled at her ear as if I had the right. "Especially when sorry is about the last thing I am."

Her breath was hot against my skin, blasting me in short pants. She buried her nose in my neck and inhaled. "This is a bad idea."

"Being roommates? No way. Best idea ever."

She giggled. Baker giggled. And it was the sweetest sound I'd ever heard. I tickled her ribs, and she squirmed in my arms, another laugh escaping her.

"Can we go home now?" I smiled against her hair, filled with something I hardly recognized.

We were in the middle of a sea of gyrating bodies, yet it was just her and me.

Baker made me forget everything else.

She shimmied, her ass brushing my cock again. Baker twirled, her eyes playful when she pushed at my chest. "You can. You weren't invited anyway."

I clutched my heart. "You're killing me here. You can't leave your roommate out."

"You do realize that 'roommate' means we live together. Not that we're attached at the hip."

I glanced where my hands gripped her. "Looks to me like we are."

Her eyes followed my gaze and her mouth did this little ripple like she wanted to argue and was fighting a smile all at once. I wanted to find out what that tasted like.

She lifted her chin, and then I was the one fighting my own grin at her defiance. "I'm not ready to go."

I dug my fingers into the soft flesh of her hip. "We both know you're only here because you were running from me. From *this*." I motioned between us.

Her throat worked as she swallowed hard, but fire blazed up at me from her eyes. "There is no *this*."

"Oh, there is so a this." I inched my face closer to hers. She held her breath and backed away. "The first time I kiss you *won't* be in a crowded club."

"I'm not kissing you." Her voice tripped over the words.

I smirked. "Yeah. You're gonna kiss me. And Easy? I'm gonna kiss you right back."

I spun Baker before I pulled her back against me. "You wanna dance? Then let's dance."

CHAPTER FIVE

BAKER

HE CAME HERE.

For me.

And he wanted me.

Down, down, down I went, consumed with how good it felt to be desired again. I hadn't been with anyone since I'd arrived at Paths, hadn't even considered it. Yet Holt had my mind going places it hadn't been in years . . . maybe ever. I could easily get addicted to this feeling, which meant I couldn't have him. Even if he wasn't my roommate, he was still off limits.

Too dangerous.

Too easy to get sucked into.

My body moved of its own volition, following where he led. My hands threaded through the back of his hair and pulled in punishment for being so damn irresistible. But it was me who paid the penance when a low rumble escaped him, his chest vibrating against mine. Dark eyes threatened me with the promise of pleasure. All I had to do was reach out and take it.

And then I remembered that he hadn't come home last night. Had probably seduced some unsuspecting woman with his sweet talk and sexy smile.

He brushed his thumb across my lips. "I thought we were having fun." The playfulness in his tone from minutes before had vanished. He didn't get to act like he cared about me. Not when he'd been with someone else less than twenty-four hours ago. Hell, less than *twelve* hours ago.

Ugh.

The thought of him waking up in another woman's bed nauseated me.

I shoved at his chest, no longer thrilled with his tainted hands on me. Holt didn't budge.

"Let me go," I hissed.

"Can't do that, Easy." He was far too calm for my liking.

"*You're* the easy one," I said petulantly, the green streak of jealousy on display for him to see.

Confusion flitted across his face. I pushed again, somehow managing to break out of his hold.

I wrestled my way through the wall-to-wall dancers, my anger propelling me forward. Stupid. I was so so stupid. This was how it had all started before. When I'd gotten myself in more trouble than I could have ever imagined.

The room spun as I made it to the fringe of the dance floor. Pounding bass throbbed until my heart matched its rhythm. All I could hear was the *thump, thump, thump,* but what I saw terrified me. I was no longer in the club, but back in the car that had been my nightmare. I'd thought it was the safest place in the world.

"We're gonna leave our mark, baby. You and me. Nobody's ever gonna forget us."

That slow grin. The way I'd believed the words he'd spoken. He'd been right. I just didn't know I'd spend the rest of my life trying to make people forget me.

I stumbled, throwing out my arm against a wall for support. Steady hands found my waist. Endless pools of concern peered down at me.

I jolted, slapping his hands away. "You—you don't get to do that." I shoved a finger into his chest, shouting above the music. *Nobody had ever heard me because I'd never put up a fight. But those days were done.*

"Baker?"

My heart twisted with the reverent way he spoke my name, but I pushed my anger toward the surface. "No. Go use your sexy words on somebody else. Maybe the woman from last night wants to hear them again."

"Last night?" He blinked at me in confusion. "What are you talking about?"

"You can't just brainwash me." There was an edge of desperation in my voice. I tried to remember techniques I'd learned in therapy to deal with stress, but they all escaped me.

I am strong. I am strong. I am my own woman.

He took me by the hand and tugged. I tried to remain rooted in place, but he was too strong. Holt stopped when he felt my resistance.

"We need to talk and we're not having this conversation here."

He waited until I gave a subtle nod before he led me down a narrow hallway. I cursed myself for giving in so easily. I didn't owe him an explanation. Didn't owe him anything. Yet I felt compelled to follow where he led.

Just like I always did.

Holt moved with determination. The music had only faded a fraction, still too loud to be heard without shouting. He pushed through a door with an exit sign lit above it into a stairwell. The echo of the door closing bounced off the concrete block walls. The music muted.

He released me and raked a hand through his hair, pacing in a small circle. "I know my behavior," he paused and looked at me, yanking on his thick locks, "hasn't been the best."

I wrapped my arms around my middle and hugged myself, staring at the ground.

"Brainwash? Baker, I don't know what to say to that. I'd never . . ." Anguish filled his eyes. "Why would you think that?"

I lifted my gaze to his. "It's what men do."

He froze. "Not all men," he said quietly.

All men, I argued in my head. Instead of saying anything, I just lifted my chin.

"Seduce you? Yeah, I'm totally guilty. And obviously I've done a bang up job of it."

"Seduce. Brainwash. They're really one in the same." I shrugged, but my insides had gone cold.

Holt's stare burned into me. "What happened to you?"

His voice was lethally low, as if he were furious on my behalf. When he figured out who I was, that anger would evaporate in an instant.

"Nothing that matters." It was a lie. What happened to me defined the person I was today no matter how I tried to get away from it. I'd managed a new start, only a few people I'd confessed the truth to.

This . . . the woman in the dress who had a dream job working at a fashion magazine? She was a facade. Nothing more than a thin veil disguising the ugly truth.

He stepped closer. "I think it does. A whole hell of a lot."

I held my ground, though I hugged myself more tightly. "I don't care what you think."

Holt recoiled as if I'd slapped him. Instant regret flooded me. Was this my new tactic? Hurt him before he hurt me?

A vein pulsed in his temple, but he nodded once. "Fair enough." He let out a frustrated breath. "Then let's get to what exactly you think happened last night."

I lifted a shoulder and painted a look of indifference on my face. "I *know* you didn't come home."

Light dawned in his eyes. "And where exactly do you think I was?"

"Never gave it a second thought." More lies. And he knew it.

"Then why'd you bring it up?"

I shrugged again, wishing I hadn't.

He edged closer to me until I felt the heat radiating off of him. "Why do you think I spent the night out?"

"Not my business."

"Because of you. *You.*"

He shoved open the door before the weight of his words settled on me. It slammed, and I jumped before sagging against the wall. *He didn't deny it.*

It was always because of me. I just couldn't figure out why I drove men to do horrible things.

I shivered and resisted the urge to go after him. Instead, I hugged myself harder and rocked until my heart slowed to a normal pace. I couldn't go home. Not after that.

I couldn't face if he didn't come home, either. I was afraid to find out that he didn't.

The shelter.

Mrs. Quinn wouldn't mind if I spent the night there again. She'd welcome me. I closed my eyes and settled a bit more at the thought of somewhere familiar. Safe. Somewhere without Holt.

No. That felt wrong.

I straightened, picked up my head, and squared my shoulders. I'd promised myself I was ready to live out in the real world. When I'd agreed to be Holt's roommate, I'd known it wouldn't be trouble-free. Nothing in life was . . . *and I'd learned that the hard way.* But I wasn't *her* any more. *"When you accept you are the strong woman who tried to do the right thing and started a new life, you'll know. You'll have the strength to take another step forward."* Another step forward . . .

Was I going to tuck tail and run every time I got scared?

Absolutely not.

Just like Mrs. Quinn had told me I'd be able to do, I was going to take another step forward.

CHAPTER SIX

HOLT

WATER.

I guzzled down half of a cold bottle and nearly spit it out with the sound of the lock on the front door turning.

Baker strutted in on her sex-kitten heels, her hair disheveled and her dress wrinkled from the night out dancing. She flicked a glance my way and kept moving straight toward her bedroom.

I'd rather she'd slapped me.

I couldn't take my eyes off her as she sashayed past. Yeah, I was pissed at the accusations she'd hurled my way, needed some space to breathe. But more than that, I was relieved she'd come home. Truth be told, I was angry at myself for leaving her in that crowded nightclub to not only fend for herself, but find her own way home. *I was raised better than that.* But coupled with that guilt? What if she hadn't made it home safely?

What if she'd hooked up with another handsy guy after I left? And she didn't come home because she was with some ass—

Shit. I'd done that to her last night. *That's what she meant.*

She and I didn't have any obligations to one another, but there was something simmering beneath the surface. A little more heat and it was going to boil over. Both of us were already burning.

I couldn't shove that word out of my head, either. *Brainwash.* Whoever had tried to do that to her, I wanted to kill. Teach them a lesson for hurting her. Because in that club, there was a moment where she'd been scared. Not of me. She hadn't even been with me for a minute. Her fear was so real, I'd felt it too.

This wasn't what I signed up for. I couldn't care about anyone else. There was just no room for it in my life. I wasn't willing to let another person leave me. She was supposed to be something new. A little bit of fun.

Except, I was unsettled. Desperate to go to her, take away her hurt. Make her smile.

Baker might need some space. Hell, I probably did too. No, maybe that was the problem. There was too much space between us.

I tossed my empty bottle in the recycling and headed down the hall. Instead of veering into my bedroom, I knocked once on her door and went on in without waiting for a response.

I nearly tripped. She was wearing one of my T-shirts, long, bare legs going on for days. Her hair was up in some sort of messy knot, a few pieces already loose in her face. And that face. It was free of makeup. She looked younger, innocent even.

She's beautiful.

"Did we not just discuss boundaries?" She busied herself with tossing her dirty clothes into a laundry basket instead of looking at me.

"Are clothes included in that? Because that sure looks like my shirt."

Her back stiffened before she turned to face me. "I didn't have any clean ones."

Little liar. But I liked the sight of her in my clothes. And that in itself was weird. It didn't equate with a little bit of fun.

I made a non-committal noise and took long strides toward the bathroom.

"Another shower?" she called through the open door.

"Nope. Toilet's not working now."

"I thought you were fixing things, not breaking them."

I couldn't help but smile. "Where'd you get the idea I'm a plumber?" I asked, flushing the toilet.

Baker crowded in the doorway as I washed my hands. "You. I got that impression from *you*."

Her mouth rolled from one side to the other in frustration. I took a step closer as I dried my hands with her pink hand towel, absently tossing it back toward the sink when I was done.

She held her ground. Something about that made me inordinately happy.

I fixed an apologetic look on my face. "Thought I'd get to work on it some this weekend, but I gotta go into the garage tomorrow. Maybe Sunday too."

She looked panicked. "Why don't we hire someone? We could both pitch in. I have a little saved." The edge of desperation in her voice had me closing the gap between us. Her head tilted back to look at me as I got a breath of her sweet scent.

I pointed in the direction of my room. "Easy, that's thousands of dollars of work if we hire somebody."

"But we can't keep doing this."

I grinned at her. "Sure, we can. I think we've done pretty well so far, don't you?"

"I guess," she conceded. Something in me swelled with an intensity I wasn't used to.

I lightly chucked her chin and winked. "You guess right. Now, I'll get out of your hair."

When she didn't immediately move, a hope I shouldn't have felt crept through me. I didn't want to leave her any more than she wanted me to go.

"Good night," she said stiffly, taking a step back.

Disappointment poked at me. I didn't want to be alone. I opened my mouth to tell her as much, then I thought better of it. Alone was what I deserved. And Baker had enough shit to deal with. No need to drag her into mine.

My phone vibrated in my pocket.

"Aren't you going to answer that?" Baker pointed toward me with her chin. "It's late. Could be important."

She was right. As soon as I saw the caller ID, I wished I hadn't. *Celia.*

I shoved my phone back in my pocket as if it had burned me.

"Who was that?" A few wrinkles formed on the top of her nose.

My jaw clenched. "No one."

"It had to be someone—"

"I said it was no one," I snapped, and she recoiled. I closed my eyes to reel in my temper. When I opened them, Baker had her arms wrapped around her middle. I couldn't take it twice in one night. "I'm sorry. It's just—I just—come here."

I opened my arms, but she didn't move. We stared at one another. Only three feet separated us, but it seemed like a mile.

"Easy." The word came out a plea.

She hesitated before she took a tentative step forward. My heart leapt, an erratic beat drumming with her next step. One more. That was all we needed.

She let out a shaky breath and closed the distance. Without hesitation, I folded my arms around her and pressed her head to my chest. A sense of rightness came over me. I clung to it because I knew I'd have to let it go. Let her go.

Slender arms slid around my back. I closed my eyes and rested my cheek on the top of her head.

"I stayed at my dad's last night."

Her hold on me tightened, and she burrowed deeper into my chest. I wove a hand through her soft hair, clinging to her. She felt perfect against me.

Peace. Light. Sanctuary.

"I'm sorry I said those things," she confessed quietly.

I tipped her chin up and was lost for a second in those open eyes staring at me. "I'm sorry too. Truce?" She nodded, and I grinned. "You owe me a roommate night."

"Oh, I do?"

"Yep. I'll cash in my raincheck tomorrow. Pizza. Beer—"

"And the Walking Dead. I got it," she finished.

"You wanna sleep in my room?" A strangled gasp escaped her and she struggled to get out of my hold. "No. No. I meant—dammit." I tried to regroup before I completely terrified her. "I have to get up early tomorrow. If we switched rooms tonight, I wouldn't disturb you when I need a shower. You could sleep in." I was rambling in an effort to make up for my huge foul. *Who did this to her?*

She relaxed, though her eyes were still wary. I suspected she did that a lot and I was only just recognizing her hurt. *But that's the Baker I first met.* "No. It's fine."

"Okay. Sweet dreams." I kissed the top of her head, both of us blinking at one another in surprise.

She released me, and I wanted to put her arms back around me. But I resisted.

"Sweet dreams."

I STRETCHED out on my bed, staring at the ceiling despite the darkness. Where I wanted to be was only a room over, but I'd done enough damage already. Pushing when I didn't really know what I was doing.

I wanted her. There was no denying that. But I couldn't have her. Baker deserved more than just sex. She deserved a guy that would treat her right. Put her first.

And I wasn't that guy.

Those lips. I'd been so close, yet hadn't touched. I fisted my dick, the pressure building too much.

Those legs. God, her body. Every inch of her sweet perfection.

I hadn't been thinking when I barged in on her shower. Didn't consider the consequences. Like how I couldn't get the sight of her wet and those feral eyes out of my head. She was wild and innocent. Fire and passion. And her body? Holy hell. She was stunning. Creamy, soft skin. Tits I wanted to bury my face in and suck. Trim waist, something I held at the club hours ago. Damn . . . every one of her perfect features rolled through my head. *Fuck. So gorgeous.* I wished I'd touched her when she was naked, the way I had at the night club. Inhibitions gone. Restraint at zero. *Want* at 100 percent. Her name.

I pumped my shaft in hard, intense strokes. "Easy."

Her name was a prayer on my lips. Torture and mercy. That woman was driving me straight out of my mind.

I looked down at my dick as I stroked, imagining her mouth around me, taking me deep. My cock swelled. I pictured her eyes, ripe with pleasure as she looked up. Hungry for me as I was for her.

My balls ached. I needed Baker. To feel her around me. To have her come apart at the seams because of me. My hand was a poor substitute, but it was the best I had.

I bet when she let go she was beautiful. I could almost hear her crying my name in bliss and that was my undoing.

"Easy."

Thick ropes of my release shot to my stomach. I pumped until there was nothing left, sinking into the mattress.

Moving in with Baker was both the greatest and worst idea I'd ever had.

And damn her, my dick twitched back to life. But it wasn't my own touch that would do. Hers. I had to have it, and I couldn't.

My phone buzzed on the nightstand, lighting with an incoming call.

I lolled my head to the side, my arm too heavy to reach for the phone.

Celia.

Why now? It had been months. I had started to forget.

No. Baker had distracted me.

She made it so simple to forget what I'd left behind. I'd practically vanished from my old life. Left it like I had the intention of going back. I'd led my family to believe I might.

There was no way. I'd tried to stay until I felt like I was crushed to the point I couldn't breathe anymore.

One lone buzz signaled a voicemail.

A knot formed in my stomach. I didn't care what she had to say.

Yet . . . I reached for the phone anyway and held it to my ear like a desperate fool.

"Hey . . . it's me. I know it's been a while . . . Crap. Just call me back. I-I miss you, Holt."

Her voice turned me inside out, just like it always had. I listened to the message six times before I buried the phone under my pillow. I turned on my side and punched the goose down, which did nothing to squash my anxiety.

Weak.

It took all my strength not to call her back. She missed me?

Truth of it was, a part of me missed Wyoming . . . and her. When I moved there, I'd been running from New York. All these years later and I'd run right back here.

Running. Always running.

I rolled to my other side and tossed back to the same position. Would I ever find the place where I belonged?

All I wanted was to be accepted. I'd never had it here. Sure, my family loved me, but my mother's abandonment had caused this deep rooted sense of unsettledness. Made me question if anybody really wanted me around. The last year had only cemented that insecurity.

I was sick of living with a shadow of doubt constantly hanging over my head. Problem was, I didn't know how to get out from under it.

"Holt?" Baker's roughened voice broke through the darkness.

I rolled over. Light from the hallway spilled in, her shadowy figure huddled in the doorway.

I sat up straight, on alert. "Everything okay?"

"I can't sleep." She rocked back on her heels, eyes trained on the floor before they found mine. The turbulence in them made something inside me ache. She was begging for me to make it better, and this was her way of doing it.

I slid over and pulled the covers back. "I can't, either." She scurried across the floor before she lost her nerve. "Wait," I said when she was at the edge of the mattress. "I, uh, can you give me a sec?"

Her shoulders deflated. "I can go."

"No." I reached for her hand when she turned to leave. "Hang on. Figure you probably wouldn't appreciate that I'm naked under here."

She appeared amused. "When are you not naked?"

I tilted my head as if considering. "Fair point." I lifted my chin toward the dresser. "Problem is, my sweats are over there."

Even in the dim light her amusement was visible. "Are you getting shy now?"

"Maybe a little," I teased, easing out from under the covers. Shit. I still had come all over my stomach. I swiped a shirt off the floor and discreetly cleaned it off as best I could.

I felt her eyes on me, slightly embarrassed that she probably could see the evidence of what I'd been up to. Couldn't help it. She did this to me.

Baker crawled into bed, and I made the mistake of looking over at her. The sight of her there in my T-shirt had my body at full attention again.

What the hell? She turned me on. No point in hiding it.

I tossed the shirt on the floor and stalked to the chest of drawers, pulling out a pair of old sweatpants.

"I need some water. You want some?"

"Yeah." I swore I heard disappointment in her voice now that I had some clothes on. Or maybe I just wanted to.

I hurried to the kitchen, rinsed off the rest of the mess on my stomach, and returned to the bedroom. Baker was propped against the headboard. A little more of her hair had worked loose from the knot it was pulled in.

This was where I wanted her.

My steps faltered at the thought. I shoved down the truth and forced the cocky swagger to the surface that I'd learned as a disguise.

Her eyes were all-knowing when they met mine.

She saw me.

She saw everything. *Hopefully she didn't hear everything too.*

I unscrewed the cap on the water bottle and passed it to her. She took a drink, but I guzzled most of the liquid when she gave it back to me.

"Lights on or off?" I motioned toward the hallway.

"On."

I rounded the foot of the bed and slid in beside her. "Come here."

She hesitated, eyeing me warily before she crawled into my arms. I settled her head against my chest and stroked her hair, the finest silk between my fingers. Her breath was warm on my skin and when she slung her arm around me, something right clicked into place. Something I'd never felt.

"Want to talk about it?" I asked against the top of her head.

"No." She clung to me a little tighter. I didn't want her to hurt, but it gave me inordinate pleasure to know when she needed someone she'd come to me.

I kissed her hair and ran my hand up and down her spine. She sighed, her body already growing heavy with sleep.

"Holt?"

"Yeah, Easy?"

"Maybe we should forget the boundaries."

CHAPTER SEVEN

BAKER

"BAKER."

The sleep-roughened voice that spoke my name made me want to stay in my dream. I was in strong arms. Safe. Content.

"Baker."

A soft kiss pressed to the top of my head sent warmth melting through me. No, I definitely didn't want to wake up.

"Easy, I don't want to get up, but I've got to go to work."

Easy. Hmm. I thought that sounded like Holt's sexy voice. I clung more tightly to the dream, though it felt as if it was slipping away.

A laugh rumbled in my ear. I screwed my eyes shut, desperate not to let this go. "I'm flattered. And you aren't making this easy. But I can't be late again."

"Mmm. Keep talking. But not about work," I mumbled, fighting reality.

Another laugh and I couldn't avoid him any longer. Bright eyes met mine when I blinked open. I propped my chin on his chest.

"There she is."

Whoa. His knockout smile sent me spinning. They always did, but this one was different. More . . . real.

"Hi."

He swept a piece of hair from my face. "Sleep okay?"

"Yeah. Better than okay."

Last night, I couldn't get away from the demons. All I'd wanted was Holt. I'd crossed a line by coming to him, but that didn't stop me. It was a decision I had no regrets over.

"Me too," he said quietly.

Something cool poked against my back. Blindly, I reached behind me. "What's your phone doing in the bed?"

A shadow passed over his face and I immediately wished I'd left it alone.

"No reason." He pulled me closer to him. "As much as I'm enjoying this, I really do have to get up."

I pushed at him playfully. "Go. The sooner you're out of here, the sooner I have the house to myself."

"Are you saying you're already tired of your roommate?"

"I thought you were going to be late."

He groaned and threw the covers off. "Fine." Absently, I traced a pattern across his chest. "Thought you wanted the house to yourself today?"

"I do."

"That's not the way to get it." He flipped me on my back and tickled my sides.

"Holt," I shrieked, flailing about. "Go away. Go away."

"Aww. You don't mean that."

"I do," I said between laughs. "I definitely do."

HOLT STROLLED INTO THE KITCHEN, hair damp from a shower I hadn't joined him in, with a fresh pair of coveralls on. I steadied myself on the counter, growing warm at the reminder I'd spent the night in his arms.

"I packed your lunch." I offered him the brown bag.

His startled look gave way to something that appeared in the same family as pleasure. "Thanks." He leaned a hip against the counter beside me.

"I didn't make it," I hastily explained. "Trish did."

"Yeah? So I guess I need to thank her instead."

I swatted him with a dish towel. "Go."

His eyes drifted toward the dining room table. "What are you working on now?"

"I'm still trying to figure out the lip gloss. I can't get it the shade I want."

"Keep at it. You'll get there." I gaped at him, surprised by his confidence in me. He rapped on the counter twice. "I'll see you later."

"See you," I said, almost shyly. I didn't want him to go and that spelled trouble.

He grabbed his leather jacket off the back of the sofa. Halfway to the door, he turned around and pointed at me. "Don't forget tonight. Pizza. Beer." He looked at me expectantly.

"The Walking Dead," I grumbled.

"You got it." He made a finger gun and winked at me as he pulled the trigger.

I gasped, shaking in fear, and the second the door clicked shut, I took another breath.

It was nothing, meant as a cute gesture, yet the move nearly sent me to my knees.

I stumbled to my bedroom, my heart beating so hard I could barely catch my breath. With shaky hands, I unplugged my phone where it was charging on the nightstand and dialed.

"Can you come over?" I choked out.

As soon as I got an okay, I hung up and collapsed on the bed.

TRISH FOUND me curled up in a ball where I'd been since I called her.

"Baker?" She crawled in bed beside me and coaxed me to put my head in her lap.

"Sorry," I said weakly. "You've got the food truck. And Ella."

"Andrew has it covered. Sonya and Drew are helping him out." She tried and failed not to smile at the thought of her husband with those two. But even their shenanigans couldn't make me feel better. Her smile turned kind. "I'm glad you called."

I shifted and closed my eyes as she stroked my hair. She knew everything about my past and had completely understood why that meaningless gesture had sent me into a tailspin when I spilled out what happened. I needed my best friend and was beyond grateful she'd come when I called, no questions asked.

"It was nothing," I mumbled. "But last night . . . and he didn't mean anything by it this morning."

"Did you tell Holt?" Her fingers stilled for a moment.

Panic filled me at the thought of him ever knowing what I'd been a part of. It had been hard enough to tell her. "No. I can't do that."

She paused as if collecting her thoughts. "Take it from someone who tried to hide her truth. The longer you do, the worse off you are."

"Just because he's my roommate doesn't make him entitled to my secrets."

"You're right. But I think we both know he's more than that."

I hugged my knees closer to my chest. "I'm scared."

"Falling in love can be that way."

I sat up straight, eyes bulging. "I'm not in love with Holt."

"Not yet."

I furrowed my brow and dropped my head back onto her lap. "I don't deserve to be here. Those people . . . I see their faces. I don't want to think about any of it, but it's wrong for me to forget."

I shuddered. The vision of their fear was so vivid. I tried to make them disappear now but they wouldn't.

"You feel it's your cross to carry."

"It is. I didn't do enough. I was so caught up. And Kyle. He's in my head all the time."

"He always will be," she said apologetically. "But you have control over what you do with that."

My therapist had tried to make me understand that concept. I knew what it meant but had failed to put it into practice. That was one reason for moving out of Paths. To get control over my life.

"I like to think that if I had it to do all over again, I never would. But I don't know that. I got sucked in, was so weak."

"You weren't weak. He wasn't right. It's not your fault you didn't know it."

I'd been young and vulnerable when we met and had lied to my family about his age, not that they'd cared. The second I'd finished high school, I'd been on my own. Well, Kyle had been there.

"He loved me. Too much." I fingered the comforter and stared at the wall. "It's messed up that I still miss that."

"He gave you a side of himself that you fell in love with."

"He was controlling, but I didn't mind. If I'd been stronger—"

"Don't do that."

Tears trickled down my cheeks, and I sniffled. "I can see it happening again. With Holt. It wouldn't take much for him to become my whole world."

Trish gently pulled on my shoulder until I sat up. Her eyes were serious as she looked at me. "You are strong. Your own woman. Look at how far you've come. What you've accomplished."

"I got the internship because Hayden felt sorry for me."

She frowned. "That's not true."

"Oh come on. At the shelter, we're all charity cases."

She recoiled as I lashed out. "Maybe," she said hesitantly. "But I learned a long time ago that help is help. And sometimes we just need it in any form."

I let my eyes fall closed for a brief second. "I'm sorry. I shouldn't have said that. I'm just—"

"Upset," she finished for me.

"Yeah."

"In all the time I've known you, this is the first I've seen you any less than perfect."

"I'm not perfect."

"You make it look easy. Especially when I know it's not."

"I don't know how to deal with it anymore."

"One day, one step at a time." She put her arm around my shoulders and squeezed. "I saw a mess out there on the table when I came in. I've got a little time to play test subject if you're game."

I gave her a wobbly smile. "Yeah. I'm definitely game."

CHAPTER EIGHT

HOLT

"HONEY, I'M HOME."

I balanced a pizza and a six pack of beer as I kicked the front door shut. The large living/dining/kitchen area was quiet, other than the low sound of "Only" by RY X in the background. Except the mess on the table had spread from the center space it occupied this morning to the entire surface. I smiled. Baker had been working hard today.

She emerged from the hallway wearing my T-shirt, a pair of sweatpants, and her hair piled up in that knot thing again. Something filled me at the sight of her in some of my clothes I recognized from the night before, but wasn't entirely sure what it was.

I liked it.

"I brought dinner." I lifted up the pizza box before I set it down next to the beer on the island.

She put a hand on her hip and cocked that pretty head to the side. "Maybe this roommate thing isn't so bad."

Her smile turned me inside out. Real. All for me.

She glided over to me and plucked a beer from the holder. I held the neck and opened it for her, flicking the cap on the counter.

"Thanks," she said quietly.

"I'm gonna go change." I unzipped a few inches of my coveralls, and her lips parted. "I'm dirty, Easy. Really dirty. Want to help me clean up?"

A little noise of frustration escaped her. "Do you spend all day thinking of ways to get me in the shower with you again?"

"Yep." I tossed her a wink and sauntered off toward the bathroom. No need to lie when the truth was much better.

"YOU'RE SPOILING ME." I set my beer on the coffee table and sank onto the sofa next to Baker. She already had the television show cued up, the pizza box and napkins in front of her.

"You're killing me. This pizza smells so good, and I've had to wait on your slow self before I could start."

She flipped open the top of the box and scooped a piece of pizza up. I was fascinated as she lifted the slice to her lips like I'd never seen anybody eat before. I'd never seen a mouth like hers, that was for sure.

"Aren't you going to eat?"

"Yeah. Of course."

I grabbed my own slice and devoured it in a few bites. Baker stared at me. "Hungry?"

"Starved." I took a long swallow of beer and pointed the bottle toward the dining room table. "Looks like you've been busy. You find the perfect shade you were looking for?"

She angled her body toward me and tucked a leg up under her. "I don't know. I think I'm close."

Baker abandoned her pizza and scrambled off the sofa over to her work station. She hurried back with a small container of something red in her hands.

"What's that?" I was afraid at the gleam in her eyes.

"You're the perfect skin tone to see if this looks right."

"I am?"

She laughed and if I didn't watch it, I was going to become addicted to that sound. "Are you afraid of a little lip gloss?"

"Uh, maybe."

She pried my beer from my fingers and set it on the table next to hers. A waft of her scent intoxicated me when she scooted closer.

"I bet you've fought off bears in Wyoming. This is nothing," she taunted, swiping her finger into the red stuff. "Pucker up."

"Can't say no to that."

She made a face at me. "Not what I meant."

My response died on my tongue as she ran her finger across my bottom lip. Everything in me tightened to the point I had to ball my fists to keep from grabbing her hips. With slow, torturous movement, she repeated the motion on my top lip. Her eyes were trained on my mouth, her tongue peeking out of the corner of hers in concentration.

She couldn't do that and expect me to be a gentleman. A smile spread across her lips and I was done for.

"Perfect." The triumph on her face had me grinning back.

"I knew you'd get it right."

She sat back, uncertain by my confidence. "You did?"

"Yep. Now what else do you need to test?"

Her brows shot up. "You'd let me put makeup on you?"

"Easy, I'm beginning to think there isn't anything I wouldn't let you do to me." I reached for my beer, and she grabbed my arm.

"You'll smudge your gloss." Her lips twitched, and I tried to scowl, failing miserably.

"There's plenty more there." I took a swig. "You'd better name this after me. Since I made it look perfect and all."

I stripped the container from her hands and dipped my finger into the well.

"I can't name it Holt."

"Sure you can. You made it, didn't you?" I spread the color onto her lip, and she froze. "It does look perfect." I cocked my head and smacked my lips together. "What's in this? It has a hint of something . . ."

"Honey." She blushed the same shade as her lip gloss. "I wanted it to feel good and taste good."

"For the person wearing it?" I dropped the container of gloss on the table and leaned closer. "Or the person kissing her?"

"Both," she whispered as I inched toward her, our mouths only a few breaths apart.

"We're gonna have to test that part out."

"We are?" She scooted back a little, and I followed.

"Uh-huh. I'm a very dedicated tester," I said huskily.

"I didn't know you'd been a tester before," she huffed. If I didn't know better, I'd think she was jealous.

"This is my first time. I want to get it perfect." I ran my thumb across her mouth. Heat flared in her eyes. "What else do you need to try out?"

"This." She darted from the sofa back over to the table. Relief practically poured from her.

"Should I be offended you were that happy to escape my kiss?"

Something in her hands clattered to the table. She met my gaze. "Probably."

I stifled a grin at how quickly she composed herself. "You won't evade it forever."

A blush crept up her neck. "We'll see."

It was my turn to be surprised. She hadn't shot me down. That was a start.

Hands full of I didn't know what, she piled it on the sofa in front of me and sat back down.

"I can't believe you're letting me do this," she said as she brushed something on my cheeks.

"I can't believe you make all of this."

"It's not hard."

I shrugged. "Still impressive. Have you shown anyone at the office yet?" She shook her head. "Why not?"

"I don't know." She scoured through the pile until she found what she wanted. "We work with the best of the best products."

"Isn't that what you've got here?"

"I want it to be."

"Then that's what you'll do." I touched her thigh, and she stared at me. "You can't make the stuff fast enough for the ladies at Paths."

"They're just being nice."

I gripped her chin, forcing her to look at me. "Being nice is trying something once. They're all clamoring for your stuff."

"Who told you that?"

I winked. "I've got inside sources." I lifted my chin and turned my head from left to right. "Now what do you think?"

"I think you make an excellent guinea pig."

BAKER'S EYELIDS drooped where she was curled up on the opposite end of the sofa.

"Ready to call it a night?"

She yawned and stretched. "I think so."

I nudged her in the ribs. "See. Roommate night wasn't so terrible after all."

"I guess not."

I stood and held out my hands to her. She took them, and a spark shot up my arms as I pulled her to her feet. I couldn't force myself to immediately release her. She seemed frozen as she peered up at me.

Heat crackled between us. I was desperate to pull her closer, but uncertain where the lines were that we weren't supposed to cross. She'd said maybe we didn't need boundaries, but I doubted she meant what I had in mind.

"What are you doing tomorrow?" The words were out of my mouth before I thought them through. She looked as surprised as I felt.

"I don't have any plans."

"Now you do."

Lines creased her forehead. "What are they?"

"All you need to know is they end up at Dino's for Sunday dinner with my family."

A fondness etched her features. "I like your Dad and your sister."

I pouted. "What about me?"

"Not really." Pure mischief taunted me. "Don't you care what I think about your brother?"

"I kinda hope you don't like him. That way I don't have to be jealous."

"You do realize he's with my best friend?"

"Doesn't always mean anything," I said, too cutting.

She saw too much as she looked at me, her hands squeezing mine back. "It does to me."

I forced a smile. "Big day tomorrow. We'd better get to bed."

She opened her mouth as if she wanted to protest, instead led me toward our bedrooms. At our doors opposite one another she hesitated.

"You never have to ask, Baker."

She swallowed hard, kept my hand in hers as she pulled me into her bathroom. We washed our faces and brushed our teeth. Somehow doing this normal, everyday thing together made me nervous.

She took my hand again and guided us into my room. My heart thudded when she crawled into my bed like she belonged there. Everything inside of me screamed that she did.

She watched me as I rounded the foot of the bed, shedding my T-shirt as I did. I climbed in beside her and stretched out my arm in invitation. The second she nestled against me, a peace settled in my soul.

"You're spoiling me, Easy," I said when her breathing evened out.

Although, I was sure I heard mumbled, *No. It's you spoiling me.*

It had been eight months since I'd had someone else beside me. Someone I thought I'd spend—no, I wasn't going there. I seemed destined to be on my own. Hell, maybe I didn't deserve a woman like Baker.

And that would be a dangerous thing to forget.

CHAPTER NINE

HOLT

"WHAT IS THIS PLACE?"

Baker turned in a circle, looking around the dilapidated space with curious eyes.

I shoved my hands into my pockets and kicked at some of the dirt on the floor. "I was thinking of starting my own garage."

Light clicked as she flicked her gaze toward the roll-up door and back around the space. "Looks like this would be a good place to do it."

"I can lease to own the whole building. There's an apartment upstairs. A loft with plenty of room for you to set up shop for making your cosmetics." I realized the implication of my words as soon as I said them. That whatever future I had, I imagined Baker in it. But how? How did I get to this point with a woman I'd only known a little over three months? And why had I said that out loud?

Her lips parted, an expression somewhere on the spectrum between surprised and horrified flitted across her face. I dug my hands into my pockets, despite that there was nowhere else for them to go. I hadn't expected her to jump for joy, but I didn't think she'd look at me like it was the worst idea she'd ever heard.

"Holt," she said carefully.

I spun around, pretending to inspect something behind me. I couldn't look at her when she told me no. Until this moment, I didn't realize how much her answer meant to me. Which was insane. We'd been roommates for weeks. This boundary that separated friendship and something more had barely been breached.

But when I'd found this place, I'd immediately thought of her. I'd wondered if she would even want something like this, was nervous to show it to her. Cosmetics and car repair didn't exactly go hand in hand, but that hadn't mattered.

My entire adult life had been one impulsive move after another. The decision to go to Wyoming for college. To be a park ranger. Coming back to New York. Moving in with Baker. This place.

I never thought things through, I just ran from whatever problems plagued me. But I was quickly burning through places to run. The city was where my family was. Even if it hurt being in the same vicinity of my mother, it was equally painful being away from Dad, Andrew, Marlow, and Blake.

When I'd set foot in this space, it felt right. Then again, Wyoming had felt that way too and it had turned to complete and utter shit. I should know better than anyone that things didn't just fall into place, even though New York seemed to be doing just that.

Having my own business wouldn't be easy, but I'd been working on cars on the side for as long as I could remember. I'd made decent money as a ranger and mechanic, lived modestly, and had enough saved where this wouldn't sink me. I might have to scrimp while I restored the building and built up a clientele, but it wasn't impossible. Hard. But definitely doable.

And I wanted Baker to see what I saw here.

"We could be the kind of place where women are comfortable to come get their car repaired and not feel like they need a man with them. Where they know they won't be taken advantage of. And the ones that wait might like to see your makeup." I was rambling, yet couldn't seem to shut up. It kept her from flat out rejecting me. Because I didn't think I could take that.

I wandered over to the space customers would see and pointed to the long wall. "Here. We could display your products." It was easy to envision one of those lit up counters like at a department store. "A mirrored wall might be nice."

I turned to look at Baker. She was rooted in the same spot, staring at me with an unreadable expression. My confidence took a nose dive. I'd hoped if she saw this place, the potential, that she'd share my vision.

"What about your job in Wyoming?"

I swallowed hard. That was about the last thing I'd expected out of her mouth. "I had no idea you were so anxious to get rid of me."

The bitterness of my words caught me off guard. I'd never given it a second thought to show her this place. Lay out my dreams. Even if she didn't want any part of it, I'd wanted her to see me. Wanted her opinion first, even before my family.

"You're the one who keeps saying you're on leave. I take that to mean this is temporary," she said curtly.

"Does this look temporary to you?" I spread my arms wide.

"Looks to me like a man who doesn't know where he wants to be."

"What are you talking about?" I stared at her incredulously, though her words had a ring of truth in them. One I was going to ignore. At some point I had to stop running. "I'm showing you what I see for the future. I'm not the one who doesn't know that they want."

Her shoulders rounded and she folded her arms around her middle. Damn it. I couldn't stand it when she tried to hide from me. Like I was the enemy.

I crossed the space that separated us in quick strides. "Easy, I already signed the papers. I want to be in New York. As strange as it may seem, I like my roommate. And I could see us . . . moving apartments. Staying here rather than where we are now."

I'd sworn I'd never be vulnerable again, but something about her made me stop thinking. Deep down, I was tired of running. With roots—property, a business, her—I couldn't just pack up and leave on a whim.

"So I'm just supposed to go along. The decision's already been made." The disappointment she felt in me was palpable. I just didn't understand it.

"This place feels right." I wanted to reach for her, but she was too far away despite standing right in front of me. "It seemed perfect. Soon you'll outgrow the apartment. You won't be able to make the quantities of product you'll need." I couldn't stop myself from peeling her hands away from her body and taking them in mine. "If this isn't the right place, then we'll find somewhere you like."

"You already signed the papers," she said.

"This will be my shop. I meant if it wasn't the right space for you to build your empire, then we'd find somewhere that is."

"Empire?" she squeaked.

I squeezed her hands. "Empire."

"It's just a hobby. I don't know what I'm doing."

These moments of vulnerability were night and day from the woman who put lipstick on me without asking. I liked the soft side of Baker, but I wanted her to have confidence in her abilities. I certainly did.

"I don't know what I'm doing, either."

"You know how to fix a car. Trish told me about what you did for Delores."

Something strange happened when she took up for me. I liked it. More than I should.

"That's the easy part. I don't know how to run a business. Be a property owner. Find customers."

"I'm beginning to question if you know how to fix a bathroom too."

I pressed my lips together to keep from smiling and pulled her against me. "Oh yeah?"

"First it was just the shower that was broken. Now it's the toilet. I'm not sure I should let you in my bathroom anymore." There she was. The one who let stuff roll off her back. The one who had no problem using me as a guinea pig.

"Can't have it both ways, Easy. Either you live with me smelling like a grease monkey or you let me use our shower."

"Our shower? There is no *our*."

"Sure, there is. We're both using it."

She slapped at my chest, but at least she was smiling now. "All right, Grease Monkey. Show me around."

AFTER WE'D WANDERED the entire space, she swiped off some of the dirt from the front counter. "I think you might be on to something about a repair shop that's friendly to women." She glanced around what could be the waiting area for customers. "I remember my mom feeling like she'd been screwed by a mechanic. She never took the car into the shop again."

She rarely mentioned any family. I wanted to ask more. When had that happened? Was she close with them at some point? They didn't seem to be now.

"Did it ever happen to you?" If it had, it wouldn't again under my watch, but we could draw off of her experiences to make things better for customers.

She looked embarrassed. "I've never had a car. Never had a license."

"My dad and brother haven't had cars in years. I don't know if either of them have a driver's license either," I said, trying to make her feel better. There was nothing to be ashamed of. Our conversation had been going so well I didn't want to derail that, so I carried on. "I want a reputation of being honest and fair."

"That'll come with time." She wandered over to the long wall where I'd suggested her cosmetic counter go. "What if we made an inviting space for customers? Maybe modern with a touch of femininity. And we need to make sure there are plenty of power outlets and USB ports for easy charging of electronic devices. Oh, and a tea and coffee station too."

"I like it." I moved over to her and tried to see things through her eyes. "That should be the first project. The inviting customer space."

Baker grinned at me. "You could also talk to Mrs. Quinn to see if one of the girls at Paths has customer service experience. She could be your eventual office manager, part-time, but also be the first face customers see." How did she keep surprising me with her intelligence? Cleverness. "Although . . . shouldn't we get the equipment you need to fix cars first?"

"I suppose that would be the place to start." I rubbed my chin as if considering.

"Holt?"

"Yeah, Easy?"

Her eyes were wary when she looked at me. "Isn't this going to be expensive?"

"Yeah. But if we go in stages, it's doable. We'll do the garage and where the customers will see. The back office can wait. The apartment isn't pressing at the moment. And the other space"—I met her gaze— "is up to you."

She didn't say anything for a long time, simply taking in the garage.

Had I made a mistake showing her my dream? Including her?

"I—I don't have the money to set up an operation here. It takes every spare cent just to get the materials I need." She looked uncertain.

Admiration filled me. She didn't give herself enough credit for what she'd accomplished.

"I'm not asking for any money from you," I said. "I'm sorry if I gave you that impression."

"I can't let you pay for this." Her protest was almost feral. "I don't want another handout."

I recoiled. "It's not a handout." I wasn't entirely sure why I wanted to help her reach her dreams, whatever they may be, but I did. Even if it meant sacrificing something I needed for my own business.

She released a long breath. "I don't let myself think about this beyond making lip gloss in the living room."

Why? The question was on the tip of my tongue. It was the perfect time to find out more about the inner workings of the woman who intrigued me.

"And for now, that will remain the same. You have your job at the magazine, and the makeup is your side project. Down the road, you might want to make that your main focus. Why don't we keep options open?"

"That makes sense." She paused as if digesting my words. "One of the women from Paths, she's an apprentice to an interior designer," she said before I had a chance to open my mouth. "Oh, and Leesa's working with an architect. Do we need an architect?"

Her newfound enthusiasm was an abrupt change, but I'd take it. Maybe it meant she'd warm up to the idea of the building being ours.

I shrugged. "I'm not sure."

"Maybe they'll help us. I'll go by there on the way home."

Her enthusiasm was contagious, but that wasn't what filled me with that strange feeling which only happened around Baker. "That would be great. If they would help *us*."

She blushed, but lifted her chin. "There's a lot of potential here."

I wasn't so sure we were just talking about the garage. "I think so too."

CHAPTER TEN

BAKER

"ARE YOU GOING TO TELL THEM?"

I slipped my hand into the crook of Holt's arm after he locked the door to his new garage.

He tensed, his expression wary when he glanced at me. "Normally, my family would be the first to know." He stopped walking and turned to face me. "Is this crazy? Do you think it'll work?"

"Only one way to find out."

He searched my eyes, and my heart beat in triple time. I clutched his arm and confidence filled him.

"It's going to be hard for a while. Especially without my steady salary. But this lady came into Ed's the other day. A garage down the road tried to screw her and I just—I want somewhere people can come and be confident they're getting what they pay for." He covered my hand with his. "When I saw the building, it felt like my chance to do that."

I barely knew Holt, but his heart—he was a decent man. It would be nice to be part of something worthwhile, even if I didn't deserve to be.

We strolled along the sidewalk in no hurry. I took in the neighborhood, noticing Holt's building was in the worst shape. An eyesore, if I was completely honest. But the place had good bones.

I wanted the space upstairs with a vengeance. And I was still reeling from the fact he had me in mind when he bought it. We were nothing more than roommates, yet it seemed as if we were headed toward something bigger. A something neither of us had expected. I wasn't sure either of us were truly ready for it.

Once again, it seemed that choices about my life were being made for me. I'd vowed to never let it happen again. This was different than it had been with Kyle. Holt wasn't trying to manipulate me into doing something I didn't want.

I flicked my eyes to an elderly man and woman on the opposite side of the street. Their position mirrored ours. *How long have they been together? What have they survived? What would it take to make it that long?*

Trust.

A whole lot of trust. Which was the one thing Holt and I would never have. Not when I couldn't tell him the truth about who I was. When I couldn't trust his motives, not because he wasn't genuine, but because I'd always have a little kernel of suspicion in the back of my mind, especially when it came to men.

I'd meant what I told him. Men manipulated. I was evidence of it. I'd never had a driver's license, for God's sake, because Kyle wouldn't let me. If I couldn't get over what was ingrained in my head—which I wouldn't—then we weren't going anywhere.

"We had pizza last night. I didn't think we'd be going to Dino's."

I lifted a shoulder and lowered it. "I could eat pizza every day."

He grinned. "Me too."

"Is Marlow going to be here?"

Holt held open the door to Dino's, and I stepped inside.

"Never know with my sister."

He took my hand and led me toward the same table we'd sat at when I'd come with Trish. Everyone was here, except Mrs. Quinn. The surprise guest was Patrick, who was seated next to Marlow. Her wine glass was already nearly empty.

"Did you know Patrick was coming?"

"Nope."

"Think he invited himself?"

"If he thought it would rub Marlow the wrong way, definitely."

"I'll take my whiskey hand delivered," Patrick said to Andrew. Holt's brother looked over his shoulder and made a face. "Roommates to lovebirds in less than six months."

"I'll have it to you by the weekend."

Apparently they'd made a bet on what would happen between Holt and me. *Would any of us ever grow up?*

"Why are you here?" Holt asked before first kissing Ella and then Trish on top of the head.

"Considering Andrew and Trish are practically married and this is the Dixon family Sunday dinner, I'd say that explains itself." Patrick pointed at Ella. "You know she can't talk, right?"

"I meant you." Holt stuck out his tongue at him.

"If I'm not family, I don't know who is."

Andrew laughed and shook his head. "He invited himself."

Patrick clutched his heart. "All of you want me here."

"Especially my sister," Holt said, squeezing Marlow's shoulders. She flipped him off.

"Could we limit obscene gestures to the confines of our homes?" Mr. Dixon stood. He bent and kissed my cheek. "Hello, love. Glad you could make it."

"I wouldn't miss this for anything."

I grinned at him, and a satisfied smile spread across his face.

"Son." He reached around me to shake Holt's hand, so much meaning in just that one word.

I looked back at Holt, who gave nothing away. "Dad." He pulled him in for a hug. "I thought you might've invited Mrs. Quinn. Maybe patched things up."

Mr. Dixon scowled.

"Don't start," Marlow said. "I already asked, and he won't say a thing."

I had no idea what was going on, only that Mrs. Quinn and Mr.

Dixon both seemed miserable now that they weren't speaking. Her absence was notable, and I missed her in general. I'd promised Holt I'd go by the shelter to rally some help with the garage, but I hoped to catch Mrs. Quinn too.

I dropped into the empty seat next to Patrick, and Holt took the one beside me.

"Sandwiched between two beautiful women. Life doesn't get any better." Patrick flashed me a disarming grin. One I found myself mirroring back. I tried to wipe it off my face, but couldn't.

"Hands to yourself," Holt warned.

He held his up in surrender. "I see she's your woman."

"I am not his woman," I blurted out, instantly wishing I could take it back.

A flash of hurt crossed Holt's face, but he quickly smoothed it over. "She's her own woman."

Everyone around the table relaxed as if they'd braced themselves for a fight between us.

"No. She's yours. Even if she doesn't know it yet." Marlow took a healthy swig of wine and stared at both of us unapologetically.

"How many glasses have you had? Cause you're veering into territory that isn't your business," Holt said as if he barely had control of his temper.

His sister snorted. "Please. There's no such thing as privacy in this family."

"Then why don't we talk about Jack?"

"Holt." Andrew gave him a look to shut his mouth.

Marlow pushed up from the table, her chair scraping as she did. "You're an asshole."

She stormed toward the bathroom.

"Should I go check on her?" Trish asked.

"No. I will." Patrick bolted from the chair and followed the same path as Marlow.

"You crossed a line," Mr. Dixon said, leveling Holt with a look.

"She keeps it all bottled in. Like if she doesn't talk about it, nothing happened." Holt straightened in his chair, his tone defensive.

"That's her choice."

"She's my sister. I'm not gonna sit here and let her keep rotting from the inside out," he said through his teeth. "*That* would make me an asshole."

"She's still hurting. You know that." Andrew took Trish's hand as if he needed the support.

"Yeah, and I can't stand it. I lived with her a few weeks, remember? I've cried more in my life than she has, but I heard her every night. So if you two want to keep skirting the issue, fine. But I can't keep watching my big sister slowly die." Holt glanced around behind us. "What does it take to get a drink around here?"

He shoved out of his chair and went straight to the bar.

"You're all right," I said, the two Dixon men blinking at me with the same surprise I felt. I should stay out of this, yet I couldn't help myself.

"I agree." Trish backed me up, and I gave her a grateful smile.

"This isn't the time or place to dredge it up," Mr. Dixon said with a sigh. He looked toward the restrooms and clenched his fist around the stem of his wine glass. "It kills me to see my little girl hurting."

"Wonder where she learned to keep it all in?" There was no malice in Holt's tone as he dropped back into his seat.

He slid a glass of red wine toward me and took a long pull from his beer.

"If she doesn't come back soon, we're all gonna have to go get her out of that bathroom," Andrew said, looking like he was ready to do just that.

"Here she comes." Trish pointed her head behind me.

Neither Marlow nor Patrick appeared particularly happy as they returned to the table. She plunked back down in her seat and gave us all a glare to keep our mouths shut. Everyone except Holt. She refused to look at him.

"This wasn't the place to bring him up," Holt said.

The look she fired at him was nothing short of lethal. "Then why are you doing it again?"

"Because I love you."

She fisted her napkin in her lap, her pain palpable. "I love you too." The words were spoken through gritted teeth, but the truth was in them.

"How's the makeup line going?" Mr. Dixon leaned forward and looked at me.

I shifted in my seat, surprised and pleased by his interest in me. I'd always felt invisible with my own family. We'd been lucky if we sat down at the holidays. Both of my parents had high-ranking government jobs and that was all they cared about. I'd have given anything for this kind of attention.

"Pretty good. I'm still learning, trying to find my footing."

"The women at Paths can't get enough. And I can't keep the lip gloss in stock on my truck." Trish beamed at me.

"Have you formed a company yet?" Patrick popped a piece of a garlic knot into his mouth. "I know a good lawyer to set you up." He winked at me.

"I thought that was a Dixon move." I winked back.

He shrugged. "Guess it is."

My breath caught at the implication. I wasn't a Dixon. And neither was he.

"No, I haven't even thought of it. It's just a hobby," I brushed off.

"Don't do that." Holt gripped my thigh.

"What?"

"Diminish your business. Maybe it's small now, but you're going places." His expression was so open and honest, I had to look away. I craved his confidence in me, but it was too much.

"Want me to give out samples to the women at church?"

All eyes went to Marlow.

"You go to church?" Andrew asked incredulously.

"Sometimes." She stole the remains of a garlic knot off Patrick's bread plate.

We all stared at her like we'd never seen her before.

"I'd like to go with you." Mr. Dixon gave his daughter a soft smile.

"Sure. I'll let you know."

"I'll come too."

Now everyone looked at Holt like he was a stranger.

"Might as well text the memo," Andrew said.

"Leave me out of it." Patrick held up both of his hands.

"You scared you might disintegrate if you set foot inside a church?" Marlow cut her eyes over to him before she polished off the rest of her bread.

"I can't rule it out as a possibility."

Holt snorted. "Anyone ever notice how we end up in the strangest conversations at Sunday dinner?"

A server delivered mozzarella sticks, bruschetta, and stuffed mushrooms to the table.

"Considering you've missed most of them in the last decade, I don't think you're an authority in that arena." Marlow scooped a few mushrooms onto her plate as she delivered the dig. She lifted her gaze to Holt. "What did you and Celia talk about at your Sunday dinners?"

Holt tensed beside me. *Who is Celia? And why does she elicit this reaction from Holt?*

"Marlow." Mr. Dixon's searing tone cut across the table. All movement ceased.

"Oh, he can bring up—" She swallowed hard, unable to finish her sentence.

"Tit for tat is not how this family operates," their father scolded.

"No, we just go straight in for the kill." Marlow held up her wineglass to a passing waitress.

"Actually, avoidance is what we do best." Andrew dunked a mozzarella stick into marinara sauce.

"Enough," Mr. Dixon admonished.

An uncomfortable silence enveloped the table. Trish and I exchanged helpless looks, uncertain what to do or say.

Holt drained his beer and immediately began to peel the edge of the label. He concentrated on the bottle and left his plate of appetizers untouched.

I moved my hand to his thigh before I thought better of it. It pained me to see him so upset, but I didn't know if he wanted my comfort.

. . .

THE REMAINDER of the meal didn't get any better. Awkward silence stifled my appetite. No one was really eating. Mostly we pushed food around on our plates. But I'd take that any day over no family dinner at all.

Mr. Dixon settled the bill and stood. "I want this stuff cleared up by next Sunday at dinner."

Marlow tossed her napkin on the table. "I don't know if we're coming."

Hurt flashed in her father's eyes. He bent to pick up Blake and cradled him to his chest. Mr. Dixon simply nodded once.

"Why do you do that?" Holt glared at Marlow. "This is the only thing Dad wants from us and you can't give him a couple hours of your time."

"I'm not the one who ran away to Wyoming. You're really not in a position to lecture me." She slung her bag onto her shoulder.

"Just because you're miserable doesn't mean you have to make the rest of us that way," he said, his voice rising.

She shoved in her chair and rounded the table, prying her now crying son from Mr. Dixon's arms. "If it weren't for you, we'd have had a mother at all these Sunday dinners you missed."

Whoa. That was unbelievably harsh.

Holt recoiled.

"Marlow." Andrew had been mostly silent, letting his siblings argue, but I'd never heard such a severe tone.

"Why don't you say what you really mean?" Holt asked as if his brother hadn't interjected.

"What? That it's your fault Mom left us. Or that you should have stayed on the other side of the country. Because I could go with either."

"That's enough," Mr. Dixon hissed, stepping between the two of them.

Holt's fists clenched at his sides as he glowered at his sister. Hurt and anger radiated from him, but he held his tongue.

I touched his arm, and he flinched. "Let's go," I said softly.

For a moment, he didn't move. I gripped his bicep and gently tugged. Holt relented and stormed toward the door without a word to anyone else. I gave Trish a look over my shoulder, conveying we'd talk later. She nodded once, her hands knotted in front of her.

"You okay?" As soon as I said the words, I wanted to take them back.

"Why wouldn't I be?" Holt asked stiffly.

His strides were long and quick. I struggled to keep up, somehow holding on as he led me down the street.

"A lot of awful things were said back there."

"Truth hurts, doesn't it?"

CHAPTER ELEVEN

HOLT

BAKER WANTED TO PUSH.

I felt it.

Yet somehow she kept from doing it. I was too pissed off to fully appreciate that.

I unlocked the door to the apartment, held it open for her, and shut it with a satisfying slam. The one beer I'd had at dinner didn't even scratch the surface of my need. I went straight to the fridge and pulled out two bottles.

I untwisted the cap, offering it to Baker. Reluctantly, she accepted. I opened my own and downed half of it in one swallow.

She stared at me as I wiped my mouth with the back of my hand.

"Whatever it is you want to say, now's not the time," I warned.

She bristled before she straightened. "If you want to talk about it, I'm here. If you don't, I'm here too."

I flashed a saccharine smile across the kitchen at her. "You know what I want? A long, hot shower. If you want to join me, I won't lock the door."

Her lips parted, a satisfying little gasp of air escaping. She didn't bother to remind me that I still hadn't repaired the door and it *couldn't* lock. I polished off my beer and set the empty bottle on the counter. My eyes dared her to follow me before I shoved off the cool granite.

As I moved down the hall, I shed my shirt. Damn my sister. She'd be the first to admit she was a bitch, but this was a new low. I'd never once doubted our relationship. Now?

I didn't know where we went from here. Sure, we fought like all siblings. We'd both said things we didn't mean before. But I'd never seen today coming. She'd never attacked so viciously. Why now after all these years?

I pushed my jeans and boxers off my hips. Her words were on replay in my head, and even as I dipped my head under the lukewarm spray of the shower, I couldn't turn them off.

"Goddammit." I pounded my fist on the wall.

Anger had made me lose my mind. I never should have said those things to Baker. Hell, it was the truth. I wanted her wet, naked body in this shower with me. Needed to hear her scream my name until my sister's voice was muted.

Instead, I was stuck in a perpetual hell where Marlow had confirmed my worst fears. What my father would never admit.

They all blamed me for my mother's departure.

I hadn't been able to stay in Wyoming, but I shouldn't have come back here. Where I wasn't wanted.

I wasn't wanted there, either. Celia and I hadn't had Sunday dinners. We'd done Saturday nights with our best friend Cameron. Grilling out. Beers on the tailgate by the creek. It had all been perfect. And Marlow knew what had happened, even if I'd never talked about how I felt. For her to use that against me . . . in front of Baker? For the first time ever, the stirrings of loathing for my sister swirled. It was an emotion I was all too familiar with.

I braced both hands on the wall in front of me and let the spray rain down on my back. My breaths were harsh as I pulled air in and pushed it out of my lungs.

A soft thud of the shower door made me stiffen. She stepped behind me. The water splashing on the tiled floor was the only sound.

I sensed her movement and closed my eyes.

"If you don't want me to touch you, then get out now, Easy," I ground out through clenched teeth.

Her fingers splayed on my back, and I hissed at the contact. Fire blazed up my spine. I was torn between reaching behind me and holding her hands in place and throwing them off of me. She shouldn't do this to me now. Not in the state I was in.

Her lips drifted up my back, and I pressed my hands into the wall so hard I was certain I'd crack the stone. I fought the urge to turn, pin her against the wall, and fuck her senseless. Through the haze of anger, my desperation to see what her next move would be won out.

She peppered soft, tender kisses on my skin as her hands explored. They cascaded over my sides, around to my abdomen, up my chest. She was everywhere at once, too much and yet not enough.

Her body pressed into mine, and I groaned when her teeth grazed the back of my neck. She wrenched me closer. Hard beads of her nipples surrounded by soft flesh pushed into my back. The woman was trying to kill me, my restraint already dead.

Her hands skated down my stomach. I grabbed her wrists just before she reached my dick, holding her in place. She gasped, and I exhaled heavily.

"Are you sure about this? Because once I start, I won't stop. Not today. Not tomorrow. Not—"

"*Yes.*" She emphasized the point by kissing my shoulder.

"I want to see you." My voice sounded gruff to my own ears.

I released my hold on her, and she eased around, squeezing between me and the wall. Her eyes were clear as she looked up at me. I forgot everything else for a minute.

"I'm sorry and I'm not sorry about the other day. The shower. I didn't have the right, but damn it woman."

"Do I seem mad?" Her hands drifted up my chest and locked around the back of my neck.

"I don't normally do that." I couldn't find the proper words to explain.

One corner of her mouth curved up. "I'm glad to hear that."

My lips mirrored hers, an overwhelming feeling of *something* came over me. I dropped my forehead to hers. "I need you. So goddamn much."

The confession tumbled out, and I had no desire to take it back. Just being close to her . . . it was more than I'd ever had.

I tried to hold on to the remaining thread of my control.

It snapped.

My mouth crash-landed on hers. She tasted like her lip gloss, honey and sugar and perfection. I caged her in with my body as she pulled me closer at the same time.

Her whimper had my already hard dick stiffening between us. I rocked against her as I captured her mouth. Or hell, the truth was, she captured me.

Everything inside of me swelled as she clung to me like she couldn't get enough. Her tongue fought to get to mine. Her hands held me like she'd never let me go.

I couldn't stand not touching her a second longer. My fingers stroked her hair with a reverence I didn't know I was capable of. As my mouth ravaged hers, my hands memorized every inch of her that they touched. She shivered as they skimmed her sides, down her hips. This woman, enigma that she was, deserved to be worshipped. Like Trish, she'd probably overcome something far from trivial to end up at Paths. I wanted to be the man to help her . . . whatever she needed. I was more than happy to be the man to do it.

I feathered kisses along her jaw, nipped at the column of her neck. She leaned her head back against the wall, yielding to my touch.

"So pretty," I murmured against her skin.

I bent, sucking a nipple between my teeth and flicking it with my tongue. Her breasts were heavy in my hands. I kneaded them as I licked and grazed. My name fell from her lips, and I loved it.

Her fingers tangled in my hair, urging me south even as she held me against her chest. She wanted everything, and I was going to give it to her.

I tilted my hips and nearly came undone as my hard length slid through her slick folds. "Feel what you do to me, Easy?"

She grabbed my wrist and pressed my hand against her sex. "Feel what you do to me?"

I'd planned to take my time, but as soon as my fingers touched her smooth skin, I couldn't. I ran my index finger up her slit, and her knees buckled. I caught her by the hip, and she gripped my shoulders.

Her clit was swollen. The hiss of pleasure as I circled it nearly sent me over the edge. I slid my finger through her folds, teased the tight entrance to her sex, and pushed inside.

"Holt."

Hips bucked. Fingernails dug into my back. That beautiful face relaxed in ecstasy.

Because of me.

I crooked my finger, pressing against the rough flesh of her inner walls. An intense cry pierced the air. Her lips parted, and I couldn't resist a taste. I kissed the edge of her mouth as I slid my finger out of her and slowly pushed it back in.

Her body melted into me as I pumped, adding a second digit to her tight pussy. Those bright green gems glazed over as I drew her closer to the edge.

I dropped to my knees without missing a beat. Her clit throbbed as I sucked it between my lips. She tensed before all her energy released on a low moan.

Baker trembled. I withdrew my fingers and extended them toward her face. "Suck."

Her eyes widened, but she clasped my wrist in her delicate hands and lowered her head. She darted her tongue out and flicked it over the tip of my finger.

I buried my face against her wet heat, though I kept my eyes locked on hers. She popped my finger in her mouth. I slipped my tongue inside of her. My first taste of her had my dick so hard I thought I'd come all over myself.

Easy sucked on my finger and my dick wept in protest. The urge to bury myself deep inside of her became almost impossible to ignore, but I forced myself to focus on her. She'd come by my mouth before we left this shower.

She chanted my name. I'd never heard a sweeter sound. Never tasted anything better. I'd been addicted before I ever touched her. Now, she owned me.

"How?" The question was a breathy rasp. Her eyelids were leaded as she watched me in fascination.

I didn't stop to answer, fueled by the twinge of pain in my scalp where she fisted my hair. I licked her from ass to clit before delving back into her.

"Falling," she whispered as she came on my tongue.

I lapped until my face was coated in her, and it still wasn't enough. My fingers dug into the flesh of her ass, holding her to me. She lifted her hips, begging me for more with her body.

I kissed her sex until her orgasm receded. She sagged, her weight on me for support. My lips trailed up her stomach, her sternum, her neck, until I reached her mouth. I claimed it, and she yielded.

I cupped her face and tenderly touched my lips to hers. "So perfect."

Her mouth curved into a satisfied smile. "Is that what you planned when you stormed into my shower?"

"I may have thought about it once or twice." I winked, and she snickered.

Making her come had nearly made me forget about my cock, but when she laughed, I quickly remembered.

"Are you going to make a habit of it?"

"Absolutely."

She pressed on her toes and stole a kiss. A warmth spread over me from the inside out that I didn't understand. I only knew it was unique to her.

Her grin was pure seduction when she peeled her lips from mine. "My turn."

She slid down the wall to her knees before I could stop her. "Baker . . ." All thoughts died when she took me in her hands and flicked her tongue in my leaking slit. "Shit."

Her lips closed around the head of my dick, those doe eyes staring up at me as she pumped my shaft. Jesus. I wasn't going to last long. Not with her on her knees, my fantasies come to life.

"That mouth . . ."

She bobbed, taking me a little deeper every time. One of her hands cupped my balls while the other jacked me off. "You're spoiling me, Easy," I rasped as I hit the back of her throat.

Her teeth grazed my sensitive length as she released me. She sucked on the head before plunging down again. Her eyes never left mine.

Powerful.

That was what this connection was between us.

I caressed her cheek and thrust my hand out to the wall for support. Like an avalanche, my orgasm built, starting in the backs of my thighs. Lightning raced up my spine. My balls drew up and my dick swelled.

"Do you want it? In that pretty mouth?"

She sucked harder, faster until I exploded into her mouth with a grunt. My hips pumped until I was spent, and she swallowed everything I had to give like she couldn't get enough.

I dropped down to the floor and scooped her into my arms. She settled against me, and I kissed the top of her head.

Her fingers traced a pattern on my stomach, and I prayed she'd never stop touching me. Lukewarm water sprayed our legs. I had to get her out of there before it turned cold, but couldn't find the energy to move.

She scraped a fingernail down my chest. "You're gonna be so late for work every day."

CHAPTER TWELVE

BAKER

I'D LOST my mind getting in that shower with him.

But I couldn't stand his pain and wanted to do anything to stop it, even at the risk of my own psyche.

I was more attracted to Holt than I'd ever been to another man. I hadn't expected *that*. The power of his touch. The intensity of the orgasms he gave. The addictive taste of him.

As I lay in his arms, back in his bed for the third night in a row, I couldn't find it in me to get up. I didn't want to. Here, I was safe and anything but, all at the same time. I'd known he was risky. That I'd get caught up in him in an instant if I didn't watch it.

I'd been careful, and it still wasn't enough.

The second I'd stepped into the shower, he'd become everything. Holt was all I could see, but his pull on me was a thousand—a million —times worse than Kyle's. I wanted more nights like this.

More mornings like the last two.

More showers.

More roommate nights.

More family dinners, even if they turned to shit like the one tonight.

I wanted that empty warehouse with his garage on the bottom

floor and my shop upstairs. I wanted to remodel that apartment. Fight over paint colors. Have make-up sex in another shower—one that belonged to us.

I wanted it all. I wanted it with Holt and only Holt. *Which was so dangerous.*

But this was exactly how I ended up so broken. Because I couldn't see past Kyle. Couldn't stand on my own two feet.

I thought I'd made headway. The internship. The makeup line. A friendship with Trish. An honorary aunt to Ella.

Holt had sucked me in from the second he'd given me that lazy smirk and called me easy on the eyes. Despite my best effort, I'd never escaped his vortex. I should have known that the second I lost my mind when he didn't come home.

He shifted beside me, a possessive hand splayed across my back even in his sleep.

"Easy." His voice was rough as he pried his eyes open. "You okay?"

The concern that met me twisted my soul into a heart-shaped knot.

"Yeah." I touched his cheek. "Go back to sleep."

The semblance of a smile I offered was enough to placate him. He rolled onto his back and pulled me on top of him.

"Holt."

He ran his fingers up and down my spine. I closed my eyes and rested my head on his solid chest. Just one more night. Or maybe two. Or maybe I could do a few nights and not lose myself.

I held him a little too tightly. No. It was already happening. My mind was already altered because of him. I wasn't strong enough to stop it, so after tonight—no, tomorrow—I'd have to distance myself. Which was going to be nearly impossible since I lived with him.

"Don't tell me you're okay when you're not."

"I'm—"

"Your heart is going at a million miles an hour."

"I just can't sleep. It's nothing." This was the lie I'd been telling for nearly three years. It was stale and bitter on my tongue.

"I'd prefer you tell me you don't want to talk about it than lie to me." He sounded more awake now, his voice somber.

"Today. It was . . ." I was uncertain how to put it all into words.

The garage.

The dinner.

The shower.

The feelings.

"Yeah. It was." He drew circles on my lower back with one hand and massaged my scalp with the other.

"Why'd your sister get so angry with you at dinner?"

Holt tensed. "Jack, her husband, was killed in Afghanistan. She'd told him she was pregnant the day before."

The way she'd lashed out made more sense. How could anyone get over that?

"At least he knew he was going to be a dad." That was a stupid thing to say. A boy would never know his father. A wife would never get over losing her husband.

"That's what I said when I found out. Marlow didn't take too well to a positive spin."

We were quiet for a long moment, a heaviness in the air. There was nothing to make the situation any better.

"It's killing her. She loves Blake, but I don't think it's enough." He wrapped both arms around me and buried his nose in my hair. "I shouldn't have brought him up. Not like that."

"You don't want her to hurt anymore."

"No. I'd take his place in a heartbeat if it would take her pain away. My nephew deserves a dad."

"And what about you? Don't you deserve a life?"

"He was a great guy. Looked after Marlow. Made her happy. He'd have been a great father too. Jack was more of a man than I ever hope to be." A hint of self-loathing I'd never heard before from Holt tainted his words.

"Nobody's perfect."

"Well, he was damn close. Died fighting for his country. That takes the kind of guts I'd never have."

"Bravery comes in a lot of different forms," I said quietly.

He gently moved me off him and onto the mattress. "I need some water. You want anything?"

"No."

Holt picked up his sweatpants off the floor and pulled them up over his hips. Instead of heading toward the kitchen, he crossed the hall to my bedroom. I rolled over on my side to face the door.

IN A FEW MINUTES HE EMERGED. I expected him to return immediately with a bottle of water, but as I waited, my lids grew too heavy to keep them open. The bed was cold without him.

And so was I.

CHAPTER THIRTEEN

HOLT

I'D JUST GRABBED my keys off the kitchen counter when Baker appeared.

Her hair was in that messy bun. She wore only my T-shirt, and my eyes betrayed me, running up the length of her body, when I was supposed to be headed for the door.

Damn it.

"Trying to sneak off?"

She flashed me a teasing grin, but there was uncertainty in her voice. Well there should be because, yes, I was most definitely sneaking off.

"I need to be on time. Knew if you ended up in the shower with me, I definitely wouldn't be." That was at least the truth.

She closed the distance between us and placed both hands on my chest. "I didn't pack your lunch yet."

My throat worked, and I felt what little control I had slipping as she stared up at me. I grasped the edge of the counter. If I touched her, it would be all over.

"Still spoiling me, Easy."

"Hmm. Seems to me I'm falling down on the job."

I white-knuckled the granite when all I wanted to do was rip that shirt straight down the middle.

"I gotta go." Even I didn't believe me. And I really did need to leave.

"Give me two minutes." She held up her fingers in a V.

I regretted the second her hands were off of me.

She sauntered over to the fridge and bent over in search of something inside. A peek of her ass cheeks teased me. Now that I knew what they felt like in my hands, I only wanted more.

"There ain't much in that refrigerator, Easy."

She tossed a look at me over the shoulder. "View not to your liking, Grease Monkey?"

"The view is most definitely not the problem."

She turned back around and resumed rummaging. "Oh no?"

"Nope. The problem is that I don't have time to show you how much I appreciate it."

Baker straightened and kicked the refrigerator door shut with her heel. "Then you better hurry up and become the boss so you'll have time to do whatever you want."

She turned her back to me and stuffed a box into a brown paper bag. She began to close it, abruptly stopped, grabbed a couple of bottled waters from the fridge, dropped them in the bag, then strutted back over to me.

She held it out to me, but didn't let go when I latched onto the fold.

"Thank you."

Her eyes smoldered. I was two seconds away from saying to hell with everything and staying home in bed with her.

"Have a good day."

I pulled on the bag and still she didn't let go.

"This for me or you?"

"You."

"You gonna let me have it?"

She smirked. "Depends."

"On what?"

"What you're willing to do to get it?"

I swallowed my groan. Anything. And she damn well knew it.

"Easy, if you want something from me, all you have to do is ask."

She cocked her head to the side. "I don't think I want to ask."

"I don't need you to anyway."

Her lips parted. I knew what she needed. Better than she did.

"I don't think I want something from you. I think I want to give you something."

I prepared myself for whatever she had in mind. Mischief was in those pretty eyes.

She rolled up on her toes, wound her arms around my neck, and kissed me like she'd never have the chance to again.

I dropped my lunch on the counter, hoisted her up by the hips, and set her beside it. She locked her ankles on my lower back. I threaded my fingers through the base of the knot on top of her head and slanted my mouth over hers.

Her moan vibrated through me. I deepened the kiss in response, unable to stop whatever this madness was.

She slid to the edge of the counter. I pressed my erection against her center, cursing the fabric that separated us. Baker fumbled with the zipper on my coveralls, had it halfway off my arms when I came to my senses.

I grabbed both of her wrists with one hand. "No time," I panted.

"I need you."

It was a soft plea that shot straight to my heart. How was I supposed to say no to that?

"Easy."

I was torn between my need to please her and going to work.

She buried her forehead against my chest. "Go to work," she mumbled.

Her legs fell to my sides, and she wrestled until I released her wrists. She straightened my coveralls while I looked on in irritation.

I clasped her face and kissed her hard. "I gotta go."

I snatched my lunch and slammed the door harder than necessary on the way out.

"Shit. Shit. Shit," I said as I stepped inside the elevator.

"Must be trying to live with a beautiful woman."

I snapped my head up to find Daniel Elliott propped against the wall. I held the lunch sack in front of my crotch. He smirked, knowing damn well what I was doing.

"You have no idea," I muttered.

"I've got a pretty good one."

His wife was stunning, and from what I'd seen, she didn't put up with any shit. But my landlords seemed happy. More than happy.

I grunted in response and stared at the mirrored wall ahead.

"Apartment okay?"

"Yeah. It's great. Baker and I both appreciate you letting us lease the place." Now I was speaking on her behalf? This shit was getting out of hand.

"Have you had a chance to work on the remodel?"

"Not yet. Can't seem to find the time."

"I'll have a plumber come by."

"No," I said quickly. One brow lifted. "I want to do it myself. Least I can do for the discounted rent."

"It's no problem."

"I'll take care of it," I insisted.

He shrugged. "Suit yourself. But if you change your mind—"

"I won't."

"Come for dinner soon. The invitation is standing. We start at six thirty."

I got the impression I wasn't meant to turn him down. "Sure thing. But I haven't been getting home until after seven lately. I'll tell Baker though."

"Let your family know too."

The elevator doors slid open, and he gestured for me to go first.

"Thanks."

"Would you like a ride?"

I glanced down at my stained coveralls. "No. I'm good. I appreciate it."

He nodded at the doorman as we exited onto the sidewalk. A black car was waiting at the curb.

"When it comes to your roommate, you might as well stop fighting it now. You'll save yourself a lot of trouble down the road."

"Fighting what?" I played dumb, and judging by his smirk, he saw right through it.

"Have it your way. But I promise, one way or the other, you'll end up with her."

"I can't imagine why you'd think that."

"Because I've been in your shoes. Doesn't matter how much you deny that you need her. The truth is the truth. And it always comes to light."

He slid into the back of the car, and I stared after it as the vehicle moved into traffic.

Denial.

I wasn't denying anything. I knew exactly what Baker did to me. The problem was I didn't know how to keep her.

She'd leave just like everyone else did.

"We drifted apart, Holt. You were always working."

I'd asked myself a million times if that were true. If the problems had been my fault. I didn't think so, but I wasn't totally sure.

Regardless of who was to blame, I'd been hurt, and I couldn't take it if Baker left me too. I'd planned to keep it casual, but that was shot to hell somewhere between the time I'd met her and when we'd agreed to be roommates.

"Fuck."

This morning . . . what man wouldn't want a send-off like that every day of his life? She was doing a lot more than spoiling me. Baker gave me hope for things that weren't possible. Not for me.

"THERE'S somebody here to see you." Ed jerked his thumb over his shoulder toward the office as soon as I stepped inside the bay.

"You recognize them?"

"A woman. That's all I know."

Baker? Nah. There was no way she beat me here.

Marlow? Maybe my sister wasn't as stubborn as I thought. I smiled at the thought of her coming to apologize. If she had, I'd let yesterday go. Give her an apology of my own.

The door squeaked when I moved from the garage to the waiting area. I froze in the doorway when she pivoted.

"Hello, son."

CHAPTER FOURTEEN

BAKER

"WHAT'S THIS ABOUT A MAKEUP LINE?"

I sat up straight at the architectural desk, layouts spread before me. Hayden leaned over my shoulder and pointed to one.

"That's quite good, don't you think?"

I turned to her and grinned. "It's my favorite."

My boss returned the smile. She was an icon in the publishing industry. She'd started the magazine while she was in college and built it from zero subscribers to the millions we had today. Hayden was tough, but she had respect for people I admired.

"Let's make that photo the cover."

"Already in my pile of possibilities." I moved it to the top corner of the desk to make sure it stayed separated.

"Let's get a coffee. We haven't had a chance to talk lately. Crazy busy, right?"

Her time was limited so when she gave me so much of it, it meant more than she knew.

"Always."

"I could use a change of scenery."

. . .

WE WALKED in silence a few blocks to the small coffee shop we frequented.

Hayden blew on her cappuccino before taking a sip. She looked at me over the mug, astute eyes studying me.

"The ladies at Paths are all abuzz about this makeup made by someone I *thought* would share it with me first."

I shifted uncomfortably in my seat, the heat on my cheeks nothing to do with the coffee. "I'm still testing. And Annmarie is the one who showed me how to make lip gloss. I've researched to expand into other things."

She rifled through her purse and pulled out a small container I recognized. "The product is good." She unscrewed the lid and dabbed her pinky into the shade I knew to be Grease Monkey. "The texture. Color. Longevity. Feel. It's all very good. Especially for something homemade."

She spread the gloss across her lower lip, and I realized she was already wearing it.

My mentor uses my cosmetics?

I blinked a few times in disbelief.

"How long does it take to produce this?"

"I'm making thirty at a time. I can do it in about a day."

"What's the shelf life?"

"Six months. The blush and mineral foundation don't expire as long as they don't get wet."

I'd researched every component that went into my products to make them the best they could be.

She rolled the round container in her fingers. "That's impressive. Let's have an independent lab verify. Never can be too careful, especially when it comes to potential lawsuits down the road. We'll have to get licensing. We can chat with my attorney about setting the business up as iron-clad as possible." Hayden smirked.

All that kind of thing seemed daunting. I didn't know where to start. "Everything I use is natural."

"Which is perfect. We have to figure out how to produce it on a larger scale. With the right branding, this has incredible potential. You've really got your finger on the pulse of what women want today."

I blushed. "The idea of making my own appealed to me. Turned out it was fun."

"You are your own consumer. We can use it as a backstory to grow the sense of community." The more she talked, the more animated she became. "What do you think about using the ladies of Paths as models?"

I slumped in my seat. "I don't know about that. Some would probably be okay with it, others . . ." *Like myself, not so much.*

She winced. "That was insensitive of me. I didn't think."

"No. It's okay. That place, the people, they mean everything to me. I'd love to involve them in any way possible, just maybe not so much in the public eye."

She nodded, but still looked uncertain. I covered her hand with mine, temporarily forgetting this woman was my mentor, a giant in our industry. For the moment, we were just two friends, making big plans.

"Okay. We'll keep an open mind about that." She took another sip of her coffee. "You've done some test marketing—"

"I haven't done much of anything," I interrupted, panic flooding me.

"Sure you have. The women at Paths are crazy about these products. Crazy enough to talk to strangers about it." She pointed to herself and grinned. "We need to sample more of the market, but indications are good."

"They want to support me." *Just like I would any of them.*

"You're too modest." She glanced at my barely touched coffee. I lifted it to my lips and took a long swallow. "Where do you want to place your product?"

"Umm . . ." The lobby of Holt's garage popped into my head. It didn't make sense to have beauty products in a garage, though I loved the idea of a boutique space. That took money I didn't have. An online store made the most sense, but I hadn't let myself think of that.

Having dreams of any kind wasn't something I deserved, yet I couldn't seem to help myself.

"How much are you selling the gloss for at Trish's food truck?" Hayden carried on before I could give a proper answer.

I gaped at her. How did she know all of this? "Two dollars."

Her mouth dropped open. "Two dollars? For this? You're losing money."

I had no idea. The point was the enjoyment I got out of making my own makeup. An image of Holt with lip gloss and powder on popped into my head. I liked my guinea pig too.

"Who did the logo?" Hayden forged ahead, examining the cap for the gloss.

"Cricket."

"The quiet girl?" I nodded. "She's talented. This is a great start."

"I told her to make something that conveyed natural and feminine."

"You've got the foundation. We just have to build on it. And I'm going to help you."

"You don't have to do that. Thank you, but you have the magazine and . . ."

Like yesterday, becoming overwhelmed sent me spiraling into a panic that closed my throat.

"I want to do this. I want to be part of it." She frowned. "Have I inserted myself here without invitation?"

"No. I'm grateful for your enthusiasm. I just—this has blown up into something I didn't expect." The confession lifted a weight off my chest.

Her expression softened. "Do you think I planned to build one of the most powerful magazines in the world?"

I nodded. Yes. I absolutely did.

A faraway look glazed her eyes as she glanced out the window. "I loved fashion. I loved products. I loved women's issues. And I loved to write. So I did it. Somewhere along the way, I discovered I had a knack for presenting all of those things."

She reached into her bag again and slid a worn out group of pages bound together by plastic comb binding.

"That's the first magazine I ever produced."

The photographs were cut out polaroids pasted onto a thick paper. The articles were done in the same fashion.

"Did you use a typewriter?" I asked, thumbing through the short magazine. It was rudimentary, but there was something about it I loved. The magazine now was just a glammed up version of this very thing.

"Early eighties, baby," she said with a grin. "When you look at that, do you see what we have today? No way. And neither did I."

"Maybe not, but this is the magazine." I paged through it again.

"That's the work of a kid who loved what she loved and thought other girls might too."

"It's obvious in these pages." I squinted at a photograph. "Is that you?"

"That's me." She motioned toward the image of her younger self. "Think I should do my hair that way again?"

"Yes. Definitely. If you do, the rest of the world will follow suit." I laughed and slid the magazine back over to her.

"My mother always told me to dream big. Truth is, I never really understood what she meant." She tapped the cover of her old magazine. "Not until much, much later. That's what this was. Except, it had more of hold on me than I did on it."

"That's exactly how I feel," I said quietly. And hearing Hayden talk about the inspiration her mother gave her . . . it connected so many dots. She'd been one of the first mentors to come speak at Paths. Afterward, I remember being nervous to approach her, but that had disappeared in seconds. We'd clicked, and if it weren't for her support, I wouldn't have made the progress I had. Sometimes I wondered if I'd still be hiding away in my room.

Her face turned somber. "I wouldn't give up the magazine for anything. It's me. Who I am. Without it, I'm not sure what's left." She fiddled with her coffee cup. "But that isn't right for everybody. And you'll have to give up some things you might not realize you didn't want to give up until it's too late."

The flash of pain in her eyes tore me apart. "I just like experimenting with the products. Seeing what a dash more honey adds or a bit less color. When I'm mixing up lip gloss, it quiets the noise."

"Knowing that will make it a lot easier to decide how to move forward so you have control of your brand instead of it controlling you."

"A friend of mine . . ." A streak of doubt slashed across my chest. "He-he bought an old building. One he wants to revitalize into a car garage. It has a huge upstairs space and—" I was at a loss for words, overwhelmed by what Holt had done.

"And?" Hayden asked the question like he hadn't suggested something life-changing.

"He offered it to me to make my products. He'd even mapped out a display area for them in his lobby." The magnitude of what he'd offered and that I'd immediately rejected it hit me hard.

"So what's the issue?"

Was it that easy to simply say yes to Holt's proposal? She seemed to think it was.

"When he showed it to me, it felt like he was taking away my choice. But now, I'm not so sure." I glanced out the window as confusion descended.

"Want my advice?"

"Please."

"Keep doing what you're doing. Keep tweaking, improving, loving what you do. You'll know if you want to push to the next level or stay where you are now."

I nodded. "That makes sense."

"Whatever you decide, I'm behind you. You have a place at the magazine, but if you want to pursue cosmetics, I'm with you as soon we have the lab verify it's safe."

"I'm happy right now." As I said it, I realized that was the truth.

"Let's chat about this again in . . . a month? Would that give you more time to see what sort of line you'd want to start with? Complete the products to be ready for testing?"

"I'd like that."

Gratitude for Hayden coming into my life filled me. Knowing I had her support and friendship eased my stress.

She grinned at me over her cup. "Now tell me about this man who's offering you space in his garage."

CHAPTER FIFTEEN

HOLT

"WHAT ARE YOU DOING HERE?"

Inwardly, I cursed at the nervous edge in my voice.

"I didn't know how else to reach you." My mother stayed rooted in her position by a worn-out chair and dusty end table littered with magazines that were at least five years old.

"How'd you find me?"

"You wouldn't answer my calls."

"Maybe I didn't want to talk." The words were hollow, even to my own ears. I'd wanted to speak to her all my life . . . more than anything.

She grasped the back of the chair, a gold bangle bracelet glinting in the light. Her pale pink slacks were pressed flat, the collar of her white blouse flipped up in a way she made work. My mother didn't look anywhere near the sixty-something she was. Somehow that disappointed me.

The life she'd left us for had obviously treated her well.

"I'd like to speak with you." She glanced around the space. "Somewhere more . . . private," she finally settled on. "Could we meet for lunch? Or dinner perhaps?"

"I don't know."

She'd presented the opportunity I'd been waiting for my whole life, yet I wasn't sure if I could take it. Sometimes the not knowing was better. She had the power to confirm my worst fears. I didn't think I could take being responsible for robbing my father of a wife and my siblings of their mother.

She reached in her purse and handed me a cream business card, a phone number the only thing written on it. "When you do know, you can reach me at this number."

Before I could respond, she disappeared, almost as if I'd dreamed up the whole thing.

"You know her?" Ed wiped his hands down the front of his coveralls. He and Dad had been friends for a long time, but post-divorce.

"Not really."

Not so long ago, I'd been determined to talk to *her*, even against Andrew's wishes. It was one of the reasons I'd returned to New York, to get the very chance she'd just given me. Had she stopped by because I'd reached out to her? If she were as eager to reconnect as I was, why did it take her so long? Months had gone by since I'd messaged her on social media.

I flicked the card in the trash. My brother was right. She'd abandoned us. That was her choice. Now I'd made mine.

"DID YOU SPEAK TO YOUR SISTER?"

Baker stood in the kitchen, already changed into my T-shirt and a pair of sweats. Her hair was piled on top of her head and her feet were bare. My first thought was strip her down and get lost so I didn't have to think about my family or the mess I'd made of my life.

Instead, I tossed my keys on the island and kept it between us. I didn't trust myself in the mood I was in.

"No." Sarcasm seeped into my voice.

When she opened her mouth to respond, I was 100 percent sure she'd press me on the topic.

I held up my hand. "Not now."

She stuck out her tongue. "I was going to tell you about my meeting with Hayden, but I think you need some time to chill on your own."

I shrugged off my leather jacket and unzipped my coveralls. Her eyes followed the motion. My body came to life.

"I need a shower. And something to eat. And a beer. And then I want to see how that other shade of lip gloss looks on me."

Her mouth lifted a fraction. I held the edge of the counter to keep from rounding it. The ferocity with which I wanted her caught me off guard.

This morning I'd tried to leave without waking her because I needed to get away from her. From *this* . . . whatever it was.

The pressure of it still suffocated me, but I needed her. After the shit for a day I'd had, I didn't want to talk. I wanted to park it on the couch, play guinea pig, and find any excuse I could to touch her.

"Dinner, beer, and lip gloss; I've got it covered."

No longer able to resist, I rounded the island and tapped her on the nose. "Spoiling me."

She tilted her head back to look at me where I towered over her. So close, yet not anywhere near close enough.

Baker wrinkled her nose, though her eyes smoldered. "You stink."

The words were husky, a tease, and my body reacted as if she'd given me a compliment.

"And you smell like heaven."

I ran my nose up the column of her neck, inhaling like a man possessed. Honey. My new favorite scent.

I grazed my teeth on her earlobe, and her hands flew to my shoulders.

"This is a bad idea," she rasped as I feathered my lips down her jaw.

"I thought we were past that."

I pressed a kiss to the corner of her mouth. She rocked her hips into mine. "I thought you wanted dinner." Her fingers slid under my coveralls, shoving them off my shoulders.

"I'd never choose food over you."

"That's a strong statement to make, Grease Monkey." The tease coated her words, but the vulnerability in her eyes was unmistakable.

"I don't say things I don't mean."

Her hands framed my neck. "I think you did yesterday. To your sister."

She was right, but I didn't bother admitting it. I just wanted to forget it all.

"I'm going to take a shower." I couldn't think about yesterday right now.

I brushed my lips across hers and pushed off the counter. She grabbed my hand in silent support. Briefly, I closed my eyes and squeezed back.

Baker didn't let go until our arms were stretched as far as they could reach.

"LOOKS GOOD." I moved straight to the fridge and grabbed a beer. "This your poison?" I held up a bottle of white wine to Baker.

"Yes." Her eyes lit, but she wasn't looking at the wine. They wandered from my damp hair, across my chest, and down to where my sweats hung off my hips. "I ran into your dad at Trish's truck today."

"Oh yeah?"

"He had your nephew and Ella in tow. It looked like they were getting the best of him."

"She's an infant."

"Have you met her? The girl is the loudest human being I've ever known," she said fondly. "And Blake is the only one spirited enough to match her."

"Bet my brother never tells them they're not blood cousins." I unscrewed the cap and flipped it onto the counter.

She narrowed her gaze. "What do you mean?"

"Oh come on. Like you don't see the match they are. My nephew knows all of two words, and all she does is scream, but it's like they're speaking the same language."

"True," she said carefully after a moment of consideration. "Why would Andrew care if they end up together? And by the way, that's pretty far-fetched."

I tipped my beer toward her. "Mark my words, Easy. They'll end up together." She frowned like she knew I was right. "My brother isn't going to let little Ella date until she's fifty."

"Did he say that?"

"Didn't have to." I pulled a wine glass down from the cabinet. "Don't tell me you haven't noticed how protective he is?"

Baker grinned. "Yeah. Of both my girls." Her eyes went soft.

She deserved that too. The kind of happiness my brother and Trish had. And I prayed she found it.

You could give her that.

I gulped half my beer. *Where did that thought come from?*

"What else do I need to carry?" I asked, balancing her wine glass and my beer in one hand.

"This." She held out a paper carton filled with what appeared to be scalloped potatoes.

I took it and followed her to the living room. Carefully, I set everything on the coffee table.

She settled on the sofa and handed me a fork.

"Another Trish specialty?"

"Actually, no. Well, the potatoes are. But your dad made the chicken."

I paused halfway to digging into the food. "He did?"

"Yep. He said it used to be one of your favorites."

I peered into the other carton. Pieces of his famous drunken chicken were piled inside.

"I don't understand. Did you meet him on purpose?"

"He was going to bring it over to us later. Since I ran into him, and he doesn't live far from Trish's, I went with him to pick it up."

I forked some potatoes. "Did we make plans I didn't know about?"

"No." Her features brightened when she tasted the chicken. "That's so good," she said around a bite.

"I've got good taste," I said smugly.

"Apparently, you do." She reached for her wine and took a long sip. "Your dad tried to put up a good face, but he's worried. Trish got it out of him that Marlow barely spoke when he picked up Blake this morning."

I dropped the carton of potatoes on the coffee table. "Thought you wanted to talk about your day."

"That wasn't an attempt to get you to talk about yesterday." She picked up the abandoned potatoes. "You're close with him. I thought you'd want to know."

I polished off my beer and went for another one, an obvious attempt at escape. Was she trying to get me to open up about yesterday? Even if she wasn't, the mention of my sister was still picking at a fresh wound.

I was always the one having to give answers, yet Baker managed to stay on neutral ground. She hadn't told me a damn thing about her past. Maybe I didn't have a right to know, but I wanted to.

And that was the problem. No matter how I promised myself I wouldn't get close to another woman, I couldn't seem to stop trying. Inviting—no, wanting—her to be part of the new building was all on me. There was this constant push and pull I kept getting dragged into. I couldn't help it.

It was as if my attraction to her was beyond physical, and that wasn't wise. It was so confusing. I wanted her with me, and I hadn't been lying when I said I wanted to continue the living arrangements once the apartment above the workshop was ready. But after the last two days with Marlow and then my mother, I didn't have the capacity to work through this. And that ticked me off.

When I dropped onto the sofa, I slouched in the corner and nursed my drink. We were slowly pushing past every boundary. If she got to know my problems, I wanted to know some of hers.

"What were you doing in that shelter?"

The fork fell from Baker's fingers and clattered to the floor. She hurried to her feet and knocked her glass over, a river of wine snaking to the edge of the table.

Baker staggered around the sofa, gripping the arm as she passed. "None of your business," she whispered.

A door slammed. I immediately regretted hurting her. But had I asked the question for her sake? Or to push her away because she was too close?

CHAPTER SIXTEEN

BAKER

I COLLAPSED on my bed and held a pillow to my chest.

The sheets were cold, deepening the chill setting in my bones.

I'd overreacted. The question was inevitable. One I didn't want to answer. One I couldn't bear to answer.

If I told him the truth, he'd want nothing to do with me. And that thought scared me.

I was getting used to having him in my life. After speaking with Hayden, and then daydreaming about a future with my makeup line, I'd felt so excited about the building. It showed he was a good man. Willing to include me in his plans.

But the one question I didn't want to answer had come far sooner than I'd hoped. My overwhelming desire to avoid answering had little to do with the shame for what had landed me in the shelter and everything to do with how Holt would react.

Even though he thought he wanted the answer to that question about my presence at the shelter, he didn't. No one did.

THUMP. *Thump. Thump.*

I sat up straight in bed, drenched in sweat. Quiet surrounded me, though I could still hear the music in my nightmare. I'd been trying to turn it down when I woke up.

I took a few deep breaths to steady the erratic drum of my heart. In the darkness, I reached out. No Holt.

And then I remembered.

I'd waited on him while curled in a ball. He never came. I was too chicken to go to him, my bravery officially spent.

In only a few days, I'd grown used to sleeping with him. It was more than that. I'd gotten accustomed to his presence. How acutely I felt his absence frightened me. Without him, I was having the nightmares again.

A car horn blew on the street below, the city coming to life with the start of a new day. I didn't have to get up so early, but knew I wouldn't find sleep again.

I pushed the covers back and stumbled to the bathroom. As the water warmed, I undressed. Steam fogged the mirror and a heart formed on the glass.

He'd drawn it. The shape hadn't been there yesterday, and it twisted me up. What did it even mean? Holt was a mechanic. He'd been a park ranger. A man's man. In my wildest dreams, I'd never imagined him drawing hearts on the mirror.

I backed into the shower and shut out the gesture I didn't know what to make of. Wasn't I only a bit of fun for him? Someone convenient to occupy his time?

I'd convinced myself that was all he was capable of, yet he continued to prove that wasn't the truth at all.

I won't stop. Not today. Not tomorrow. Not—

I'd cut off the end of that sentence because I couldn't bear to hear how Holt would have finished it. Didn't want to listen to promises made in the heat of passion that weren't meant to be.

But my heart ate up everything he said and did. That was a problem. My heart was what always got me into trouble. It blinded me to reason. I couldn't afford to let that happen again.

I dropped my head back, letting the spray hit my face. Even showering without him felt wrong.

Needy.

That was all I'd ever been. A needy little girl. A needy teenager. And now, a needy woman. I hated myself for it.

I was frustrated with my own lies. I'd believed I was strong enough to stand on my own two feet.

But it wasn't the truth.

With every passing day, I'd grown more dependent on Holt.

Was I going to stick it out here? Prove to myself that I could handle being out in the real world? Or was I better off going back to the shelter? Where I was protected, not only from the madness out here, but from myself and my poor judgment.

Mrs. Quinn would be disappointed if I came back. I'd be disappointed in me too. Sometimes it was better to admit not being ready than to dig a deeper hole.

Would Holt care if I moved out?

I slapped myself in the forehead. "Get a grip, Baker. Get. A. Grip."

A decision didn't have to be made right now. I'd think it over. Decide what was best for *me* without rushing into another bad choice.

Except when I'd agreed to live with Holt, it was an automatic yes. My soul knew what it wanted without having to mull anything over. But I'd been wrong before. No doubt I would be again.

THE APARTMENT WAS quiet when I finally emerged from my room. Holt's door was closed, but I felt his absence.

Our dinner from the night before remained on the coffee table. The wine glass still lay on its side, though the spilled liquid appeared to have been wiped up.

Quickly, I discarded the food and loaded the dishwasher. I grabbed an apple and a banana, dropping them into a brown paper bag with the rest of my lunch.

As I picked up my keys off the counter, I found a note folded underneath them. With trembling hands, I opened it.

Gone to my father's for a few days. I think we both need the space.

Coward.

I crumpled it in my hands and tossed it back on the counter. Space? I didn't need space. I wanted him to talk to me. Or at the very least, not run when things got tough.

You mean, kinda like you "talked" to him?

I scowled as that little voice in my head pointed out how I'd been just as guilty of shutting down as he had.

Space.

I hated the word.

Screw Holt Dixon and his space.

CHAPTER SEVENTEEN

HOLT

"YOU HAVE TIME FOR LUNCH?"

A pair of feet that belonged to a familiar voice came into view.

"No," I said without rolling out from underneath the Chevy Suburban I was working on.

A foot stretched out and kicked me in the arm. "The answer is yes."

"If that were the case, you wouldn't have needed to ask."

"Your big brother comes to buy you a nice meal and you can't even tell him no to his face? I'm wounded."

Thank goodness I was hidden so he couldn't see me almost smile despite my annoyance. He knew how to push my buttons and get what he wanted all at once.

I rolled until my head was out from under the car. "No."

He scowled, his lips twisting into his masculine version of a pout. "No? Damn. I came all this way."

"All ten blocks?"

"These shoes aren't the most comfortable pair I've got." He wiggled his foot, the tassel on his oxfords swaying.

"Think you could make it to a restaurant?"

He grinned. "Of course. We'll take a cab."

I rolled completely out from under the Suburban. "I'm not exactly dressed for a nice meal."

I gestured down at my coveralls when I stood.

"Sure you are."

"I don't want to go to your woman's food truck." I folded my arms over my chest.

His expression darkened. "Why not?" He was insulted on her behalf.

"It's not the food. Or Trish."

Light dawned in his eyes. "Baker."

I'd tried and failed miserably not to think about her.

I'd needed to get away, yet it was already too far. Last night, I'd pushed her to avoid talking about myself. That was the coward's way, but I wasn't ready to face her yet.

And I'd reacted the exact same way with the Marlow situation. I didn't know how to break the pattern and I hated that. When would I stop it?

"Something happen between you two?" Andrew's brow furrowed as he slid his hands into his pockets.

"Isn't that why you're here? I'm sure Dad told you I'm crashing with him for a few days."

"Actually, he didn't."

"Well, now you know," I said bitterly. "Let's do this. I need to be back in less than an hour."

"HOLT." Trish's smile brightened when she saw me in her window. "What a pleasant surprise."

"What about me?"

Her smile turned soft. "You're a great surprise too."

I was happy and jealous of my brother in one chaotic swirl. I tried to force the envy away, but it clung tightly with its talons.

"What's good at this place?" I scratched my temple, and she laughed.

"If you came by more often, you'd know."

"I've been sampling your dishes. The chicken roll things are my favorite. Oh, and those potatoes with the cheese and I don't know what else. But they're good."

Her grin widened. "I wondered what Baker was doing with all that food she ordered."

"Spoiling me." The words were out before I could take them back. I'd had no lunch packed today. No smile or kiss before work. Hell, no messy hair and sleepy eyes to wake up to.

Andrew cleared his throat. "I'll have my usual."

Trish passed two large glasses of lemonade to us.

"And I'll have the same." I pasted on a pleasant expression, though my day was getting worse by the moment.

What was I thinking when I told her we needed space? That was the last thing I wanted. Sleeping in separate rooms last night was too much, but I'd thought we needed the distance before we pushed each other past the point where we hurt each other too badly to salvage any kind of relationship, even friendship.

"Go grab that bench. I'll wait for the food." Andrew pointed with his chin toward the empty seat.

I parked it and slouched on the bench, my legs spread wide. I should have stood my ground, told my brother today wasn't a good day for this. If I'd kept working, my mind couldn't totally focus on Easy. Now, I couldn't get her out of it.

"Here you go." My brother held out a container with my lunch. "What happened?" His ass had barely hit the seat before he started in.

"Nothing." I stabbed my fork into a piece of chicken.

He snorted. "Have it your way." He sucked down a swallow of lemonade. "I tried to call Marlow. Several times. She won't answer."

"Don't want to talk about that either." I was quickly losing my appetite.

"The only one she'll see is Dad, but he said yes or no answers is about all he can get out of her."

"Maybe she should think about the consequences before she opens her mouth."

"It's not true," he said quietly. "None of us blame you for *her* leaving."

"Obviously your sister does." I snorted, resentful and still hurt.

"You know how she is. Barely make a scratch on her and she goes for the jugular."

I held out my hands. "Well, I'm bleeding out over here." Maybe I shouldn't have admitted that, but why hide?

"She was in the wrong."

"But I am too, right?" I asked, unable to keep the bitterness out of my voice.

He let out a long sigh. "It wasn't the time to bring up Jack. Honestly, there's never a good time. And you're right. None of us are doing her any favors by pretending he didn't exist."

My shoulders sagged. "I can't stand to see Marlow hurting. I know —" I hesitated, shoving the words I was about to say back in. "I don't expect her to get over his death. Ever. I just don't want her . . ."

"To feel like you do," he finished for me. "What happened wasn't your fault."

I bristled. "You have no idea what you're talking about."

"How long are you gonna punish yourself? Cameron made a decision that cost him his life."

"And I made the one that didn't save it."

I set my food carton on the bench between us and stood. "I appreciate where you're coming from. I know you came to help me find some sort of reconciliation, but I'm not there yet. This isn't me avoiding a conversation, but rather asking you to be patient. Please."

He looked up, and I could tell he wanted to say something, but he wisely dipped his head. "Okay."

"Tell Trish I appreciate lunch." I didn't believe I could stop punishing myself. It wasn't that easy. But at least I could reach out to someone I did want in my life.

. . .

I PLOWED both my hands through my hair as I paced in front of the skyscraper. What was I doing here? I had to get back to work, but I couldn't stay away.

Screw it.

I pushed through the revolving doors and prayed it wasn't a mistake.

CHAPTER EIGHTEEN

BAKER

"THE CONTRACTS CAME in this morning. Schedule the shoot for a month from now."

I scribbled the reminder on the bottom of my notes from the meeting we'd just finished.

"Got it. Anything else?"

"Let's meet again Thursday afternoon to plan locations for the April and May editions. Hayden wants you in from start to finish." Macy, our creative director, pulled the conference room door closed as we exited.

"Perfect. I'll see you Thursday."

She jetted down the corridor toward her department. I trudged to the lobby. It was nearly two and I hadn't had lunch yet. We'd been going nonstop today, which was a blessing. My mind had only minimally drifted—

"Holt?"

His hands were braced against the reception desk. Those dark locks were a wreck. His coveralls were coated in stains. And the sight of him was such a relief I almost ran to him.

He turned, his eyes blinking a few times in disbelief before he closed the distance between us.

"Easy."

He stopped a fraction of an inch before he reached me, careful not to touch.

"I thought you needed—"

"I should have called first." He glanced at his dirty clothes. "Shit. I don't want to embarrass you."

I touched his cheek. "I'm glad you're here. And for the record, I don't want your damn space."

"I don't want it, either." He placed his hand on top of mine. "Do you have a minute? Is there somewhere we could go?"

I grabbed his hand and led him out of the elevator lobby to the stairwell. "Nobody uses these," I said with a tease.

The second the door clicked behind us, I launched myself at him. He caught me, folding me in his arms. Holt buried his nose in my hair and held me like he'd never have the chance to again.

This was the first peace I'd had since I stomped away from him last night. He smelled like motor oil and Holt. The lethal combination I couldn't resist.

"Damn it." He tried to disentangle from me, but I held fast. "I'm getting you all dirty."

"I don't care."

"You look so pretty today. I like this dress."

"I wore it for you," I confessed. When I'd slipped on the Kelly green A-line, I'd hoped he'd see it and forget how I shut down on him. "But you weren't there this morning."

"I'm sorry." He rested his forehead against mine. "There are things I'm not ready to talk about. And I shouldn't have pushed you, either."

"I don't like you hurting over your sister. I only want to help."

"I know." He nuzzled my nose. "My mother was waiting for me when I got to the shop yesterday. She wants me to have dinner with her. To talk."

I gripped his face in my hands and pulled so I could look at him. I searched his eyes, and he nodded. "Why didn't you tell me? What did you say?"

I had no idea what had transpired with his mom all those years ago, only that she'd left shortly after Holt was born. Somewhere along the way, I'd gathered she didn't have anything to do with any of the Dixons.

"She gave me her number. Told me to think about it." His fingers dug into my back. "I threw it away when she left."

"Why?"

"I don't know." He glanced away from me. "And I really don't want to talk about it."

I nodded. "Okay."

It was his turn to look surprised. "Okay?"

"Yeah. And I'm sorry about last night. What I said. The way I reacted."

He placed a finger over my lips. "No need. I'm the one who's sorry."

I gave him a wobbly smile. "Are you coming home?"

He smoothed my cheek with his thumb. "Yeah, Easy. I'm coming home." He flashed me a cocky grin. "And we're having a roommate night tonight."

"Is that so?" I teased.

"Yep."

"What if I have plans?"

"You do. With me."

"I get to pick this time."

"As long as it's pizza, beer, and—"

"Pretty Woman," I said triumphantly.

He groaned. "I guess two out of three ain't bad."

The air shifted between us.

"Why did you come here?" The question was soft and wound around us like a cocoon. But I needed to know.

Holt sighed and pressed his lips to the top of my head. "My brother insisted we have lunch. He wanted to talk about things I didn't. I got upset and ended up here."

Was it possible for a man to need me the way I needed him?

"Sounds crazy, right?" He gave me a sheepish smile.

"A little." I kissed the corner of his mouth. "But I get it."

The tension in his body released on a long exhale. "I better get back to work. Ed's gonna kill me."

"We wouldn't want that."

He banded his arms around my back. "Thanks, Easy."

I weaved my fingers through his hair, and a jolt of electricity tingled through me. "See you at home."

"I might be late."

"Then I'll see you when you get there."

Holt loosened his hold on me, and I immediately felt the loss. He captured my face in his hands and lowered his lips to mine. I whimpered in relief at the first touch, fisting his coveralls for support.

"This your gloss stuff?" He ran his tongue across my lips. I nodded. "You're gonna drive men everywhere crazy; it tastes so good."

"I don't plan on kissing anyone but you."

He grinned. "I'm definitely glad to hear that." He dipped down and brushed his lips against mine. "I meant all the women who will wear it. Men are going to write so many thank you notes we'll fill up the garage."

I slapped at his chest. "Stop it."

"I mean it." He smirked. "Except we're all going to get fired because we can't stop kissing our women."

He shrugged and then his lips were on mine again, all tenderness gone. Desperation infused the kiss. I'd never needed anyone the way I did him. It was more than physical. I was just happier when he was around. And I told him so through our kiss.

I hooked a leg around his hip. He lifted me by the waist and moved until my back hit the wall. I kneaded his hair. He pressed his body against mine. I lashed my tongue with his. He nipped my lip.

On a grunt, he ripped his mouth from mine. "Gotta stop, Easy. Or I won't."

The heat in his gaze set me on fire. "I don't want to."

Our chests heaved as we stared at one another.

"I'll see you tonight." He scowled as he spoke and made no move to let me go.

"Okay."

He kissed my cheek and took a reluctant step back. His eyes ran down my dress. He smoothed it back in place and examined his work.

"I didn't get you dirty."

"Yet." I dished out the signature Dixon wink and pushed off the wall.

He grabbed my hand and caged me between the door and his solid body. "Yet," he whispered against my ear.

Goosebumps rose on my flesh. He reached around me and pressed the bar to open the door. I stepped into the lobby.

Holt called the elevator, and I waited with him for it to arrive. He kissed my temple like he couldn't help himself. I looked down at the floor and smiled.

"What's that about?" Holt hooked his thumb under my chin.

"Baker."

I jumped at Hayden's voice. Her eyes dropped down to where Holt and my hands were joined before they drifted back up to him.

"Um, Hayden. This is Holt Dixon." I gestured awkwardly between them. "My roommate," I explained quickly. Her smile was mischievous. He flinched, but recovered quickly.

"And you're the boss," he said with ease.

"You've heard of me. I'm not sure that's good." She shuddered.

He gave her his easy grin. The one I was sure he'd drawn in many a woman with. "All good. No need for concern."

"Glad to hear it." She turned to me. "Were you heading out?"

"No. Holt just came by for a quick visit."

"Then come with me. I want you to see the process of finalizing an issue."

Holt dropped my hand and chucked my shoulder. "See you at home, *roomie*."

The stab of the word slashed my gut. He caught the closing elevator door and disappeared inside before I could respond.

We'd just gotten back on track, but it felt like we'd already derailed.

CHAPTER NINETEEN

HOLT

I'D BEEN a step away from blowing her off.

But damn it, my desire to see Baker far outweighed my irritation.

I shoved the front door open and kicked it closed. Baker jumped when it slammed.

"Hi." The greeting came out more like a question. She edged closer to the counter, her eyes wary as I stalked across the room.

Wordlessly, I dumped the pizza, beer, and my keys on the island. Her breath stopped when I stepped into her space.

"You just wanna be roommates?" The sentence was a tease. But I wanted her to know exactly how much I was beginning to hate that word.

"I—"

"Because it's completely your call." I cut her off, inching my face closer to hers.

"How was I supposed to describe you to my boss? I have no idea what we are."

"You could have just left it at my name. Instead, you tacked on a roommate at the last second like you didn't want her to get the wrong idea. Never mind that we were holding hands." I paced in the small space between the island and the cooktop. Maybe I had no right to be aggravated over that, but it was official. I definitely hated that word. Especially when it came to Baker and me.

"I—" She paused and deflated. "I don't know why I said it. As soon as the word popped out, I wanted to take it back."

I studied her face. She was telling the truth, and that relieved me more than it should.

"You know how you hate the word space. Well, I despise the word roommate. Never refer to me as that again."

"But you *are*." She threw up her hands.

"I don't want to be anymore."

She recoiled, and I realized the mistake of what I'd said.

Her chin lifted, that perfect face lowering a shield to hide her hurt. "Are you moving or am I?"

The world slammed to a stop. "Nobody is going anywhere."

"You're right," she said, a minuscule amount of relief knifing through my consuming anger. "I like this apartment. And I'm not letting you push me out of it. So if you're not happy, you'll have to be the one to go."

I stared at her, stunned into silence and proud of her at once for standing her ground. Somehow I sensed she needed that. But I meant what I said.

"I think we're both feeling our way through this," I started, trying to stay calm. She stared at me, unimpressed. "I sure as hell didn't expect this." I gestured between us.

Baker folded her arms across her chest. She saw right through my half-truth. On the one hand, I saw us coming a mile away. It was one reason I proposed we lived together in the first place. But I hadn't anticipated this clawing need I had for her. Hadn't expected how much I liked living with her. Being around her. How much I wanted to break my own rules and go all in with her. But I couldn't. And I should have told her that from the start.

"I can't give you what you want."

She tapped her foot. "How do you have any idea what I want?"

"Commitment. Am I right?"

The look she shot me made me question my rationale. All the

women I'd ever known wanted commitment, even when they changed their minds.

"No. I'm not anywhere near ready for that."

"With me?" I asked, affronted.

She rolled her eyes. "With anybody."

Somehow, that didn't sit well with me. "I guess I should have asked."

"I guess you should have." She softened. "I didn't ask what you wanted, either."

Wow. Hadn't expected this.

The woman constantly took me by surprise.

"I like coming home to you." I clamped my mouth shut after the words came out unfiltered.

"I'm not trying to force you into anything," she said quietly.

Maybe that was the problem. She was more casual about whatever this was between us than I was.

"I know." Damn it. I plucked a beer out of the six pack I'd left on the counter. I unscrewed the cap and offered the bottle to her. Baker accepted, and I watched her delicate throat work as she swallowed.

"Did some spill on my chin?" She wiped her mouth with the back of her hand while I watched like it was the most fascinating thing I'd ever seen.

"No." I shook my head a few times and grabbed my own beer. "Want some pizza?"

She gaped at me. "That's it? Now you want to eat?"

"Yeah." I shrugged one shoulder. "I guess we said our piece. I'm ready to move on if you are."

She nodded. "Okay."

I snatched the box off the counter and followed her to the sofa. She snagged a slice of pizza and eyed me suspiciously.

"What?"

"What are we going to call *roommate* night now?" She mouthed the word, a scandalous look in her eyes.

"Date night?" I tore off a bite of pizza and reached for the remote.

She paused mid-sip of her beer. I glanced over and continued eating as if I hadn't just dropped a bomb.

"That sounds awfully commity to me," she said carefully.

"You scared?"

"Nope. Date night it is." She lifted her bottle to me and we clinked. "This doesn't mean we're serious."

"Suits me." I switched on the TV. "But Baker?"

"Yeah?"

"I don't want you giving anyone else my kisses."

Her breath hitched before she leveled me with a saucy look. "As long as you aren't showering with other people, I think we're good."

I sank back in the cushions and threw my arm around her shoulders. "We're better than good."

CHAPTER TWENTY

BAKER

I HAVE WHIPLASH.

Pure and simple.

This day had been so full of highs and lows, I wasn't sure if I was at the top of the hill or down at the bottom. Lying here, curled up on the sofa with Holt snoring in my ear, was a satisfying end.

He'd barely made it half an hour into the movie before his breathing turned even. I, on the other hand, couldn't turn my brain off.

The torrent of displeasure that had come home had calmed into this. He'd not only been annoyed about my roommate comment, but insulted.

Had we really resolved anything? Neither of us wanted anything too serious, yet we weren't seeing other people. Wasn't that commitment?

His phone buzzed on the coffee table, the sound piercing in the quiet living room.

"Easy?" Holt stirred, halfway between sleep and awake.

"Your phone."

I reached over and picked it up. *Celia.* That jealousy flared as I held it out to him.

He silenced the call and tossed the phone on the floor. "Movie was good," he murmured in my ear.

"Oh yeah? What happened?"

"They lived happily ever after."

I snickered. "Lucky guess."

"I don't wanna move," he moaned, nuzzling my hair.

"You'll regret it in the morning if you don't."

Holt sat up, taking me with him. "Off to bed with you."

He scooped me into his arms.

"Put me down. You'll hurt yourself."

"I'm wounded. I thought you were impressed by my arm muscles."

I was. So, so impressed.

"I can't see them, so I've forgotten."

"Pssh. Forgotten." He carried me straight to his bedroom. "Flip on the light, please."

I turned on the bedside lamp, and he dumped me on the bed. In seconds, he'd shed his shirt. Damn, I was one lucky girl.

"I'll take it by the O-shape of your mouth you remember."

I shrugged, and he prowled over to me. He placed his hands on the mattress on either side of me and touched his nose to mine.

"I like how we can let stuff go."

I wrinkled my brow. "*Have* you let it go?"

"Yeah. I'm ready for the make-up sex part."

I shoved at his shoulders. "That's why you picked a fight in the first place."

"You *are* beautiful when you're mad." His grin was wolfish as he crawled on top of me. A growl escaped me. "See what I mean?"

My heart flipped over on itself.

"I don't like to fight," I confessed. Arguments always left me feeling raw and drained.

"Then let's not do it again."

He kissed me like it was the most natural thing in the world, an answer to the question of what we were. *This.* We were this right here. Two people who couldn't stay away from each other.

His phone vibrated again from the living room.

"Who is she?" The fear I didn't want to show slipped into my voice.
"No one."

The sharpness of his tone made me flinch. His expression softened, and he ran his thumb over my eyebrows.

"I-I'm not asking for a label, but I can't do this if you're with someone else."

"I would never cheat. *Never*."

"Okay." I felt the conviction in his words, but a seed of uncertainty took root.

He cupped my jaw with his hand. "You know my mother left us after I was born. But did you know it was for another man. One she'd been seeing behind my father's back."

"I didn't," I said quietly. "But I had my suspicions."

"Andrew thinks it was for years. Dad won't talk about it. But I've seen firsthand what cheating does. Nothing good comes of it, I promise you."

I might not have known exactly what infidelity was like as he did, but it was easy to see what it had done to his family.

"You all deserved more."

He diverted his eyes for so long, I wasn't sure what he was going to do. When his gaze finally landed back on mine, the intensity stole my breath.

"Do you think I look like my family?"

My lips parted and then closed. The hurt he'd carried his entire life pressed on my chest. "Yes."

I searched his face, fingered a lock of his hair. His was more of a caramel shade of brown compared to his father's and brother's. Marlow's was nearly black. There was a slight wave in Holt's, where the rest of theirs was straight. But I'd never seen his mother. And those differences alone were hardly cause to believe he was only half their blood.

Mr. Dixon and Andrew weren't clones, though when the two of them were together, there was no mistaking they were father and son. His sister was a little more difficult to tell. I'd never really considered them that closely.

"Are you saying . . ."

"I'm not one hundred percent certain Dad is my biological father."

What? Oh no. How did he deal with the weight of that?

"Why would you think that?"

"My mother had an affair. I'm pretty sure she was sleeping with someone else at the time she got pregnant with me."

"You don't know that."

"Just putting two and two together."

"Sometimes that doesn't equal four."

He turned his mouth down in a bitter frown. "The facts don't lie."

"Have you ever talked to any of your family about this?"

"They'd deny it."

I hesitated before speaking. "Your mother would know better than anyone."

He rolled over, taking me with him. "I need to know," he started, pushing a lock of hair from my face. "But I'm not sure I want to."

I tried to think about what I'd do in his situation. What I'd want, how I'd feel. I came up confused and empty.

"I've got a family who loves me unconditionally, which is more than some people ever have." His fingers traced circles absently on my back. "She *left* us. Left me. I should just let it go. Be thankful for what I have."

At least he realized how fortunate he was to have the family he did. Not everyone's family stuck by them, wanted them as an active part of their lives. What would I have given for even one parent to have Sunday dinner with every week?

"Would it change anything? If you found out your dad wasn't really your dad?"

"No." He shook his head vehemently. "He's the only father I have, even if my DNA says differently."

"Wouldn't it hurt him to find out otherwise?"

He closed his eyes, his features fraught with concern. "Badly."

"And you don't want to do that."

He shook his head, eyes turbulent when he opened them. "For years, I've struggled between being happy with what I have and my curiosity. I thought I wanted a chance to talk to my mother as much as I'd ever wanted anything. But when the chance presented itself, I wasn't so eager. In fact, I'm not sure I want to speak to her at all."

"Then don't." I understood the need for truth, but that woman had had a lot of years to make things right with her children. Why now?

"Would you? Want the truth, I mean."

"The truth isn't always what it's cracked up to be." I folded my hands on his chest and rested my chin on them.

"No. I guess it's not." Knowing was in his eyes, and I didn't think it had a thing to do with his family situation.

"Let's just say you met someone. And hypothetically speaking, their past was ugly. Something that had you known from the beginning, you'd have had nothing to do with them. But you don't know. And you like them. Like the person they are. Would you want to know the truth?"

"Is it something that defines them? Is it part of who they are that they're hiding from me?"

"It could go both ways, couldn't it? Maybe it's part of their life they want to escape."

He was quiet a minute. "I think if it's just something that *happened* to them, then I'd be okay without knowing. But if it was something they *did*, I'd want to know. Even if it hurt."

I shifted uncomfortably. He'd want to know the truth. And I wasn't sure I could ever tell him. Because it *would* hurt him.

"What about you?"

I gave him a wobbly smile. "That old saying, ignorance is bliss, there's a lot of value in that."

"Yeah. There is."

"I'm not sure what I'd want," I said truthfully. Sure, if I'd known Kyle was who he was, things could have been different. But what if they weren't? What if I'd been with him anyway?

Those were the thoughts that had plagued me for three years. Was I a bad person? Or was it circumstance that caused behavior I'm so ashamed of? I still didn't know the answers, after all this time. I could see why Holt was struggling with this with his mom. Wanting to know the truth, but hesitant. Life wasn't always so easy. Or black and white. Either way, he needed to know peace, and I hoped he found it one day. Even if I didn't.

"I'm gonna go see my sister," he said after a long beat of silence.

"Want me to go with you?"

He stroked my hair, a tenderness in his eyes. "Thanks. But I think this is something I'd better handle on my own."

"Whatever happens, I'm here."

CHAPTER TWENTY-ONE

HOLT

I LIFTED my fist to knock on the door and hesitated.

She was my sister, for God's sake. We'd fought and gotten over it more times than I could count. But this was different.

More personal.

Screw it. Somebody had to make the first move. I'd come all the way to Jersey, and I wasn't leaving without some sort of resolution.

I pounded on the door and peered through the small glass squares that lined the top.

No movement inside.

I stepped back and shoved my hands in my pockets. This was a decent neighborhood. A good one for a kid to grow up in. Blake had a backyard and the widow next door adored my nephew.

But my sister belonged in the city with the rest of us. I got why she'd never leave this place. It was the home she and Jack had made together. He haunted these walls and that was exactly how she wanted it. Who was I to judge her for that?

The door opened a crack, and my sister's stunned expression greeted me.

"What are you doing here?"

"You know. Now are you going to let me in?"

She contemplated for a moment, and I stared at her incredulously. If she'd showed up at my place, I wouldn't have thought twice.

Finally, she opened the door.

"Where's the little monster?" I glanced in the living room to find it empty.

"In the kitchen."

I faced Marlow. "Look, I crossed a line on Sunday. That wasn't the time or place."

"And I torched it." Was this my sister? Because this definitely sounded like some semblance of an apology. "I was pissed at you for bringing up . . ." She looked down. "That didn't give me the right to lash out at you."

"I know what it feels like to suffer in silence," I admitted. "It's one thing for me to do it and completely different for my big sister to hurt alone."

That was the crux of it. I couldn't stand her pain when I understood it far better than most.

She shrank in on herself. "There's not a thing you can do to make it better."

I placed my hands on her shoulders. "I know. Doesn't mean I don't want to try."

"What I said . . . I didn't mean it. If I were you, I wouldn't forgive me for it."

"Are you asking me to?" She nodded. "Then we'll forget about it."

I took her in my arms, and Marlow clung to me. "I'm sorry."

"Me too." I closed my eyes and rested my cheek on top of her head. The distance between us over the years was more my fault than hers. I'd missed my sister. I hoped we could fix that.

"I'll come to Sunday dinner if you will," she said, a mischievous smirk on her lips.

"You're not going to tell Dad, are you?"

"Nope. He'll like the surprise."

"HOOOOWW!"

I shoved my finger in my ear and shook my head at my nephew's shriek. "Is somebody else here?"

I pointed my chin in the direction of the kitchen at the muffled voice.

"Umm . . ."

I grinned. "Patrick hiding in there? I know you like him." I tugged on her hair and took off.

She grabbed my arm. "Holt. Wait."

I glanced back at her over my shoulder. "You don't have to hide it from me." I winked.

"*Holt.*"

I ignored her urgency. "Patrick. You dog—" I stopped dead in the doorway to the kitchen.

Patrick wasn't the one holding my nephew.

I looked back at my sister.

"Holt . . ." Remorse filled her eyes, though I wasn't sure if it was only because she'd gotten caught.

"How could you?"

I stared in disbelief at our mother sitting in a chair like she was right at home.

"It's not what you think."

I spun on Marlow. "No? Then what exactly is this? Because it sure as hell looks like you've been hiding something from your *family.*"

Her face turned red.

I steamed ahead. "What does Dad think?" And then I turned back around. "What are you up to? Nearly forty years of radio silence and now you're everywhere." I glared at the woman who gave me life.

She looked at me with the confidence of a person who held all the cards.

"I've been here the whole time."

My mouth gaped open as I stared at my sister. "What does she mean?"

Marlow fumbled as she tried to speak and came up short.

"*Answer me.*"

"If you want answers, ask me." My mother was a different woman than the one who had showed up at the shop only a few days ago. This one was less demure, more in command. Like placating me was no longer important. Like . . . she'd won the battle to tear us apart, just in a different way. What was Marlow doing?

I pointed at her. "Stay out of this."

My sister placed a hand on my shoulder. "Holt. Please."

My head was literally about to explode. "Please what? I know I've been a stranger, but I have no idea who you are. You've been lying to all of us." I sniffed and looked away in disgust. "Except on Sunday. Guess you knew what you were talking about after all."

I marched over to my nephew and kissed the top of his head, careful to avoid touching my mother. "Love you, little man."

"HOLT."

I blinked at him in surprise. "That's right, buddy."

"Holt. Holt. Holt."

I gently pinched his chubby cheek. "Blake. Blake. Blake."

Reluctantly, I pulled away from him. I ignored my mother and frowned at my sister as I moved toward the door.

Without a word, I brushed past her. She grabbed my shirt as I stormed down her hallway.

"Wait. Holt."

"I don't know how you can do this to Dad. He's been a rock for you. For Blake. But this? I can't hide this from him. It's not right," I said without stopping.

She pulled harder and followed me out the front door. "Don't. It'll kill him."

I spun on the front stoop. "You should have thought about that before you betrayed him."

"We shouldn't have to choose between them."

"We don't," I said, my voice rising. "*She* chose. Or have you forgotten she walked out on us. *All* of us."

"Please don't tell him. I'll find a way. Just let me do it in my own time."

I crossed my arms. "I can't do that. I'm sorry, but I can't."

She clutched the sleeve of my shirt. "I can't lose him."

"Do you have that little faith in the man who raised us? All on his own?" I stared at her. "What's happened to you?"

I stomped down the sidewalk without waiting for an answer. She'd betrayed all of us and put me in the terrible position of having to keep her secret or hurt our father. I didn't want to do either. And I didn't want to lose my nephew. But right now, I could hardly stand to think of Marlow, let alone consider being in the same space with her.

How long has this been going on? Why had she kept it from all of us?

My brother would have never condoned the relationship, but he wouldn't have tried to stop her if this was what she wanted. Dad wouldn't either.

Dad.

How was I going to tell him Marlow had been seeing our mother? I didn't know, but there wasn't a choice. He deserved the truth.

CHAPTER TWENTY-TWO

BAKER

"WHERE'S THE LITTLE LADY?"

Trish was empty-handed when she opened her door.

"Andrew is picking her up from his dad on his way home." She stepped to the side to let me in.

I hugged her tightly.

"Hope leftovers from Delores are okay for dinner. I'm bushed."

"I'm not picky, especially when it comes from your food truck. And as long as I can take something back for Holt."

Trish gave me a strange look and a secretive smile. "I think that can be arranged." She linked her arm through mine and led me to the kitchen. "Speaking of, how's the roommate situation going?"

I widened my eyes in mock-horror. "Do *not* use that word in front of him."

"Why not?"

I filled her in on the whole fiasco.

"So let me get this straight. You're not seeing other people, but you're not exclusive?"

"That about sums it up." I threw my hands up and shrugged.

"Do you want to be?"

Trish transferred food into serving dishes. She looked back at me when I didn't immediately answer.

"No." I knotted my fingers together. "Well, I mean, I don't want him to date anyone else, and I don't want to either. But I'm not ready for commitment." I rested my arms on the kitchen table and dropped my forehead on top of them. "I'm not sure I'm ready for what we're doing."

"Most of us rarely are."

"I think I might have agreed to live with him because I didn't want to look like a chicken." The confession came out in an annoyed huff. Not with him, but with myself.

"You agreed to live with him because it's what you wanted to do," she corrected.

"My brother driving you crazy?"

I popped my head up. Andrew strolled across the kitchen, Ella in his arms. He kissed Trish's temple.

"Hey." She touched his cheek, then ran a hand over her daughter's baby soft hair.

A pang of longing nearly crippled me, even as happiness for my friend spread. She deserved this kind of love, especially after everything she'd been through.

"So, my brother? Is he behaving?"

"Does he know how?"

"Nope." He pointed toward the fridge. "Tea?"

"I'm good." I held up my half empty glass.

"You need anything, Bright Side?"

"I'm good too." She popped a couple of the baking dishes in the oven. "How's your dad?"

Andrew sighed. "Stressed about the tiff between Marlow and Holt."

"Tiff?" I asked incredulously. That seemed far too mild to describe what was happening.

"His words, not mine." He reached for a glass from the cabinet and poured himself some iced tea.

"He's going to see her." I held out my arms, and Andrew placed Ella in them.

"He is?"

I nodded. "I offered to go with him, but he wanted to do it on his own. Since I haven't heard from him, I don't know how it went."

"I wonder if that's why she didn't need Dad to keep Blake today."

The doorbell rang, and we all looked at one another.

"Are you expecting company?" Trish tensed.

"No. It's probably Patrick." Andrew disappeared from the kitchen.

"I know it's crazy, but every time someone shows up unannounced, I always think the worst."

"He's not coming back. Ever again," I promised her. "Patrick is going to make sure of it."

She'd been through hell with her ex-husband. The fear didn't just disappear, even though she and Ella were safe.

"Slow down."

Trish and I looked toward the doorway at the sound of Andrew's voice.

"I don't know what to do. How am I supposed to tell Dad? How could she do this to us?"

I stiffened at Holt's panicked tone.

"Take a breath, man."

"I can't—" He froze when he saw me. "Easy?"

I bolted from the chair and stopped short of throwing my arms around him. "It didn't go well."

He gave his head a slight shake and took me into his arms. I snaked mine around his waist and buried my face against him. The scent of motor oil and Holt settled my racing heart.

He tangled his fingers in my hair and pulled my head back.

"What happened?" I whispered.

His eyes were turbulent. "*She* was there." The words were pained as he choked them out.

"Your sister didn't accept your apology?"

He was quiet a moment before he finally spoke. "She did."

"Then I don't understand."

"My mother was there."

Holy crap. *Why would she have been at Marlow's?*

"I thought . . ."

"That none of us had anything to do with her," he finished. "Me too."

He dropped his chin to the top of my head. His pulse throbbed at the base of his neck. I clutched his shirt in my fists and held him close.

"Here." Andrew handed Holt an open bottle of water.

The oven timer beeped, and we disentangled to help Trish set the table.

Once we were all settled around it, our plates filled, Andrew cleared his throat. "What the hell happened?"

Holt downed some water and picked at the edge of the label. I touched his knee under the table where it bounced in a restless rhythm.

"I thought it was Patrick. But *she* sat at the kitchen table, holding Blake like she fucking knew him." Holt glanced at Ella. "Sorry, Trish."

"It's okay," she said softly, giving him a reassuring smile.

"She said she's been here the whole time. What does that even mean? Has she been in Marlow's life all along?"

Andrew's face went blank. "I don't know."

"I have to tell Dad."

He gaped at Holt. "Is that a good idea?"

"Your sister didn't think so." Bitterness threaded Holt's words.

"Let me talk to her."

Trish touched Andrew's arm. "Holt's right. Your dad deserves to know."

He grimaced. "This is going to hurt him."

Holt shook his bottle at Andrew a few times. "What is she up to? She's after me. You. Marlow. Dad. Why now?"

"It makes no sense."

"I swear it's like she was watching Dad, saw he was happy with Mrs. Quinn. Then *she* shows up and everything goes to hell." Holt pushed his plate away.

"You should've seen him the day she'd come by to see him."

Andrew's fork dangled from his fingers. "He was as distraught as I've ever known him to be."

Holt stopped peeling the label. "I wonder how often she calls him."

He couldn't even say Mom. Neither of them could. I didn't blame them one bit.

Andrew pushed back from the table, the chair making an awful noise as it scraped across the floor. He tossed his napkin down.

"She's been in contact with him again? And you didn't think to tell me this?"

Andrew's anger over a phone call took me by surprise, but it was a testament to just how deep that woman had hurt all of them.

"I thought you knew." Holt stood and grabbed another beer from the fridge. He held up the wine bottle to me. I nodded emphatically. He filled both my glass and Trish's.

"I *didn't*. Is everybody in this family keeping secrets from each other?" Andrew spat as he paced in front of the oven.

Trish went to him and slipped an arm around his waist. He clutched her to his side and absently kissed her head. Like he needed the comfort.

"Why won't she just leave him alone?" Andrew muttered.

I sat awkwardly, uncertain what to do. This was bad. All of it so, so bad. Holt's pain was palpable. Both brothers' were.

"I wasn't trying to keep anything from you," Holt said. "I hadn't said anything because, well, I didn't want to talk about it."

Andrew plowed his free hand through his hair. The move reminded me so much of Holt.

"I know. It's just—"

"A lot to take in."

"I'll call him. Let's get this over with now." Andrew pulled his phone from his pocket.

"You should think about this," I said quickly. "Make sure it's what you want to do."

Holt's brow creased. "This about last night?"

"Yeah. Blissfully ignorant."

"The truth isn't always pretty, but it's always the best," Trish said reasonably.

We exchanged a look. Her experience had been that hiding the truth didn't end well. She didn't want the same for me. But our situations weren't close to the same.

Holt sank back in his chair. "I don't want to do it."

"Neither do I." Andrew sagged against the counter. "Maybe we should sleep on it. Decide in the morning."

"Maybe Marlow will tell him and you won't have to," I offered, knowing full well she wouldn't.

"Hell would freeze over first," Holt said. "But you're right. Let's think it over."

CHAPTER TWENTY-THREE

HOLT

BAKER TWINED her fingers through mine as we left Trish and Andrew's.

"I'm sorry."

I stared down the street. "I can't make sense of it. When she said what she did at dinner, I thought she was just lashing out. Now, knowing she's had our mother's voice in her ear, I'm pretty sure she meant it."

"I wish I had the answers, but I'm not going to lie. The whole thing stinks." She sounded pissed on my behalf. It felt like the first time in a long time someone was automatically in my corner.

"You really think I should keep this from my dad?"

She shrugged. "Honestly? I don't know. I like him so much, and I don't want him to hurt."

"Yeah." My shoulders dropped. "Sometimes I think coming back here was a mistake."

Her steps faltered. "Why did you? I don't get the impression it was something you really wanted to do."

"I didn't," I confessed.

"Just go back." Her words were almost robotic.

Ouch. It wasn't that simple. Coming home to be closer to family had been the only thing I could think to do. "I can't."

She untangled her fingers from mine, and a chill shuddered through my bones.

"Did you quit your job?"

"No."

"Because you plan to go back." It was an accusation rather than a question.

"I don't know what I'm doing."

"If you leave, you can forget about all the crap here." She waved her hand in the air. "Like it never happened, right?"

She sounded as if she was speaking from experience . . . and it hadn't worked.

"If I didn't know better, I'd think you want me to go." I tried to stay cool, but was pretty sure a trace of the hurt at her words came through.

"Don't make this about me. You're pissed off about your sister and mom. I'm just not sure what you want. On the one hand, you have a job back in Wyoming you could go back to, yet you made a financial commitment to stay here. Offering me a place for my business and for your own. So, why? Why'd you buy the garage if you never had any intention of staying? Why offer me that space?"

Because I wanted you to want me to stay.

But I couldn't say that to her. We'd told each other we weren't committed to each other. I didn't know what her history was. We were on fragile ground, hiding things from each other. And I was still too angry at my sister for what she was doing to our family.

"You're not interested in the truth, Easy. Seems to me like you want to avoid it." She looked hurt, but damn. I couldn't win.

"The truth gets in the way of the person I want to be."

I pulled her flush against me and fisted her hair so she had to look at me. Fierce eyes met mine.

"I couldn't have said it better myself."

Her lips parted. This woman got me in ways she didn't even know. Yeah, we pissed each other off. Miscommunicated like nobody's business. But somewhere, down in the deepest, darkest depths we under-stood one another perfectly.

There was a time I would have been scared of that. And it did frighten me just how well we knew each other without really knowing one another at all. But mostly, she gave me the comfort I'd been looking for my whole life.

This song and dance that she didn't care if I left was a lie. I felt how much she'd miss me, even if she didn't really know it herself.

"Don't ask me," she pleaded.

"What if telling each other helped?" Had I lost my mind? No way did I want to confess the truth. That I'd always come up short. Never been good enough for anybody to stick around.

She shook her head, wisps of dark hair fanning around her face. "People know. It doesn't make a damn bit of difference."

I couldn't argue with her. But I wanted to bear some of her burdens. Not some of them. *Every. Single. One.*

"Wanna go home?"

"Yeah. My feet are killing me."

I glanced down. She had on another pair of those sex kitten heels that drove me insane. Their effect was only slightly marginalized by the wide leg trousers she wore.

I released her, turned around, and bent my knees. "Hop on."

"I'm too heavy."

I gave her an unimpressed look over my shoulder. She latched onto me and jumped. I staggered around like I couldn't carry her.

"See. Let me get down."

I laughed and gripped her thighs, hoisting her on my back. "Hang on, Easy. This is going to be a rough ride."

Her lips whispered against the shell of my ear. "It better be, Grease Monkey."

I DIDN'T PASS Go. I didn't collect two hundred dollars. I went directly to my bedroom the second we got home.

She laughed when I tossed my keys toward the island as we passed. They bounced and hit the floor with a clang.

"What's your hurry?"

"The thought of you. Naked. Coming on my face."

I strode through the bedroom door. Her legs tightened around my waist as she gasped. I turned once I was beside the bed and patted her thigh, indicating for her to let go.

Instead, that mouth was on my ear again. "No shower?"

Her voice was straight up seduction. I turned my head, though I couldn't see her very well. "I want you dirty."

She dropped to the mattress with a soft thud. Propped up on her forearms, thighs parted, Baker was everything I'd ever wanted and more.

I balled my fists at my sides, drinking her in.

"You're a vision. So damn beautiful it makes me ache. Right here." I pounded my chest.

She blinked at me. "Sometimes you're so honest. I don't know what to make of it."

"I get tired of all the bullshit, Easy. Can you handle it? You and me. Raw."

"Real," she whispered.

"Real as it gets."

The corner of her mouth lifted. "I can handle it."

"Good. Because I don't want to hide. Not from you. From this."

"Then don't."

I crawled on top of her until we were nose to nose. "Then right here, when it's just you and me, we strip it all down."

"Raw."

I nodded and nibbled her bottom lip. "We've got a problem."

Lines creased between her brows. "We do?"

"You've got *way* too many clothes on." I winked at her, and she laughed. I'd never get used to the sound or the way it turned me inside out.

"That's an easy fix," she tossed back, pushing at my chest.

I let her flip me over on my back. She unzipped my coveralls and slid her hands underneath, the heat from her palms scorching me through my T-shirt.

"I said *you've* got too many clothes on."

She pressed on my bottom lip which I'd poked out in a decided pout. "I'm in charge."

"I can't argue with that."

She gave me a strange look before she was right back with me. I waited impatiently to see what her next move would be. Ever so slowly, she bent at the waist until her lips almost touched mine.

Her eyes swirled with need and something else I couldn't define. But I felt it. All the way to my core.

I stopped breathing, my eyes locked on hers the moment she kissed me. Heat, white hot, streaked through me. I gripped her hips to keep from taking over. She needed to run the show, and I had no problem letting her.

The kiss turned from tentative to intense in a nanosecond. Desperation took hold. We nipped and clawed at one another until we were breathless.

Somehow she'd gotten one of my arms out of my coveralls. Her blouse was over her head, but stuck in front of her where we'd refused to let go of each other.

She pulled on my shoulders until I was sitting up straight. With one hand she relieved my arm of the coveralls. With the other, she whipped my T-shirt over my head. Baker ran her eyes over my bare chest hungrily.

She scooted back and pressed gentle kisses into my shoulder, across my pecs, against my neck. I groaned at the feel of her soft lips, the scent of honey and all things my girl filling me.

With a playful push, I fell backward, and her mouth worked lower. I held my breath as she licked down my stomach. She reached for my chest, and a noise of frustration escaped her when she couldn't because she was restricted by her shirt.

Baker sat up, ripped it off of her arms, and tossed it over her shoulder. She resumed her path down my body.

I slid a finger under her nude bra strap and caressed her shoulder. "So pretty," I murmured.

She stopped, looked up at me, and I got lost for a second. I didn't want to leave this moment. Where it was Easy and me and whatever this powerful thing was between us. Because I'd never feel the way I did with her when I was with anyone else.

And when she took my hand and kissed the back of it, something I didn't fully understand filled me. This woman was slowly unraveling me.

I lifted my hips when her fingers slipped under the waistband of my boxer briefs. She freed me of the rest of my clothes and settled back on my thighs. With delicate hands, she fisted my shaft, which was painfully hard. It throbbed with need, the head swollen to the point I ached.

Deliberately she teased, jacking slowly up and down my length. Just when I got used to the rhythm, she licked the slit. My hips jerked off the bed.

She grinned up at me. "I could get used to this being in charge thing."

"Me too," I said hoarsely.

Baker dipped her head and took just the head into her mouth. She sucked hard enough to make my hips jerk again. The smile I felt around my dick had me nearly coming completely undone.

Her happiness became my own—more important than mine—and I wanted to do anything to make sure she stayed that way.

She fisted my cock and took me deeper into that mouth. My hand wound through her hair, and somehow I maintained the control to let her dictate the pace. As much as I wanted her to suck me faster, harder, I realized I was more turned on by not knowing what she would do next.

I didn't expect her to kiss the head of my dick or how that simple gesture would make my need for her escalate. And I sure as hell didn't expect for her to lick me until I was slicked with her saliva.

When she took my hands, placed them on her breasts, and leaned forward, I swallowed hard. She slid my dick between the tight valley of her tits. Hands covering mine, she lifted and lowered, pumping me with that creamy skin.

Those eyes swam with lust. I ran my thumbs over her taut nipples. She hissed in pleasure, and my balls tightened.

"Not like this, Easy." Her glazed eyes sharpened. "I want to come inside of you."

She released my hands and sat up. I tweaked her nipples. Her thighs gripped mine as she splayed her hands on my chest.

"We can come more than once."

"You're going to." I dragged my finger through her soaked slit. She clenched when I pushed the tip of my thumb inside of her.

"I want more. I want this." She gripped my dick and gave a none-too-gentle tug.

"There's something we need in the nightstand."

Baker crawled over me, her breasts swinging in my face. I took a nipple in my mouth and sucked. She seized in surprise before her body went slack. I gave the same attention to her other breast, running my tongue around her stiff peak.

"Those condoms aren't that hard to find," I teased.

A rustling sound came from behind me. "Don't use your mouth for talking."

She dropped her hips and ground against me. She was soft and wet, her lower lips cradling my cock.

"Holt."

My name on her lips was the best thing I'd ever heard.

"Say it again." I grazed her nipple with my teeth.

"*Holt.*"

Her full weight came down on me. I took her in my arms and recorded the moment in my memory. Baker wasn't the first woman I'd cared for, but I'd never felt closer to another human being. She did that to me every time we were together.

That beautiful face hovered above mine.

"You make me want to try." The confession escaped me like a roughened cry for help.

Understanding molded her features. "We're here. That's all that matters now."

I clasped her cheeks in my hands. "I won't make you promises I can't keep."

"I'm not asking for more."

Disappointment and relief mixed inside me. I wanted her to. Wanted her to demand all of me. But I couldn't give it to her. Wasn't sure I ever could. The way she got me made me want to try.

We stared at one another for a long moment. When she brushed my hair back from my eyes and kissed each of my cheeks, I'd never felt more cherished.

She winked at me before placing the foil packet between her teeth and ripping it open.

"You constantly surprise the hell out of me."

Baker slicked my cock with her desire and slid down my body. "Gotta keep you on your toes, Grease Monkey." She rolled the condom down my length and straddled me.

"I'm happy with being on my back." I tossed a wink at her.

She answered me with a grin as she positioned her center with my dick. In slow motion, she lowered, her smile twisting into pleasure as I filled her.

"Fuck, Easy."

Just my head was inside her, yet I was electrified. As she eased down my length, I lost my breath. When she was fully seated, I lost my mind.

She wiggled to accept me, and I struggled not to take control.

"Am I hurting you?"

She was tight, and I was stuffed to the hilt.

Baker shook her head, but refused to look at me. I covered my hands with hers, which were splayed on my chest.

"Easy? Look at me."

"It's—" She struggled for words.

"We don't have to do this." I threaded my fingers with hers. "I don't want to hurt you."

"It's here." She touched her chest with our joined hands. "Powerful. Already."

I drew in a deep breath and exhaled. "Raw. Almost too raw."

She nodded. "It scares me."

I kissed the backs of her knuckles and met her haunted eyes. "It scares me too."

That seemed to settle her. Her chest filled with air and she released it. Using her thigh muscles, she lifted off me and glided back down.

Baker was stunning as she rode me. Her pace was torturous, that pussy like a vice wringing me closer to orgasm with every stroke. She shifted so that our joined hands were above my head, our bodies pressed together. How she managed to fuck me and kiss me at once, I didn't know. All of me was one giant sensation of pleasure.

We were a tangle of limbs, connected at any point we could reach.

"Touch me," she whispered against my lips, releasing my hands.

They slid down her sides to her hips until I cupped her ass. I pinched, and her walls clamped around me.

"Not gonna last much longer."

I slid a finger down the crack of her ass, pressed against that forbidden knot of muscle, but didn't breach it. She tensed, though she never stopped. Her motions became fractured jerks the closer to coming she came.

I skimmed a hand up her spine into her hair and banded my other arm around her back.

"Kiss me while you make me come."

Her lips melted against mine. My tongue sought hers and I held her tight as I matched her with one final thrust.

"Easy." Her name was ripped from me as I spilled inside of her.

She shuddered her release and collapsed on top of me. Our chests heaved against one another's. She clutched my hair and I buried my nose in hers while I floated back to reality.

Holy shit.

Something had just happened. I didn't know what it was, only that I'd never be the same.

CHAPTER TWENTY-FOUR

BAKER

"I CAN'T FIND any of my socks."

Holt pointed toward his bedroom with his head. "You can wear some of mine."

I folded my arms across my chest. "My clothes seem to be disappearing."

He shrugged. "Think the washing machine ate them?"

I narrowed my eyes at him. "Why are you always so keen to do the laundry?"

"I can stop if you want."

He turned his attention back to the book he was reading. *No.* I absolutely didn't want him to stop. But his loungewear wardrobe was quickly turning into mine.

"You're staring," he said without looking up.

I closed the distance between us and removed the book from his hands and flipped it over before setting it on the coffee table. I straddled his lap and planted my hands on his shoulders.

He skated his fingertips up my bare thighs. I shivered. "Aren't you supposed to be at work?"

"I told Ed I was leaving at six."

"So you can work on the bathroom?" I asked hopefully.

He frowned. "So we could talk about plans for the garage."

I motioned toward the book. "I thought you might have been reading about how to remodel."

"I don't need one of those."

"You sure? Kinda seems like you're putting off fixing that shower."

"When have I had time to work on it?" He kissed the tip of my nose. "Maybe this weekend we can do it. Though Ed's already warned me that I've got to be at the shop on Saturday."

"I was going to see if Trish needed any help with the truck anyway."

"Don't forget Sunday dinner."

"We're going?"

"Yeah. Oh, and Dad's coming over tomorrow night."

"Are you going to tell him about Marlow?"

He dropped his forehead to mine. "I'm going to try. Will you be here?"

I clasped his face in my hands. "You don't have to ask."

"Thanks." He pulled me closer to him. "Now go get some socks before your feet freeze."

"I notice you didn't mention anything about sweatpants."

Holt's grin was as cocky as I'd ever seen. "If you put those on, it's harder to do this." He swiped his finger between my legs, and I gasped.

"You like a challenge."

I jumped off his lap and scampered to the bedroom.

"How am I supposed to concentrate on forestry now?" he called.

"Where are your sweatshirts?" I yelled back.

"I'll never tell."

I laughed as I rummaged through his drawers. In the top one, I found a worn pair of his sweats and slipped them on. But there was only one sock, so I ransacked through the whole chest. I put on a Forestry Service sweatshirt and moved my search to the closet.

Only a few shirts hung in it. A half full laundry basket sat on the floor. Everything in it was his.

The only place left to look was a duffle bag in the back corner. Tucked inside were Holt's park ranger uniforms, but still no socks.

"Are there any in the dryer?" I called, digging farther into the bag.

Paper crinkled under my fingers. I removed a sweater and pair of pants, revealing a newspaper article and a photo lying in the bottom.

Pain struck me. The picture was of a happy-go-lucky Holt sitting on the back of a pickup truck, beaming at a beautiful woman nestled between his legs.

He loves her.

The thought came so quickly it knocked me on my ass.

Unable to look at the photo any longer, I unfolded the newspaper article.

Veteran Park Ranger Killed In Climbing Accident

The article was dated nearly eight months ago, and the photograph of a man too young to be gone stared back at me.

"I found some." I started at Holt's voice, who stopped dead in the closet doorway. The smile vanished from his face. "What are you doing?"

He snatched the article from my hands and shoved it back in the bottom of the bag. When he noticed the picture of him and the woman, he flinched. He tossed it in the duffle and stuffed the clothes I'd removed back inside.

"Who are they?" I heard myself ask.

His nostrils flared as he went ramrod stiff. "I don't want to talk about it."

Holt held out a hand. I placed mine in his, and he helped me up.

"Did you know him?"

He walked out of the room without a word. I should have let it go, but somehow I felt I'd unearthed the source of some of his pain without even meaning to.

It didn't escape me I'd not mentioned a word of the woman. Because I didn't want to know. Deep down I already did, and I felt a stab of pain. *He's not yours.* He was a man with secrets, and one of those secrets involved a woman he loved . . . maybe still loved, even though he was sleeping with me. He told me he'd never cheat on a partner, but how did he switch off that love he had for her so quickly?

I followed him to the kitchen. He was at the refrigerator, twisting off the cap of a water.

"I said I don't want to talk about it." He lifted the bottle to his mouth, and I stepped in front of him.

"Maybe you need to."

"You really want to go there?" He lifted a brow, and my shoulders sagged.

"I'm sorry for your loss," I said quietly.

He took another swallow of his drink and absently began to pick at the label. My heart ached for him, far overshadowing the jealousy that had sunk into my soul.

"He was my best friend." My lips parted as he choked the words out. "It shouldn't have happened. It never should have fucking happened." He slammed his fist into the counter.

Water sloshed from the bottle. Holt reared back and threw it in the sink with a roar. Glass shattered followed by a deafening silence.

He stared past me into some unreachable place. I held him tight. Arms stiff at his sides, his entire body was a knot of tension.

I couldn't fix it. Couldn't take it away. But I could be there.

"I know what it's like to lose someone you love," I admitted quietly.

He went completely still. I didn't look at him, only held him tightly to me. Some piece of me healed with the admission I wasn't sure I'd ever said out loud.

Right or wrong, I had loved Kyle. That much had been innocent and pure, if not blind. Even knowing how it all ended didn't change my feelings. A part of my heart held on to the sandy-haired boy with the crooked smile who had charmed me from the first time we met.

"It's hard to let go, even when we know we should," I whispered.

That was the crux of it. I loved Kyle as equally as I hated him. Two sides of me warred with one another and neither of them would win. I was a fool stuck in the spin cycle, still believing if I wished hard enough I could change the past.

"I don't want to forget," he said through gritted teeth. "If I do, it could happen all over again."

I sighed, the truth of his words weighing heavily. It would be so easy to push the past out of my mind . . . and then it could repeat itself. "That's what I'm afraid of."

CHAPTER TWENTY-FIVE

HOLT

"CAN YOU COOK?" A hint of panic barreled through the phone. "Or should I pick something up?"

"I can take care of it." I tossed my empty lunch carton in the trash.

Baker never called me during the day. This was her way of checking on me. And she was freaking out about my father coming over for dinner. Maybe more than I was.

"No. You'll be running late enough as it is."

A semblance of a smile formed. She could heat something up like a champ, but a meal from scratch? The woman burned every piece of toast she tried to fix.

"My brother wants to come."

"Do you want him to?"

I pushed a hand through my hair. "I don't know."

"Okay. I'll plan for five of us."

"Easy. Don't stress."

"I screw up microwave dinners," she lamented. "And I won't have time to go by Trish's."

"Just make sure you have plenty of that wine you like. Dad will need it." I pushed out of my seat. "Why don't you ask Muriella for some ideas. She might know a good restaurant nearby to order from."

"You're a genius." Her tone was miles lighter than it had been only seconds ago.

"I want to hear that again later. In person."

"Go away," she huffed and hung up the phone.

I laughed. She had this way of distracting me even when she didn't mean to. I was already eager for six thirty despite dreading the conversation with my father. Baker's support was . . . eye-opening. I knew she'd suffered in some way, she'd been at Paths, but had someone she loved died too? She'd come after me, refusing to let me ignore my mistake entirely. And she'd held me. That had been incredible.

"Dixon. I don't pay you to stand around," Ed hollered over "Bring It On Home To Me" by Sam Cooke.

He was a good guy, had given me a chance, but I was ready to be my own boss. To put down roots.

I frowned. Was that what I wanted? Half the time I felt torn between New York and Wyoming. Some days I didn't think I could stay here. But I couldn't go back to the park, even though I loved it there.

I'd never wanted Baker to find those things in my bag. I'd almost forgotten the article and picture were there. Almost. And I'd been so close to unloading it all on her. But I couldn't stand to see her disappointment. I couldn't stand for the light in her eyes to dim when she looked at me.

I popped the hood to the Camry, and my thoughts shifted to my dad. Tonight wouldn't be easy on him. He'd need to know all of his family supported him.

I fired off a text to my brother to be at the apartment by seven. Hell, I'd need him too.

Phone halfway back in my pocket, I pulled it back out. There was one more text I needed to send. I didn't wait for a response to that one.

CONVERSATION HALTED the second I walked through the door.

"It would have been less obvious you were talking about me if you'd just kept it up." I hung my leather jacket in the closet and strolled over to the kitchen.

Baker and my dad had guilty looks on their faces. Neither of them denied my accusation.

"At least tell me it was all good."

A wry grin lit Baker's features. "I was just telling your dad that you're a genius."

I snagged her by the waist. "I said I wanted to hear that in person, didn't I?"

Her hands clutched the front of my coveralls. I was careful to keep a gap between us so as not to get her dress dirty. Her lips glistened with gloss, the faint scent of honey floating into my nose.

I kissed her—a thank you, I miss you, and I'm so glad you're here. Her answering one reciprocated relief that I was home. She'd missed me as much as I had her.

"You look pretty," I murmured against her mouth.

The blush that crept up her cheeks had me ready to get her alone.

Dad cleared his throat. I started, having forgotten he was there.

"Go take a shower." Baker shoved at my chest.

I couldn't resist kissing her again. She melted into me. "I can't without you," I said huskily against her ear.

Those eyes darted past me to my father and back to mine. "Holt."

Her cheeks were a crimson that I planned to put back there later tonight.

"I'm going. I'm going."

Ding dong. Ding dong.

"Are we expecting someone else?" She raised an expectant brow.

I snapped my fingers. "I knew there was something I forgot to tell you."

"Go. I'll get the door."

I SWALLOWED HARD when I stepped from the bedroom. Laughter floated down the hallway. I didn't want to be the cause of that to end.

Andrew shot a look at me when I came into the kitchen.

"What's a guy got to do to get a beer around here?" I slung an arm around my brother and kissed Trish on the cheek.

"Open the refrigerator door," Baker said smartly.

"I'm not sure I like your tone." I pointed at her and winked.

I refilled everyone's wine glass and grabbed a beer.

"Did you cook?" Trish looked at Baker skeptically.

She lifted her chin. "Is that so hard to believe?"

"Yes," Trish said without hesitation. "Sonya's better in the kitchen than you."

Baker put a hand on her hip. "If you must know, Muriella had an extra lasagna in the freezer." She grinned and clinked glasses with her best friend.

She was so resourceful. It couldn't have been easy to step out of her comfort zone to ask our neighbor for a favor.

I pulled her into my side and kissed the top of her head. Brows rose all around the kitchen, except Dad, who had a pleased-as-punch expression on his face.

He bounced Ella in his arms.

"She sick?" I pointed my bottle at my new niece. That little girl was a screamer. If she wasn't, something was wrong.

"She's learning to control her voice," Dad said proudly. "How to use it effectively."

"She's effective all right," Andrew said, looking at his daughter with affection.

"This one is going to do big things. She'll give a voice to those who have none." My father's eyes misted as he stroked Ella's cheek.

"I don't know what we'd do without you," Trish said hoarsely. "Any of you."

Baker hugged her in support. "We love both of you. But you already know that."

The unconditional and easy way she cared for the people important to her . . . it was—she was—incredible.

"It's nice to do this on a weeknight. Nice to be invited." Dad glanced at me, gratitude in his eyes.

I should've invited him over for no reason other than his company. Andrew paled. Apparently, I wasn't the only one feeling guilty.

"Mr. Dixon, you're welcome here any time." Baker beamed at him and what pieces of my heart I had left went to her. "You ever think about moving? From what I understand, there's plenty of room in this building."

"It's a little out of my price range."

Baker shrugged. "We've got an in with the guy who owns the place."

"Speaking of," I said, clearing my throat. I glanced at Baker who gave me a curious look. "I, uh, I bought a building."

Surprise registered on his features. "You did?"

"Yeah."

"I wish you'd come to me. That's my business. I could've looked out for you. Made sure you didn't get screwed," Andrew said.

I stared at him. He was a real estate attorney, and a damn good one, but I'd needed to do this on my own. Irritation bubbled up inside of me. He was just being my big brother, looking out for me, but it stung that he thought I couldn't handle myself.

"Shit," he said, plowing a hand through his hair. "I didn't mean it like that."

The apology was written all over his face, and I relaxed. Baker pinched my side, an encouragement for me to let it go.

"You're just looking out for me."

He nodded.

"In New York?" The hopefulness in Dad's voice clawed at me. "The building's in the city?"

"Yeah. Not too far from here."

"By building, do you mean an apartment?" Andrew leaned in with interest.

"It has an apartment, but it used to be a garage. Baker's going to help me fix it up so it'll be a place women feel comfortable to come to." I looked down at her. "And if she wants, there's space to work on her makeup line."

Trish clapped her hands. "This is exciting. Can we see it? Maybe before Sunday dinner?"

"Uh, sure." I hadn't expected their enthusiasm. Didn't know what to do with it.

"Just wait. It's perfect. There are enough bays to grow. And Holt's come up with the perfect place for a waiting room." Baker spoke in a rush, her free hand gesturing wildly.

"And you'll have room to make the cosmetics." Trish's eyes were bright. "You'll be able to work together."

"I haven't taken him up on it yet," she said quickly, though she seemed to be warming to the idea.

"What do you need me to help you do?" Andrew asked.

"I'm not sure yet, man. Maybe set up an LLC or—hell, I don't know." I lifted a shoulder and lowered it. "We're a long way off. There's so much work to be done."

"I know a contractor. If you want me to call him, I will." The stress lines that had creased around Dad's eyes had smoothed. "Once you get open, I know a guy who's a pretty good receptionist." He winked at me. "Though he'd have to bring two assistants."

I laughed. "Ella and Blake are too young to work."

"They'll enchant the customers," Dad said.

"There aren't any customers yet," I pointed out.

"There will be." He clapped me on the shoulder. "I'm proud of you, son."

"It takes guts to do your own thing," Andrew chimed in.

"We're right here with you," Trish said. "Anything you need."

I looked at my family, overwhelmed with gratitude. I swallowed thickly. "Thanks." It was all I could come up with, words failing me.

The oven timer beeped three times. Baker peered inside. "It looks ready?"

I stifled my smile. My girl didn't have a clue.

Trish wandered over and took a look. "It's ready."

It was odd to see Easy with oven mitts on, but she handled the hot pan like a pro as she deposited it on the stovetop.

Horror filled her face. "I forgot the bread."

Trish touched her shoulder. "We'll put it in now while the lasagna cools."

Baker nodded. Dad winked at me. Andrew sipped his wine like nothing out of the ordinary took place around him. I guessed it wasn't.

I took a second to appreciate what I hadn't felt maybe since I'd left New York all those years ago. I'd made my own life in Wyoming. Found friends and had people I cared about there. But it wasn't this. Family.

Things weren't perfect. I still struggled to find my place. A sense of rightness settled in me, and I wondered if I'd been my own stumbling block all along.

Andrew slung his arm around me and spoke low in my ear. "Maybe we should wait."

Before I could reply, the doorbell rang again.

"I'll get it." I set my beer on the counter and immediately wished for the label underneath my fingers.

I hesitated with my hand on the doorknob. I'd arranged this without thinking things through, a decision I questioned the wisdom of.

Best to rip the Band-Aid off now and get it over with.

I threw open the door. Marlow stood on the opposite side with Blake cradled in her arms.

She glared at me. "You win."

CHAPTER TWENTY-SIX

BAKER

HOLT INVITED HIS SISTER?

Mr. Dixon leaned against the edge of the counter while Andrew's grip on his wine glass tightened. Trish absently kneaded an oven mitt in her fist.

The levity that had been in the room only seconds before evaporated, and a thick tension replaced it.

"I didn't know the whole family would be here," Mr. Dixon said as Marlow trailed Holt into the kitchen. "I've missed my grandson."

Without hesitation, he pushed off the counter and moved toward his daughter. He planted a kiss on both her and Blake's head. She stiffened, and Mr. Dixon flinched, but quickly recovered.

"I've missed you too."

Marlow glanced away and clutched her son at her father's admission.

"It's awkward as hell being the unexpected guest." The attempt at humor fell flat.

I cleared my throat. "We're glad you could make it. You're just in time." I smoothed the surprise into something I hoped resembled pleasantry. "Wine?"

"Please." Her shoulders rounded even as she shot me a grateful look.

ONCE EVERYONE HAD SETTLED in around the table, Mr. Dixon looked at his three children.

"I see I wasn't invited strictly for my dazzling company," he said, though a line of worry creased his forehead.

"Dad—"

"That's exactly why you're here." Holt cut off Andrew and discreetly dug into Marlow's thigh under the table.

They both appeared caught off guard, but Marlow covered quickly. "We're trying to work things out." She touched Holt's arm, genuine remorse in her eyes.

"I figured if everyone was coming over for dinner, it wouldn't be right to exclude my sister just because we got into a little argument." Holt bumped shoulders with her and flashed a disarming grin.

Mr. Dixon appeared uncertain, but hope beat out his skepticism. "I'm glad to see you two working past your differences."

"I didn't even have to referee," Andrew said, pointing his fork at his siblings.

What was happening? I thought we were here to deliver the bad news. In the last thirty seconds, we'd made an abrupt U-turn from that plan.

Holt nudged my hand. "You went to all this trouble to make dinner and now you're not going to eat?"

I glanced at my untouched plate. "I was letting you go first. You know, in case something happened."

"You trying to get rid of me, Easy?"

"Maybe. It shouldn't be too hard to find a new roommate."

"You can't replace me."

"Looks like the living arrangements are working out." Marlow slugged back a swallow of wine as she eyed Holt and me.

"Better than I imagined." Holt threw his arm around my shoulders.

"You didn't think it would?" I wriggled out of his grasp.

"I sure as hell didn't." Andrew pointed at his brother. "I've lived with the guy."

"Just because he's a slob doesn't make him a bad roommate," Marlow argued.

"I'm not a slob," Holt protested. "Tell them I'm not."

His eyes bored into me.

"Not a slob, just . . . untidy." I winked at him, and he scowled.

Marlow snorted. "She really likes you, little brother. You better figure out a way to keep her around."

"Don't look at me for advice on that." Mr. Dixon carried on eating, oblivious he'd sucked all the air out of the room.

"Any word from Mrs. Quinn?" Andrew asked, successfully avoiding the topic of their mother.

Mr. Dixon set down his fork. "No. And I still don't want to talk about it."

"I went by the shelter today." One corner of Trish's mouth turned up in sympathy. "She looks miserable."

He slumped in his chair. "I did what was best for both of us, so no one gets hurt."

Marlow reached across the table, her palm up. Mr. Dixon placed his hand in hers. "You're already hurt. Tell her you're sorry and an idiot."

He frowned. "How do you know I was an idiot?"

She shifted uncomfortably before lifting her chin. "You're a man. Translation: you do stupid things."

"I hate it when she's right," Andrew grumbled.

"I miss her." Mr. Dixon looked down.

"Dad, if we'd messed up, you'd tell us to apologize." Andrew reached for Trish's hand. "You'd also tell us to forgive."

"She's the kindest person I've ever known," I said quietly.

"Me too." Mr. Dixon clutched his wine glass.

"Go talk to her, Dad. A phone call isn't good enough." Marlow patted his arm. She had a hard exterior, so this softness caught me unaware.

"Baker, would you be tremendously offended if I cut this evening short? I'm afraid if I wait, I'll lose my courage."

"Go. Go." I shooed at him. "We'll do this again sometime."

"I'll bring dinner," he promised as he stood.

We all got up with him.

"Good luck, Dad." Andrew shook his hand.

"Let us know how it goes." Holt rounded the table and embraced his father.

"If it gets desperate, use that lady killer wink." Marlow demonstrated for effect, and he laughed.

"I love you all." He blew a kiss as he left.

"I hope they work it out," I said as I grabbed my glass off the table.

"Ten bucks says he calls when he's outside for a pep talk."

Holt high-fived his brother. "Make it twenty."

I refilled everyone's wine and grabbed Holt another beer.

"Why'd you change your mind?" Marlow pinned him with a stare.

"Because I couldn't let him down." Holt picked at the label on his old beer.

"How long have you been talking to *her*?"

I shivered at the menace in his tone.

Marlow glared at him. "She's my mother. There's no law that says I can't speak to her," she said petulantly.

"Like hell there isn't," Andrew shouted. "She left us. Did you forget that?"

"No, I didn't forget. I'm just not sure I care anymore."

Holt's lips parted like she'd punched him in the stomach. "Did she tell you she left because of me?" His voice was deathly quiet.

Marlow paled. "Holt. I told you, I shouldn't have said that. I was lashing out. It was an awful thing to say."

"Answer the question."

She popped up from her chair and took her wine with her over to the window.

"What the hell? Dad gave up everything to take care of us. What if he'd abandoned us too?" Andrew followed her. "How could you betray him like this? Betray all of us?"

Trish glanced at me, her expression helpless, just as I felt.

"I didn't betray any of you," she yelled.

Ella shrieked back, a series of sharp wails in succession. Trish was halfway out of her seat when I motioned for her to sit.

I lifted Ella from the carrier and bounced her until she quieted.

"What was I supposed to do? Refuse to give her a chance?" Marlow stared out the window.

"Yes. That's exactly what you should have done." Andrew folded his arms across his chest.

"You still haven't answered my question." Holt's voice had a quality I'd never heard. There wasn't only hurt and betrayal, it was as if he'd turned off the part of him that felt.

"It doesn't matter—"

"It does to me." He slammed his bottle on the table.

"Yes. She said she left because of you, okay?" The second the words ripped from her mouth, Marlow covered it with her hands.

Wordless, Holt stood. He grabbed his keys off the counter.

"Holt. Wait up, man." Andrew streaked across the room, but he wasn't fast enough.

I jumped when the door slammed. Stared at it as Andrew followed after him.

Slowly, I pivoted toward Marlow. With measured steps, I crossed the distance between us.

"I understand arguments. Saying things you don't mean. But that —" I pointed toward the door, my hand trembling with rage. "What you just did. I will never, ever understand. And if you can't be more respectful, you aren't welcome in this house."

I turned away, unable to look at her a second more. Blake wailed, no doubt affected by the tension. Ella screamed in response, and I passed her off to Trish before I doubled back.

I poked my finger into Marlow's shoulder. "He loves you. He's been there for you his whole life. And you think *she's* worth more?" I threw my hands in the air. "What you've got is rare. And you're a damn fool not to see it."

I'd almost reached the kitchen when her words stopped me in my tracks. "You don't know anything. About me. About Holt. About Celia. About Cameron. About my family. So don't you dare judge me."

"I don't have to know everything. I *feel* it. If I had what you do, I'd never throw it away." I tried and failed miserably to keep my anger in check. "And Marlow, an apology isn't going to cut it. Even if Holt forgives you, I don't know if I ever will."

"I don't give a damn what you think of me. I finally have a mother, and I don't have to justify that to you or anyone."

"I hope she's enough, because you may have just lost the rest of your family."

Marlow sank her teeth into her lower lip and straightened her shoulders. "Thanks for dinner." She picked up Blake's carrier and her bag.

For the second time tonight, the door slammed. Ugly words had flown all over the place, and it was becoming difficult to figure out which ones were meant and which were just lashing out.

"It keeps getting worse," Trish said softly.

"I should've gone after him." I paced between the island and the row of cabinets.

"Andrew will make sure he's okay."

"Why did she say that to him? If there was ever a time to lie, that would have been it."

"I don't think she knows how to handle her emotions. Her immediate response is to attack."

"Well, it's a terrible way of dealing with stuff." I braced my hands on the counter and dropped my chin to my chest. "I don't know if he'll get over it."

"I wouldn't blame him if he didn't."

"How do I fix it?" I willed her to give me an answer I was desperate for.

"You can't."

CHAPTER TWENTY-SEVEN

HOLT

"DON'T SAY A WORD."

The warning didn't stop my brother from following me into the stairwell. I jogged down each flight on autopilot.

My worst fears were confirmed. I'd ruined my family's life. She'd left because of *me*.

"Will you slow down? I'm not as young as I used to be."

I ignored my brother, who wasn't even out of breath.

"Marlow . . . hell, I'm not even going to make excuses for her."

I stopped on the landing and whipped around. "You don't have to. She pretty much said it all."

I'd nearly made it to the next step when his hand clamped down on my shoulder. "Ask me who I'd rather have in my life."

I flinched, refusing to look at him.

"Ask Dad if he'd choose you or *her*."

"I'm not getting into hypotheticals."

"We're not. If having a mother meant losing you, she wouldn't be worth it."

"Don't lie to me," I whispered.

"I wouldn't dare." He shook my shoulders.

"I drove you crazy when we were kids."

"And I wouldn't trade a single second of it for anything. Especially not *her*." He pulled me in for a hug, but I shrugged him off.

"I messed up everything for Dad. If it weren't for me, she would have stayed with him."

"Do you really believe that? How are you so sure she'd not feeding Marlow lies? Because I'm not. *She* was cheating on him well before you came along." Bitterness etched his face.

"They might've worked it out. You and Marlow—"

"We had you and Dad. I couldn't ask for anything more."

I shoved at his chest. "You never wished we had a mother? Promised whoever's up there that you'd be good if she'd just come back." I waved toward the ceiling.

"Yeah. I did. But somewhere along the way, I realized if she didn't want us, I didn't want her." He pressed his lips together in a flat line.

"You hate her. If it weren't for me, you wouldn't have had to live your whole life with that."

"How I feel toward her has nothing to do with you. She chose to leave. And she would have whether you came along or not." Andrew scowled. "The sooner you see that, the better off you'll be."

"She wants back into your life. You can have that. I promise I won't get in the way."

His expression was resolute. "I don't want anything to do with her. Ever."

"You don't mean that."

"There is no apology or excuse she can make that would change my mind. I won't let her poison Trish and Ella with whatever game she's playing. Look at what she's doing to Marlow. She's not going to take you or Dad or Marlow away from me either."

I leaned against the wall and hung my head. "If Marlow wants a relationship with her, I don't blame her. Hell, I've spent most of my life wishing for the same thing." I looked at Andrew. "It's the fact that she's been sneaking around. I'm starting to think it's been for years."

He rested against the railing opposite me. "I honestly have no idea what to do. But you made the right call tonight about Dad. He was happier than I've seen him in quite some time."

"I couldn't do it. We were all together, and he thought—hoped—it was because we wanted to be. Nothing else." I gripped the handrail. "I couldn't take that from him."

"Maybe if he and Mrs. Quinn get back together, she'll soften the blow about Marlow."

"Maybe."

I hoped so. Dad deserved happiness. And more. Not betrayal. Was Andrew just saying all that about our family to make me feel better? Did he really feel that way about me? I felt like an all-round failure. *Should I have stayed in Wyoming?*

He lifted his chin at me. "I'm proud of you. About the garage."

"I bought the building. Haven't done anything yet."

"You will."

I looked at him in surprise, and he nodded. "I wasn't just saying things for you to feel better. You're my brother. You made our family complete."

"I'll need time to believe that, but thanks. And I'm sorry for running out like I did. No idea where I was going, but couldn't be in the same room as a sister who'd turn her back on me so easily."

"I'm not sure why she did that. Don't listen to those words."

"Thanks. For coming after me." I shrugged.

"Anytime, brother."

"You need to get back to your girl." I began the ascent back up the stairs.

"Trish understands."

I wanted that. Someone who understood what I needed the way I understood them.

Easy.

I stumbled at the realization I had that.

Andrew's hand steadied me. He grinned. "You finally figuring out you've got yourself more than just a beautiful roommate?"

I pointed at him. "Don't insult her with such a menial term."

I picked up the pace, his footsteps right behind me.

"What did I say?" He sounded perplexed.

I smirked just before I opened the stairwell door. "Better not let her hear you call her a roommate."

"THANKS." I spoke into Baker's hair as I pulled her onto my chest. "For being there."

She touched my face in the darkness, her fingers sure. "I might have done a little more damage," she confessed.

"I don't see how that's possible."

"I told your sister she was a fool and not welcome here if she's going to treat you that way."

I lifted Baker's head to look at her despite I couldn't see in the darkness. "You did?"

"I mean it. She can't come here and hurt you. I won't put up with that."

I can't breathe.

This woman . . . she was so much more than I deserved.

"Easy."

"She was pretty pissed off when she left, but I was pissed off too." Her breath was harsh against my chest.

"The Man" by The Killers blasted from the nightstand.

"It's my dad," I said, blindly reaching for it.

"That's your ringtone for him?" Amusement wove through her voice.

"It's apt. Hey, Dad," I kept an arm around Baker while I pressed the speaker button. "There are ladies present."

"Here too."

Baker popped up, her eyes wide in the glow from the phone.

"You mean?"

"She's speaking to me again."

"That's fantastic news." I grinned at Baker. "Tell Mrs. Quinn to go easy on you."

"Not a chance," she said.

"Oh. Hi."

"Hi, Mrs. Quinn," Baker said, propping her chin on my chest. "Glad you two worked things out."

"I don't know that they're all worked out per se, but we're talking through it."

"I can't believe it," Dad said, wonder in his voice.

"If you'd picked up the phone, we could have done this a lot sooner," Mrs. Quinn said.

I snorted. "Think there's a chance you'll forgive him?"

Dad coughed. "You don't have to answer that, love."

"We'll see." Mrs. Quinn was a careful woman. I liked that about her. For my dad's sake. He deserved someone he could trust.

"Hope we didn't wake you, but I—"

"Was excited," I finished for him.

Baker snickered. "Will you be at Sunday dinner, Mrs. Quinn?"

"I haven't been invited yet."

"I just did."

"I'll check my schedule."

"AT LEAST SOMETHING WENT RIGHT," Baker said when we'd ended the call.

"I can't take that from him. Not right now."

She snuggled into me. "You did the right thing."

"Don't make me out as someone noble. I didn't tell him mostly because I'm a coward."

"Not from what I've seen." She scraped her nails down my chest.

I shivered. "If you want to distract me, I'm game." I skimmed my fingers up her spine.

"I'm trying to tell you I support you. Whatever you want to do," she huffed as her hands drifted lower.

"I'm glad to hear that. Because right now, I want to make you come."

CHAPTER TWENTY-EIGHT

BAKER

"The three year anniversary of a shooting spree that left twelve people—"

I SWITCHED off the TV and tossed the remote on the sofa.

"Not a fan of morning television?" Holt stared at me, coffee in hand.

"The day clogs my head with enough noise as it is." The truth of that was startling, though I was getting better.

He handed me his mug and filled another. "You look pretty."

"You can't say that every day."

"I can if it's true."

"I thought you were going to be late." I perched against the island opposite him.

"Have time for lunch today?" He looked down. "Never mind. Where could we go that's acceptable for me to look like this and you like that?"

"I'd love to," I said, waiting for him to meet my gaze. "Can I text you? I have a meeting at ten and I'm not sure how long it will last."

He gave me a sweet smile. "Sounds like a plan."

"If you get hungry, don't wait for me."

"I'll take a snack." He picked up an apple and tossed it in the air.

"Don't forget your nuts." I motioned toward the baggies I'd separated out for us to grab and go.

He set down his coffee and grabbed my hips. "I'm nuts?"

"No, silly. The nuts behind you. The ones you eat." I canted my head. "You might be a little of that kind of nuts too."

"I can't believe it." He swooped down and captured my mouth. "I'll wait. Even if you get home late."

"Okay." I slid my hands up his chest. "Walk me out?"

"And have a pretty lady on my arm? Hell, yes."

"THE MAN who was here the other day wouldn't have anything to do with that bright face, would he?" Hayden gave me a surreptitious smile as I exited the elevator.

I looked down. "Um, yeah."

We'd parted ways almost a half hour ago, yet I was still giddy just thinking about him. Today of all days and he'd managed to distract me.

"I need to find a roommate like him." She held open the door for me. "Shadow me this morning. Executives from a cruelty-free product brand will be here soon. They might have something of use for your products."

"Sure. Let me drop my bag off at my desk."

"I'm thinking about doing a new feature. One that includes women who are trying and succeeding to do what you do. To do what I've done. Something relatable and encouraging. An 'if I can do it you can too' message. What do you think?" She stopped walking.

"It could work. Maybe we could test a feature online first to see the response before we put it in the magazine." I clutched my purse. "Our readers are the type who would like this. They come to us for recommendations, to find out what's hot. Why wouldn't they want stories of inspiration?"

She pointed her finger at me. "Yes. I love the idea of putting it on the website first. We have a different kind of reader there, but we won't find a better test market."

"How will we find these women? A submission form?"

"I thought we'd start with you."

"Me?" A knot formed in my throat. "But I'm nobody. Just getting started."

"This would be a boost."

I put my hand to my neck. "I appreciate the thought, but I'm not the right person."

"It doesn't have to be personal."

"I'm sorry. I can't do it."

I rushed to my cubicle and dumped my bag in my desk. I dabbed my damp eyes with a tissue. No way could I expose myself like that. It was just the opportunity I needed if I wanted to take the makeup line to the next level, but it was one I couldn't take. Hayden didn't know the damage it could cause to her magazine. Her brand.

"Baker." A gentle hand touched my shoulder. "I didn't mean to upset you."

At the look of worry on her face, I pulled myself together and turned around. "Exposure like that wouldn't be great for me."

Understanding flashed across her features, though no one could truly comprehend how it felt. I was trying to move forward while being held back by the past.

Shoving down my disappointment, I tried to brighten. "Trish might be a better candidate."

Hayden nodded, though her concern was evident. "Maybe so." When she looked at me, I was so grateful to have her as a mentor and a friend. "Baker, don't shut the door on everything. Right now may not be the time, but things could be different down the road."

I doubted it, but appreciated her sentiment. "I'll try."

She gave me a satisfied look. "Let's get ready for our guests."

HALFWAY TO HER OFFICE, Tracey, the receptionist, caught up. "I'm sorry to interrupt, Hayden, but there's a delivery here for Baker."

Me? I hadn't ordered anything.

"Meet me in my office," Hayden said before she hustled off.

I was nauseous by the time we reached the front desk. A spray of wildflowers in a glass vase sat atop.

"Those are for you."

"They are?"

I approached the flowers with caution, like they were a trick of some sort. A card was nestled in the bouquet. Tentatively, I reached for it.

We agreed to lunch, but I was hoping we could have dinner too.

Holt. When had he had time to do this?

Balancing the vase in one hand, I pressed my phone to my ear.

"Easy."

"They're beautiful. Thank you."

"Does that mean we're on?"

"We're on. But lunch might be off."

"Oh?" His disappointment tugged on my heart.

"Hayden wants me to shadow her this morning, which means it could turn into all day."

"We can do it tomorrow then."

"No," I said quickly. "I mean, I want to try today, but—"

"You're a busy woman. Just let me know."

"The flowers. They made my day." I set them on my desk and admired the bright colors. Usually, I'd be in bed on this day, reliving the pain. Holt had made it easier to bear and didn't even know it.

"I'm glad. I'll either see you at lunch or see you at home."

CHAPTER TWENTY-NINE

HOLT

Can you do 2?

THE TEXT TURNED around my sour mood in an instant. It was after noon. I'd already resigned myself to the fact we wouldn't get to do lunch. Now that it was on, I whistled as I changed the battery on a Ford Taurus.

I'd spent the night with Baker—I spent every night with her. Shared coffee this morning, walked her to the train. It still wasn't enough. I wanted lunch with her and had no logical reason why. Although if I was honest with myself, it did make sense. Baker had shown more loyalty and genuine concern for me than I'd ever experienced before outside my family. Even Celia hadn't ever connected with me so instinctively. I never let her see the real me, but I'd loved her superficially. And she allowed that. Whereas Baker demanded more of me, and gave more to me as well.

Meet me at the new garage. I'll bring the food.

That earned me a thumbs up emoji followed by a big smiley face. I checked the time again. Only three minutes had passed. Ninety more to go.

"HOLT?"

Baker's voice echoed through the empty space.

"Up here." I leaned over the loft railing. "I'm coming down."

I thundered down the stairs, hustling until I reached her.

"What were you doing?"

I lifted her onto the reception desk, placing her on my jacket.

"Forgot there are no chairs." I offered her a taco.

She scooted over, and I perched beside her.

"What are we doing here?"

"It's a quiet place to eat." I popped a nacho in my mouth.

"And . . ."

I shrugged. "I'm not sure I can do this."

She set her half-eaten taco on the wrapper in her lap. "What? The garage?"

"Yeah. I bought this place on an impulse. Which was stupid. I don't know if I can get any business, let alone run it."

"I'm not sure it was an impulse."

I offered her a nacho. "I can afford it. That's not the problem."

"Then what is?" She licked a string of cheese from her finger.

"I don't know shit about running a business."

"Lots of people don't when they start one." She touched my arm. "Word is you're a pretty good mechanic."

"I can fix the hell out of a car. Or food truck." I smirked, and she wiped a crumb from the corner of my mouth. "But I don't know how to do bookkeeping or about tax laws."

"Hire an accountant."

I shifted, angling my legs toward her. "Did I ever tell you how I got into fixing up cars?"

"You loved them?"

"I am a sucker for old ones. But I like figuring out how things work. I was the kid who took apart the VCR."

"What's that?" She grinned, and I chucked her chin.

"My point is I'd be that way with accounting or whatever else it is. It's hard for me to hand that stuff over to someone else. I want to know how to do it myself."

"Talk to Vivian. She's an accountant. She could teach you the basics." Our neighbors had been more than willing to help us out. I hated to ask for something from anyone, especially when they were already so generous with the rent. But Baker was right. It wouldn't hurt to talk to her.

"What if I get sidetracked? I'm always chasing shiny balls."

"If that were true, wouldn't you have had a million jobs? All you've ever been is a park ranger and mechanic, right?"

"I was in college for six years because I couldn't decide what I wanted to do."

"I didn't even finish." She reached into the bag for another taco, but refused to look at me.

"It's not for everyone."

"But it was for me," she said, her voice rising.

"Go back now."

"How? In case you hadn't noticed, we have no rent or bills. If we did, I couldn't afford them."

"They don't pay you at the magazine?"

"They pay me, but I don't have anything. I was at the shelter almost three years." She snapped her mouth shut as if realizing she'd given away something she didn't want to.

"And before then?"

"I had nothing. I have nothing. Moneywise anyway."

"Why didn't you finish school?"

She was silent so long, I didn't think she'd answer. Her hands fisted a paper wrapper until she finally tossed it in the bag.

"When my boyfriend found out I'd been going behind his back, he made me quit." My mouth dropped open. "Yeah, I know. It should have been a clue to get away from him."

"Not necessarily," I said, choosing my words carefully. "It's always easier to see our mistakes after the fact."

"Some we should see coming."

"What did you want to study?"

"Chemistry."

I perked up. "That's why you like concocting your makeup."

"I-I never thought of it, but I guess so." She swung her legs and her heels banged against the desk.

"Ever think about going back?" I tossed the idea out there casually when I was anything but indifferent.

"Not really." She stared at her swinging legs. "So why a park ranger?"

"I worked on a ranger's truck while I was in school. We got to talking about it. I needed to decide on a major or I'd be on a seven-year plan. It sounded interesting and turns out it was."

"That's it?"

"Not the glamorous story you hoped for?" I nudged her shoulder with mine.

"I pictured a hike to a top of a mountain and inspiration struck."

I held my arms out wide and looked to the ceiling. "Aah," I sang.

Her laughter bounced off the walls. "That's more like it."

I offered her another taco. "Might be a while until dinner."

She accepted and peeled back the wrapper. "Do you miss it?"

"The park? Yeah. But I couldn't stay." All at once, the food wasn't so appealing.

"Because of him?"

Just the mere mention of Cameron hurt to the point it nearly crippled me. "Partly."

"And the woman who called? She's the other reason?"

Stop running. Tell her the truth. But I could barely admit it to myself.

It's too risky. Baker was different. Which made opening up even scarier.

"Yeah." I shoved my trash into a paper bag. Admitting that didn't make me feel one ounce better. I held out my hand for her empty wrapper. She looked as if she wanted to say something but didn't immediately. I wasn't sure if I was relieved or disappointed.

"Are you okay?"

I jolted at the question she finally settled on. There was no demand of who Celia was to me or what happened. What mattered to Baker was how I felt. I leaned forward and kissed her lips softly, thankful again she was in my life.

"I'm not sure. But I'm working through it." If swinging between throbbing anger and unbearable pain could be counted as such.

She nodded. "That's all we can do." She touched my cheek. "I'm not completely sure I want to hear all the details, but if you need to talk about it, I'm here."

Knowing that made me feel better. "Thanks. I'm not sure I'm ready to relive it yet. But I'm glad to know you'll be listening when I can." I slid to my feet. "I hate to cut this short, but I gotta get back to the shop. Mind locking up?" I took the key off my keyring and pressed it into her palm.

"Hang on. I'll leave with you." She scrambled off the desk and collected her bag. "Oh. Your jacket."

She held it out to me.

"Thanks." I shrugged it on and grabbed our trash.

She slid her hand into mine and everything clicked into place.

I wanted more.

More of her body. More of her light. More of her soul.

Her heels clicked on the concrete as we moved toward the door.

I hesitated before I turned the doorknob. "It's a two-way street. If you need to talk, I mean."

She went rigid for a moment, as if the idea was hard to handle. Then she relaxed and squeezed my hand. "I appreciate that."

I held open the door and followed her through. Maybe we hadn't gotten anything out in the open, but I was confident if I needed to talk, she'd be there.

As I locked up, her mouth grazed my ear. "Same place tomorrow?"

CHAPTER THIRTY

BAKER

I LINGERED at the office as long as I could get away with.

I didn't want to go home to an empty house, and Holt had already texted he was going to be late.

The silence was a comfortable one when I pushed into the apartment, but still too much for me to bear. I put on "I Feel Like I'm Drowning" by Two Feet and collapsed on the sofa.

My mind had been at war all afternoon between Holt and Kyle. One or the other had demanded my attention. A ghost and the man who was slowly but surely mending my broken pieces.

A soft rap on the door jolted me to my feet. The neighbors had a tendency to drop by whenever they felt like it, something I was still getting used to.

I checked the peephole before I opened the door.

"Mrs. Quinn." I gave her a quick hug and stepped aside. "What brings you by?"

She held up a box of tea. "I miss seeing you every day."

I welcomed her inside, and we caught up on the latest at Paths as I heated water and searched for cups.

Full cups in hand, we settled on the sofa. "Somehow, I don't think that's the only reason you're here."

"Thought you might like some company. Especially today."

I choked on a sip of tea. Of course, she wouldn't forget.

"I'm good," I said once I found my voice. "Better than usual, I guess." And that bothered me. Did it mean I was forgetting? Or that I'd become numb to what happened?

Mrs. Quinn nodded once and hid behind her cup. "I didn't come by so we could talk about it. You've relived what happened enough."

"It's getting easier and harder," I confessed. "I'm finding my place. Have more good days than bad. And I don't deserve it."

She touched my leg. "You didn't do anything wrong."

I stiffened. "How can you say that? I-I don't want to talk about this."

"We don't have to." She glanced away, fiddling with the handle on her tea cup. "Have you seen the news today?"

"No. I've intentionally avoided it."

"Someone leaked that he didn't act alone."

I bolted to my feet. "What do you mean?"

"I'm afraid they're going to dig. The reporter claims it was a woman—"

"They promised to protect me," I shouted.

"Everything okay?"

The front door clicked shut behind Holt, who looked between Mrs. Quinn and me.

She smoothed a polite smile on her face. "Hello, Holt. I hope you don't mind I dropped by for a cup of tea with Baker. I find Paths to be a bit lonely without her."

"I hate to be the bearer of bad news, but you can't have her back." He strode straight over to me and kissed me.

Motor oil and Holt only marginally settled me.

"I'm glad to hear it."

"Is this a ladies-only conversation or can I join you once I change clothes?"

Mrs. Quinn held up her near empty cup and stood. "I need to be on my way."

"Hot date with an old man?" Holt winked at her.

"Something like that."

"I'm glad." He turned to me and said, "I'll shower and then we'll have dinner, okay?"

"Sounds good."

After another kiss to my forehead, he headed toward the bathroom, and the sound of the shower started not long after Holt disappeared. Mrs. Quinn's expression turned serious.

"I'd like to speak with Daniel Elliott about this. He would be the person to help us keep it quiet."

"How is this happening?" My heart pounded as panic threatened to overtake me.

"I don't know." She touched my shoulder. "Don't forget I'm here. We'll get through it, whatever may happen."

"Do you think they know my name?"

"If they do, they didn't mention it. I've searched every article I could find and there's nothing."

My eyes stung. "It will never be over, will it?"

"No," she said, her expression solemn. "I'll let you know what Daniel says."

I nodded and she folded me in her arms.

"I thought I could disappear," I whispered.

"You don't have to. You've got people here who love you. Don't forget that."

I HUDDLED ON THE SOFA, the tea cup in my hand trembling as I brought it to my lips.

"I didn't mean to run her off." Holt sank down next to me and took a long slog of water. "Why haven't you changed?"

"I haven't been home long. Mrs. Quinn dropped by and . . ." I swallowed past the lump in my throat.

"You're shaking." He set his water down and took my cup from my hands.

He opened his arms, his fingers flexing like he wanted to reach for me. But he gave me the choice. I crawled across the sofa and burrowed into him.

"I've got you."

I clutched his sides, fisting his T-shirt. All I wanted to do was weep. For the people who'd suffered. For the girl I'd been. For the boy who'd been so lost.

Holt stroked my hair and feathered kisses along the top of my head. "Want to talk about it?"

I shook my head, though I suspected he probably already knew the answer to that.

"This isn't about me? This afternoon?"

I sat up and furrowed my brow. "No," I said hoarsely as I searched his face.

He relaxed into the sofa. "Do you want to do this thing, Easy? For real?"

I pressed my palms into his thighs and stared at him. "Kinda feels like we already are."

He brushed my hair back from my face. "I know what I said. That I can't." He looked down. "I don't know if I'm capable of full trust. But you make me want to try."

My heart stopped. We'd been doing this dance around commitment, and that he wanted to make a go at a relationship was thrilling and terrifying at once.

"I don't want the past to get in the way. Can we pretend like neither of ours ever happened?"

His lips twitched. "Another reason why we're perfect for each other."

I snuggled back into him. "I've been thinking about the garage. About your offer."

"Yeah?"

I played with the hem of his T-shirt. "I want to take you up on it."

He grasped my arms and pulled me so he could look at me. "You do?"

I nodded. "Let's get the garage running first. We can clean up the upstairs space after. Then think about remodeling or whatever."

"What changed your mind?"

"I'm not sure it changed really, but after my meeting today, watching everyone work together and how inspired they were to be pursuing their passions, I realized I could have that too. I mean, I do at the magazine," I quickly corrected. "But I could have more."

He gazed down at me, his face lit with happiness. And knowing he wanted us to do this together excited me even more.

He flashed a cocky smirk. "You want more lunch dates."

I grinned. "I definitely want more lunch dates."

CHAPTER THIRTY-ONE

HOLT

"Hey. It's me. Please call me back. I need to talk to you."

FOUR DAYS in a row Celia had called. Today was the first message.

My finger hovered over Block Number, but I couldn't go through with it. Instead, I darkened the screen and dropped my phone back in my pocket.

"Sorry I'm late." Dad's face was flushed as he shrugged off his coat.

"Mrs. Quinn wasn't too keen to say goodbye?"

He cleared his throat and took a seat. "Not really."

I handed him a soda. "Your other son hasn't made it yet, either."

He glanced to the scoreboard hanging above the ice rink. "Still five minutes until puck drop."

I tossed a piece of popcorn in my mouth. "We could've asked the ladies to come."

"Next time." He scooped a handful of popcorn out of the bucket. "Feels like we never hang out anymore. Just the guys."

"Because neither you nor Andrew are as interesting as they are."

Dad smirked before he pointed at me. "Oh, before I forget. A Rob called me on the way here. He said he was your landlord back in Wyoming."

Rob? Why would he call Dad? Unease slithered through me. "What did he want?"

"Said he'd been trying to reach you, and I was your emergency contact on the lease. Your rent is due." Dad sipped his drink as if indifferent, but I felt his tension. "He also wanted to know what to do with your things if you weren't coming back."

I sagged and rested my head on the back of the chair. "I'll call him."

Had I been in New York four months? That was how long was left on my lease when I took off. The thought never occurred to me I might not go back. Now, I couldn't imagine it.

"What are you going to tell him?" Dad's tone was cautious.

"To go ahead and rent it out. I'll figure out what to do with the stuff."

He exhaled in relief. "Want me to go with you to pick it up?"

I took a pull off my soda. "Me and you? A cross-country trip?"

"Might be fun." He shrugged. "Or you could take Baker."

"Sorry I'm late." Andrew waded through the aisle and dropped down in the seat next to Dad.

"I've already heard that once tonight," I said with a wry look up at the ceiling.

"One minute to spare." I passed him a soda, and he accepted. "Thanks."

"How's Ella and Trish?"

He lit up. "Keeping my life interesting."

Dad snorted. "I bet."

The arena darkened and the team skated out to flashing lights and smoke. We got to our feet, hooting and whistling with the rest of the crowd.

"HOLT'S GOING to get his things from Wyoming," Dad said once the puck had dropped and the noise died down.

"I didn't say that."

"Don't you think Baker should go with him?" Dad asked my brother. Great. Now the whole family would be in on my decision.

Andrew scooped popcorn from the bucket. "Not if he wants to stay with her. They already live together. A car trip could be the kiss of death."

A knowing smile graced Dad's features. "Your mother and I drove to Virginia once. A spur of the moment getaway. I wasn't sure who was going to file for divorce first when we got back. Me or her."

Andrew and I exchanged a look. Dad didn't talk about *her*, let alone when they were together.

"Ended up being one of the best trips we ever took. Once she stopped telling me how to drive, problem solved," he continued while my brother and I stared. "I can talk about her. I just don't like to."

"It wasn't that long ago I mentioned I'd run into her and you took off." Andrew pointed his cup at him.

"I'm trying," Dad conceded.

"What's the weather like out there this time of year?" Andrew leaned forward and cursed when our goalie let the puck get past him for a score.

"Pretty nice most of the time. Cooler than here. Maybe an early snow. I haven't checked."

"Think there's a good spot for a wedding?"

I coughed and spluttered soda down my shirt. I wiped my mouth with the back of my hand. "Yeah. What are you getting at?"

"I'm ready to get married. I think Trish is. Maybe we could make this trip out west a family affair."

"You're shitting me. Seven adults and two toddlers? In one vehicle? Count me out." I spread my legs and rested my drink on my knee.

"No way in hell. We'd fly." Andrew looked at me like I was nuts. "I want to *marry* Trish. Not drive her away. We're barely surviving Sunday dinners."

"Those causing problems between you two?" I'd been the center of those fights and the thought of that overflowing into their relationship made my stomach turn.

Andrew waved his hand in front of his face. "No. No. She doesn't like that we aren't all getting along, but we aren't arguing over it."

"Good."

"When do you have to have your things out of your place?" He tossed a piece of popcorn into his mouth.

"I haven't talked to Rob yet."

"Let me know when you think you're going. I'll talk to Trish. See if she wants to get married out there."

"I need to know too. I'm sure Audrey will want to be there."

I scrubbed my hand across my forehead. "Yeah, sure."

"Think Baker will be down?"

I wasn't even sure if *I* was. This whole thing had spun out of control in the span of a few minutes.

"What about Marlow?"

"I thought you worked things out," Dad said, eyeing me suspiciously.

"Uh, well . . ." I looked to Andrew for help, but he hid behind his drink. "Things got ugly after you left. She said some things, and I'm not anywhere close to over it."

Dad gasped. "Why didn't you say anything?"

"Because you and Mrs. Quinn are figuring things out. This is the first time in weeks you've seemed like yourself. No need to bring you down over something you can't do anything about." I polished off my drink. "Anybody need a refill?"

I stood and stepped my way over legs and feet to the main aisle. I jogged up the steps and once I reached the concession stand, the line wasn't near long enough to my liking.

I loved my family, that we were close. But sometimes it felt like I was suffocating. All I'd wanted was to belong, but I guessed that meant at my own standards. I appreciated their perspective, but there was no chance in hell I would let Baker set foot in Wyoming.

I had to figure out how to put the brakes on this plan. Pronto.

CHAPTER THIRTY-TWO

BAKER

"IT TOOK us long enough to get together, right?"

Trish pushed and pulled Ella's stroller with her foot while we lazed on a park bench.

"I feel like I haven't seen you in forever," I said, relieved to finally have a moment with my best friend. Work at the magazine had been crazier than usual. One of the public figures we were supposed to profile had been in a motorcycle accident and wanted to push back her feature. We'd been scrambling to rearrange. And . . . I'd been spending every spare moment with Holt.

A little jolt went through me at the thought of him. We'd spent lots of late nights making plans about the shop. I'd let myself think a lot about the future lately instead of dwelling on the past.

It still scared me, but excited me too.

"We can't let a week go by again without talking," Trish said solemnly. "I honestly don't know where the time goes. Only that it's been a whirlwind."

I held out my pinky like the kid I wasn't, and she met mine with her own. We hooked fingers. "Pinky swear."

"Pinky swear." We grinned at each other. "I have news that was too important to share on the phone or in a text."

She paused pushing Ella. "Andrew and I are getting married."

"That's terrific." I automatically glanced at her left ring finger, genuinely excited for her, but prayed my voice didn't betray the unbalanced way I felt. *This is great news. Trish deserves this.*

"No." She laughed. "No ring yet. That will happen. We were going to wait, but the time is right. Ella and I belong with Andrew." A wistful expression shaped her pretty features. She reached for my hands. "I want you to be my maid of honor."

"You do?" I'd never been close enough to anyone to be asked something like that. It meant so much.

She nodded. "Of course I do. I can't get married without you by my side."

A few minutes ago I'd felt that tickle of being unwanted and now the pendulum had swung to the other side . . . a side I liked much better.

"I'd love to be your maid of honor." I twisted to face her. "When's the big day?"

"Next weekend. In Wyoming. Unless you can't make it," she said quickly. "Then we'll wait."

"Wow. That's fast." She was moving forward with her life and deserved all the joy that had seemed impossible not so long ago. But Trish had always had a light, a positive attitude I admired, even if I struggled to do the same. "I'll figure it out," I promised. And I would find a way to be at the wedding, no matter what. Alarm bells went off in my head. "Wait. Wyoming?"

"Holt needs to get the rest of his things, so when he said he was going to Wyoming, Andrew thought it would be a great place to get married."

I swallowed hard. In all the times Holt had opened his mouth lately, not one word of any of this had come out. Maybe he didn't want to spoil the surprise of Trish telling me herself. "Yeah? When did this come up?"

She fidgeted with the hem of her sweater. "Last week. At the hockey game."

Hurt filled the crevices in my heart. It was an old pain mingling with the fresh wound. My family had intentionally excluded me from their lives and it was something I hadn't gotten over. This felt like that all over again.

I STUCK the key in the lock, but it wouldn't turn no matter how I jiggled. I checked to make sure I had the right key and tried again. It wouldn't budge.

I rang the doorbell. No one came. My parents wouldn't be home in the afternoon anyway.

As I pulled out my phone to call my mother, I noticed through the front windows that the living room was empty. I shimmied through the shrubs and peered through the glass.

Everything was gone.

MY PARENTS HAD MOVED without telling me. That was the high school graduation gift I received.

It still hurt to think about that gut punch.

I cleared my throat. "He didn't say anything."

She touched my knee. "Is there a chance he didn't because you hadn't mentioned the wedding and he didn't want to spoil the news?"

I lifted a shoulder to my ear. "Maybe?" But deep down, I didn't believe that. We were both working through our trust issues. "Going back to get his things is a big deal, like he's really serious about being here."

"You doubted that he was? What about the building he bought?" Trish stared at me with concerned eyes.

"I guess part of me thinks whatever it is that's happening with us is too good to be true. It started out as something fun, casual. Now? It feels like it became something more with hardly any effort. At least I thought it was." The words tumbled out as my emotions spiraled.

"He wouldn't have offered you the space to work on your products if he didn't see something long term."

"But it could be friendship. Or just sex," I protested, my voice rising. A jogger passing by did a double take, but I ignored her. "I'm leaning toward just sex. Otherwise why wouldn't he tell me he was going to Wyoming to get the rest of his things?"

She looked at me, uncertain. "All I know is Andrew worries about him. I'm not sure what happened to Holt, only that he doesn't talk about it much."

I snorted. "Trust me. *That* I do know." I rubbed my temples. "I don't want to talk about my past any more than he wants to discuss his. And that's okay for now. But purposely excluding me? When I thought we were taking baby steps forward? It hurts."

I dropped my chin to my chest. Trish rubbed my back. "Do you want to know about the past?"

I didn't answer for a long time. Yes. No. I wasn't sure. "Part of me is afraid to find out. There's obviously a woman involved and I really don't like thinking about that."

Kyle had never looked at anyone else. I'd been the center of his universe and hadn't experienced a lot of jealousy. I didn't much care for the foreign feeling, but it was definitely there when I thought about Holt sharing a life with someone else.

"And part of you is afraid one day you'll have to tell him about yours," Trish said. I loved her for her honesty, but sometimes I wanted to avoid the truth. *The truth is too horrific to discuss.*

"That's true. I thought this would be simple. But my feelings got involved when I didn't mean for them to."

She gave me a knowing smile. "They have a way of doing that when we least expect it."

Ella let out a shriek of agreement.

"She's already wise, isn't she?" I placed her plastic key ring back on her stomach.

"She is." Trish beamed at her daughter before she turned to me. "Opening up takes two. You can't ask Holt to do something you aren't willing to do."

It was the constant ripping open of old wounds that made thinking clearly hard sometimes. "I know."

"We should head to Dino's if we don't want to be late."

We stood, and she threw her arms around me.

I hugged her in return. "Thank you for talking. For asking me to be your maid of honor. I'm so excited." I practically squealed, beyond pleased for her.

She pulled back and grinned. "This means so much to me."

I sniffled. "Me too."

"YOU KNOW WHAT?" I grabbed Trish's arm as she pulled on the door handle of Dino's. "I'm not ready to see him yet. I need a minute to process."

She looked proud of me for facing my feelings and hugged me hard. "If you need me, I'm here."

"I know." I vowed to myself to be a better friend and not let our lives get in the way of talking like they had lately. I needed her.

"Promise me you'll be at the wedding. It's a big ask, but I can't get married without you." If they were getting married on Saturday, I could fly down Friday night. Hayden might let me take Friday off, so I could get there earlier. *I can do that.*

"Promise." I squeezed her. "Call you later."

I kissed Ella and waved goodbye, my heart heavy as I wandered home. Holt hadn't breathed a word of a wedding or Wyoming. I understood the wedding part. That was Trish's news to share. But he'd had almost a week to say *something* about the trip, yet he'd been silent. Silent through every lunch. While he made love to me. As he held me in his arms every night.

We were taking it slow, learning to trust, but this cut to the quick. He couldn't have known that his actions would affect me even deeper because of the way my family had treated me when I needed them most. I hadn't told him about any of that. And maybe he needed time too. I could give him that as long as we were honest. I was willing to give him a chance to open up, even it if was just a little.

"EASY?"

I remained still in the darkness, staring out the windows from my position on the floor. His footsteps passed through the kitchen down the hallway and back.

Keys rattled as he picked them up and dropped them on the counter. My phone rang from inside my purse as he no doubt tried to call me.

"Easy?" The panic in his voice bumped up a notch. His boots thudded on the hardwoods as he rounded the sofa. I hugged my knees to my chest and rested my chin on them. "Trish said you weren't feeling well."

"Why didn't you tell me about Wyoming?" The words came out in a flat tone. I wanted to scream at him.

"I—" He stood there as if he couldn't figure out what to say.

"Were you ever going to?" I carried on, all my hurt coming out in a rush. "Were you going to ask me to go? Or at least talk to me about it?"

His silence stretched long and thick between us. I waited. *Why were these questions so hard for him to answer?*

"No."

How could two letters be so painful?

"Then I can't do this anymore." Somehow I managed to make that sound normal, instead of strangled, the way I felt.

"Can't do what?" he asked carefully.

I waved my hand between us. "This." He stared at me, and I struggled to articulate what was in my head. "You purposely excluded me from something important in your life. That's happened to me before and I—I can handle you needing to talk about things in your own time. I *understand* that because I feel it myself. But you could've told me you were going, even if you didn't want me to take the trip with you."

He plowed his hands through his hair. "I told you I can't talk about Wyoming."

"And I told you I'm not asking you to right now. That's not fair when there are things I'm not willing to open up about either. But if I needed to take a trip back to DC, I would've mentioned it." I went to the refrigerator and grabbed a bottle of water, desperate to do something to dampen the intensity.

My hands shook as I unscrewed the cap and took a sip.

"You lived in Washington, DC?"

That's what he picked up out of everything I said?

"Yes." There were only a handful of people who knew that. People I trusted implicitly. I thought Holt could've been in that circle too one day.

"I'm sorry. I didn't handle this well, but I'm still just not able to talk about Wyoming. It would be too hard for you to be there."

I nearly choked. "You don't want me to go to my best friend's wedding?"

He glanced away. "I didn't say that."

But it was in his tone, in his tense posture. He couldn't handle me being in that state, even for such an important event.

That was the answer I hadn't wanted.

We couldn't move forward because the past still had us in its clutches.

"We can't live together anymore."

He stumbled backward as I gripped the counter for support. Those were some of the hardest words I'd ever spoken, but were necessary.

"You're moving out?" he asked hoarsely.

It had taken all my courage to move out of Paths Of Purpose. If I needed to go back, I could. But that would be going backward when I'd worked so hard to get to this point. I cared for Holt more than I wanted to admit, but when it came to this I had to be selfish.

"No. You should."

He blinked at me, stunned. Then he stalked toward me until he'd invaded my space. "Easy." He tried to hold me, but I shrugged him off.

This was hard enough. I needed his comfort, but couldn't handle it. Not now.

He swallowed hard. "That's it then?" I nodded. I couldn't find the right words, even though I knew that underneath his secrets and fears Holt was a good man. That he wasn't a man who played games when his heart was invested. I also knew he wouldn't fight me on this one, and that made me feel guilty. *He didn't believe he was worth fighting for.* But I didn't have the strength to fight either. "I'll go to my dad's and pick up the rest of my stuff later."

I nodded, unable to speak. If I did, I'd crumble. I was barely holding it together as it was.

He disappeared into his room and came out a few minutes later with a bag on his shoulder. A lump formed in my throat. He was really going. This was it.

Neither of us spoke as he grabbed his keys off the counter and shrugged on his leather jacket.

"I'm sorry." He held my gaze, and I believed him. But he wasn't sorry enough to try harder.

I jumped when the door slammed and covered my mouth to keep my cry of anguish from escaping. My legs gave way. I sank to the floor and hid my face in my knees. This time, I didn't see any way to mend our broken relationship.

CHAPTER THIRTY-THREE

HOLT

"FEEL LIKE HOME?"

Andrew slapped my shoulder as I slung my bag in the truck I'd left at the airport all those months ago.

Dad stared at me across the bed while I made a fuss closing the tailgate. Instead of looking at him, I shielded my eyes and took in the clear blue sky. The air was crisp as it swirled the leaves around the tires.

"No."

Dad climbed in the cab and slid to the center of the seat as I got behind the wheel.

"Think she'll start?" He patted the dashboard of my '78 Ford.

"We're about to find out." I turned the key and she roared to life.

Dad grinned. "Knew she was a good one when we bought her."

He'd surprised me on my fifteenth birthday with the skeleton of a truck that just needed a little life breathed into her. It had taken me a year of working on it every spare minute I had, but I'd gotten her running.

"I remember the first time you got the motor started. The way we acted, you'd have thought we won the lottery." Andrew laughed as he recalled the day ingrained in all of our memories.

"Can't let her go." I gripped the steering wheel as I pulled out of the parking lot.

I'd missed this. Me and my truck and the open road. I didn't need her in New York. The only driving I'd done since I'd been there were test runs of the cars I'd fixed.

"What are you going to do with her? Think she'll make it back to New York?"

"How do you think Trish and Ella would feel about a honeymoon drive across country?" I glanced at Andrew and grinned.

"She'd be down, but I'm not."

"You're no fun." I reached around Dad and slapped Andrew in the back of the head.

"You haven't been a picnic since Baker didn't show for Sunday dinner last weekend."

I smacked him in the head again.

"When's she coming out?" Dad moved my arm back to the wheel. I'd been staying with him for the last three days, but hadn't elaborated on why I wasn't going home.

"Wouldn't know." I gripped the worn leather of the steering wheel. If I was going to get through this, I had to stop thinking of the apartment I'd shared with Baker as home.

You purposely excluded me from something important in your life. That's happened to me before . . .

She'd made it clear where she stood, and I didn't blame her. When she spent Sunday afternoon with Trish, I should've known they'd talk about Wyoming. Looking back, I was surprised it hadn't come up sooner.

It was stupid. I didn't know why I hadn't told her about the trip. She and Trish were best friends. It wasn't like I could avoid the subject forever.

But I had.

Because I didn't want her near my past.

I needed her separate from this. The minute she stepped into this part of my world, she'd see everything I didn't want her to. I wasn't ready for that, even though I wouldn't get another chance with her.

"Trish says she can't make it until Friday night. Something about work."

I had treated her poorly. Maybe she hadn't said the words out loud, but her actions had told me she thought she deserved more. And she was right.

It was going to be a long weekend seeing her here with Trish, supporting Trish, but nowhere near my arms.

"Marlow will be here on Friday too."

I stifled my groan as Andrew stiffened. We both wanted her here and didn't at the same time. The three of us weren't in a good place, but I gave her credit for trying to set that aside for our brother's wedding. I'd yet to speak to her, and Andrew said his conversation to invite her had been awkward at best.

A black Yukon blasted the horn as it passed. Trish rolled down the window and waved. I honked twice. The three of us waved back. We'd put Trish, Mrs. Quinn, and Ella in the hotel's car service.

I followed the SUV to the Four Seasons and dropped Dad and Andrew off.

"We have reservations at seven." Dad leaned against my door.

"I'll see you then."

FIFTEEN MINUTES LATER, I pulled up to the cabin I'd once called home. I used to take solace in the solitude. Now, it felt lonely.

I put the truck in park and sat there for a long time, tempted to go back to the hotel. Stay with my family instead of here. But I needed to pack up. Close this chapter of my life.

With heavy footsteps, I trudged to the front door with my bag over my shoulder. I pushed inside. It was dark and cold, that scent a house got when it had been closed up a while invading my nose.

I dropped my bag and flicked on the light. The only thing different from the day I left was a layer of dust and a cobweb in the corner between the kitchen and den.

It was insane to think I could get this all packed up in a few days.

What was I going to do with the furniture? It would cost more to ship it than it was worth.

I wandered to the fridge and opened it. "Ugh."

Moldy lettuce and cheese greeted me. Past that was half a gallon of what used to be milk. I shoved it to the side and snatched a beer from the six pack I hadn't gotten around to polishing off before I left.

I untwisted the cap, flicked it on the counter, and checked my phone. Almost six in New York. Wonder if Baker was home yet?

I cursed and drained half my beer. This was for the best. I wasn't meant to be in a relationship, not with my trust issues. And I wasn't so sure she was either. Some people were meant to be alone.

The last few months I'd been here, I'd learned that lesson. New York had made me forget. Maybe coming back was a good reminder.

I might not need my brother to drive my truck to the city after all. I could haul all this stuff back and move into the apartment above the garage. It was rudimentary, but I could fix it up. This weekend would be the last I'd have to see of Baker.

Everything in me rebelled at the thought. But it had to be. If we kept at it, one of us was going to get hurt, and I had a feeling it would be me. I was tired of always getting stepped on. I'd miss her, but eventually that would go away.

Three sharp knocks broke the silence.

"Who the hell could that be?" I muttered under my breath. I hadn't been back in town thirty whole minutes.

I set my beer down and checked the spy hole.

"Son of a bitch. The rumors are true." Roman, my supervisor at the park, stood on the stoop.

"What rumors?" I moved out of the way, and he stepped inside.

"That you were back in town." He slapped my shoulder. "Thought I'd have heard from you by now."

"Want a beer?"

He followed me to the kitchen, where I pulled out two fresh cold ones from the fridge.

"Glad you're back. I'm trying to get these plants surveyed before the first big snow. Which is predicted for week after next, by the way." He grinned and tapped his bottle with mine.

"You're not gonna make it." I found myself smiling back, easily slipping into the old routine.

"Nope. You can meet me at six in the morning and we'll knock out what we can."

"My brother's getting married this weekend."

He pointed at me and pretended to pull a trigger. "Monday, then." Roman yanked out a chair and sat in it backward. "You've been gone too long. Things aren't the same without you."

"I needed to get away." I picked at the label of my beer. While that was true, I should've added I wasn't coming back, but couldn't make myself tell him. Knowing Baker and I were done made New York far less appealing.

"I get it, man. But I was beginning to get worried you weren't coming back."

The words of my resignation lodged in my throat. Quitting a job I'd loved wasn't as easy as I thought it would be.

"You up for meeting the boys tonight? If Briggs asks permission now, Suzanna might let him out of the house."

I laughed. That sounded about right. "I'm going to dinner with my family."

"After that. They can come too."

"We'll see. Pretty tired after the flight."

"Come on. You've been gone forever."

"Fine. But I can't miss dinner."

He held up both of his hands. "Of course not. I'll let the guys know."

"You're a pushy bastard. Anybody ever tell you that?"

He grinned and stood. "How do you think I got to be the boss?"

Roman put me in a headlock and gave me a noogie. I punched him in the stomach, and he let me go.

"Asshole."

We were such idiots.

"Seriously. It's good to have you back."

I nodded and walked him to the door. He stepped over the threshold and turned around, his expression serious.

"Fair warning. Celia's been asking about you."

"She can ask all she likes." I leaned against the doorframe.

"She regrets—"

"Don't give a damn." I folded my arms over my chest.

"All right. All right." He trotted to his truck. "See you tonight."

CHAPTER THIRTY-FOUR

BAKER

I'D LIED to my best friend for the first time, and I vowed it would be the last.

"Baker." A paper ball hit me in the arm. "Go to the airport."

I stared across the table at Hayden.

"I'm leaving day after tomorrow."

"You're already gone," she said with a soft smile.

I tried to focus. "I'm good. Trish doesn't need me until Friday."

"Then why did she try to convince me to let you off early when I saw her yesterday?"

I sagged in my chair. "You've already bought the plane ticket. I can't ask for more time away from work."

She waved me off. "Go. I'll get your flight changed."

I didn't move. "I can't go."

She studied me. "Does this have to do with your roommate?"

Warmth crept up my cheeks. "Yeah."

I found myself spilling how they'd planned this whole trip to Wyoming and he hadn't mentioned it to me once. How he'd begun the process of moving out, and we hadn't spoken to each other in the days that followed. That Holt and I were definitely done because he wasn't receptive to me understanding him beyond the immediate.

When I finished, Hayden tapped her pen on the desk a few times.

"This weekend is about Trish." She fired a pointed look in my direction. "The two of you have been there for each other. Don't let whatever he's doing get in the way of that."

I propped my chin in my palm. "I didn't forget that. I just—"

"It's hard."

"It is."

"I won't give advice on subjects I have no authority on." She grinned. "In case that wasn't clear, I mean men."

A smile cracked my face. "Fair enough."

"I'm not telling you to forget about him or whatever shit he's trying to pull. Just forget about it for now. Go get on a plane and be there for your best friend."

I nodded once. "You're right."

"Before you go, I have the perfect dress for you to take."

I HUDDLED in my jacket and clutched my suitcase. The airport was practically deserted and it was barely ten. The night was so quiet, it was unnerving.

I'd texted Trish as soon as my plane landed. She promised a car would be by to pick me up soon.

A taxi inched forward almost eagerly. Again, a difference from New York. If I was on a street corner there, a thousand would have passed me by.

I'd made the right decision to come. I knew that. But I'd never been on a plane, let alone this far away. City life was all I'd ever known. This fresh air and quiet had my already frazzled nerves working overtime.

I glanced to my left, headlights growing brighter as they approached. A black SUV pulled to the curb in front of me.

"Miss Holland?"

"Yes."

"I'm Gerald from the Four Seasons Hotel. Let me take your things."

He held open the back door for me before loading my suitcase in the trunk.

"Wyoming's been waiting for you," he said as he maneuvered the car out of the airport.

I snorted. Somehow I doubted that. "Funny, I never gave Wyoming any thought at all." Until lately.

He laughed. "First time?"

"Probably my last too."

"Don't be so sure about that."

WHEN HE STOPPED in front of the Million Dollar Cowboy Bar and put the SUV in park, I frowned.

"Here we are."

"This shuttle doesn't go all the way to the hotel?"

He grinned. "I have my instructions. Can't deviate."

I was on the sidewalk, staring up at the sign, before I could blink. *Trish better be in here.* I pulled on the door handle; country music, dancing couples, and people of all kinds parked at the bar greeted me.

I hesitated, scouring one side of the room to the other. Trish barreled toward me, and I met her halfway. She threw her arms around me.

"You're here."

"I'm here." I clutched her back before I held her at arm's length. "How much champagne have you had?"

She giggled. "A little."

"Looks like I need to catch up."

She grabbed my hand and dragged me across the dance floor to a row of tables. "Look who's here."

Andrew, Patrick, Mr. Dixon, and Mrs. Quinn chorused their hellos. Holt was nowhere to be found.

"Where's Ella?"

"With Marlow."

Marlow is already here? "I thought she wasn't coming until Friday?"

"She showed up too, but didn't feel up to dinner." Trish leaned in. "I think she was afraid to be around her brothers."

"Can't say I blame her."

My gaze drifted around the table. There were only two empty chairs, and I was quickly ushered into one of them. I mentally chastised myself for wondering where Holt was and focused on what Hayden had advised. Trish. I was here for Trish. The rest I'd deal with later. Or never. Whichever came first.

"How'd you get off work?" Patrick asked, pouring me a glass of champagne.

I sucked some down, the bubbles immediately going to my head. "Hayden said I was already here, so I might as well come now. What have I missed?"

"The best steak I've ever had," Trish said, leaning her head on Andrew's shoulder.

"Glad you liked it, Bright Side."

"Oh come on, Baker. I expected more from you." Patrick inclined his glass of whiskey toward me. "Ask what you really want to know."

"I did."

He tsked. "He's over at the bar with some of his friends."

Don't look. Don't look. Don't look.

"Who?" I feigned ignorance, and Patrick looked unimpressed.

"Holt." Just his name sent a spark of heat and a rush of hurt through me. "You should go say hi."

"You should stir up your own trouble," I said under my breath.

"We're glad you made it," Mr. Dixon said, lifting his glass to me.

He and Mrs. Quinn were pretty cozy, his arm around her shoulder.

"Me too," I said honestly.

AFTER ANOTHER GLASS OF CHAMPAGNE, my nerves unwound and I began to relax. Marlow, Holt, Blake, and Ella's absence were noticeable, but the mood was light. I was happy for my friend. *Friends.* Andrew was part of that now too.

The pull toward the bar became too much the more alcohol I consumed. I looked over my shoulder, disappointed dancing couples were all I could see.

One shuffled to the side, giving me a clear line of sight. To Holt.

And the woman latched onto him.

CHAPTER THIRTY-FIVE

HOLT

"TO DIXON. For finally getting his ass back where he belongs."

Roman raised his beer, Briggs and Clark doing the same. I pasted on an artificial smile and clinked my bottle neck with theirs.

Briggs slapped me on the back. "Whatever vacation you've got left, take it. There's a bunch of shit work waiting on you."

"We piled all of it on your desk," Clark said with a mischievous grin.

"I have a desk?" My brows dipped, and they all burst into laughter. I wadded up a napkin and threw it at Clark. "Assholes."

He called the bartender over and ordered a round of shots. "Should I get enough for your family?"

I glanced in their direction. Patrick waved his hands in front of him while he ran his mouth. Longing streaked through me. I'd introduced all of them and felt relieved when there wasn't a big enough table available to accommodate everyone.

Separate corners.

Two separate worlds.

"Not right now."

I slung my shot back and slammed the empty glass on the bar.

Briggs grimaced and wiped his mouth with the back of his hand. "If Suzanne asks me about this and I forgot to mention it, she'll cut me off for a week."

"You scared of your wife?" Roman asked with a smirk.

"Yeah. And if she was yours you would be too." Briggs returned his attention to me. "A friend of hers from high school moved back to town."

"No." I cut him off before it went any further.

"She's not bad looking," he pleaded.

"Tell Suzanne I'm not ready or whatever you want to." Maybe I should switch to liquor. "Or why not Roman?"

They glanced at each other, a little too nervously for my liking.

"He's uh—he's been kinda seeing someone."

"Yeah?" I punched him in the arm. "Who's the lucky girl? Anybody I know?"

"Is there anybody in this town we don't know?" Clark muttered.

"So about Suzanne's friend . . ." Briggs nudged me with his shoulder.

"What don't you want me to know?"

"Oh shit." Clark glanced past me and downed the rest of his beer. "I gotta take a piss."

"Hey."

Everything in me seized.

The soft lilt had greeted me more mornings than I could count. I thought that would always be the sound I woke to. Seeing her face was a direct arrow to my chest. Still flawless. Those lips formed a shy smile, and I scowled, knowing what they were capable of. Her hair was a blonde halo that fell halfway down her back.

I wanted to look away, but couldn't. This ache, this reminder of everything that had gone wrong in my life stared at me. Begging for forgiveness, understanding, and something else I couldn't decipher.

"Roman." I pointed a finger at him. "What the hell?"

He ignored me and touched Celia's shoulder. "I won't be far."

A look passed between them, one I wasn't sure I liked. One I wasn't sure why I cared.

I spun on my barstool to face the mirrored wall of liquor bottles. "Holt."

I stiffened. How many times had she said my name? *Why does it still affect me?*

"You don't take hints too well."

She wedged between the barstool Roman vacated and mine. Her floral scent nauseated me. Honey. That was what I craved. I edged my fingernail under the label on my bottle, ripping it down the center.

"You just left."

I whipped around on the stool and stared at her incredulously. "Why would I stay? What's left here for me?"

She stepped between my legs, and I recoiled. "Me."

I wanted her out of my space and put my hands on her hips to back her up. Stubborn woman wouldn't budge.

"I don't want you."

"I screwed up. I know that."

I glared at her. "If he weren't dead, would you still feel that way?"

She flinched. "I'm sorry. I love you."

"Don't say that to me." I peeled her hand off my arm. "You don't get to say that."

I looked away. Those words used to mean everything. I thought they did to her too.

"It's true," she pleaded. "I'm lost without you. Roman understands that."

"Roman?" I asked incredulously. *One of my friends?* The woman had no boundaries.

She paled. "I thought he told you."

"Told me what?"

"It's nothing. You're home now. We can figure this out. Get back to where we used to be."

"There is no going back," I spat.

"Please. I made mistakes—"

"Mistakes? I doubt Cameron or Roman would be too happy to hear that."

"I was scared. I knew you wanted to get married, but I was afraid everything would change."

I gaped at her. "So you got serious with my best friend behind my back?" I pushed to my feet, towering over her. "Did you know he was about to propose?"

Her lips parted, her expression as if I'd slapped her. "What?"

"When a man's dying, he confesses a lot."

"I didn't know."

"Well, now you do. His last words were how sorry he was, but he loved you and wanted me to look out for you."

She touched her throat as her eyes glassed over.

I looked away. "You loved him too."

She nodded, a few tears escaping down her cheeks. "I loved you too."

"I don't believe you. If you had, you couldn't have done that to me. Either of you."

"Holt. Please." She grabbed my arm. "Give me another chance. Let me prove to you how much you mean to me."

"I'm not a stand-in, Celia. I'm not giving you a second chance."

"We deserve it." Her nails dug into my forearm, and I shrugged her off.

"Love doesn't look like this. I want more in life than a woman who plays with the emotions of men she supposedly loves for her own gain. I'm done." I hadn't been able to see that she hopped from man to man. I'd been blinded by what I thought we had. Baker had shown me what a relationship should be, even if that hadn't ended well either.

"You love me." She'd always known exactly how to play me.

"Yeah. But not enough to let you walk all over me anymore." She reached for me again, but I stepped out of reach. "You should leave."

My feet carried me toward my family, and I didn't look back. I pushed through the crowd and froze when hurt green eyes met mine.

Easy.

She clambered from her seat and rushed toward the door. Trish and Andrew looked around to see what had spooked her when they saw me.

Trish rushed after Baker while I stood there. Frozen between past and present.

Two worlds collided.

And I couldn't move.

CHAPTER THIRTY-SIX

BAKER

"BAKER. WAIT UP."

Trish grasped my hand just before I made it to the door.

"I can't," I said. "I'm here for you, but I can't stay." My heart pounded against my ribcage, images of Holt and that woman from the picture assaulting me.

"You're not going back to New York, are you?" she asked, panicked.

"No. I just . . . need to regroup."

"I'll go with you."

I shook my head. "Stay. Everyone's having a good time."

"I'll be worried about you."

"And I'll be fine."

"Thought you weren't coming until Friday?"

My breath caught when Holt appeared behind Trish.

"Want me to stay?" She touched my shoulder.

"We're ready to call it a night." Andrew led the rest of the group, who had their coats on before I could say anything to Holt. "The hotel is sending a car over." His phone pinged with a text. "Here it is."

Mr. Dixon patted Holt's back. "You're not driving are you, son?"

He turned red. "I, uh—I can get a cab."

"Do that. It's not worth getting in an accident."

We moved outside. Before I could climb into the waiting SUV, Holt hooked my arm. He opened his mouth, but nothing came out, so he closed it. I slinked out of his hold.

"Guess it would have been hard to juggle two women in the same place at once." I crawled into the third row of seating without waiting for a response.

I tried not to look back as we pulled away, but his magnetism was too strong. He remained in the same spot on the sidewalk, hands in his pockets, staring after us.

Patrick let out a low whistle. "You two are like fire and ice. One second you're hot for each other, the next it's bitter cold."

"Like it's any different with you and Marlow," I said.

"Actually, it is. Marlow's always cold. Always."

"I can't argue with you there."

"She's had a hard time since Jack died." Mr. Dixon turned around from his position in the front seat.

"She's had more support than anybody knew."

Andrew shot a warning look at me over his shoulder. I stared out the window.

"She seeing somebody else?" Patrick asked, a hint of anger behind the question.

"I have no idea," I said honestly.

"It sounds like you know something."

"What she does is none of my concern." I clutched my purse on my lap. "The only Dixons that matter to me are Trish and Ella."

Trish gave me a sympathetic look, seeing right past the lie. If I kept telling myself I didn't give a damn about Holt, maybe one day it would be true.

————

"WHAT'S on the agenda for today?"

I picked at a piece of bacon, but it was like cardboard in my mouth.

"Andrew wants to move the wedding up to tomorrow since everyone's here." She blushed and fiddled with a lock of her hair. "I want to too."

I tried to be upbeat. The travel and lack of sleep had my enthusiasm at a low level, even though I was genuinely happy for my friend.

Ella screamed, drawing the attention of the whole restaurant. I scowled right back at the woman next to us who had a look of disgust on her face.

I tickled Ella's tummy. "You always say what you think, okay? Never let anyone silence you."

"The hotel wedding planner wants to meet at ten, but it shouldn't take too long. They've arranged everything."

"So we're free to hang out in the spa all day?"

"I was thinking we could all go on a hike. It's not supposed to be too cold," she said.

"I'm game."

"Even if Holt comes?"

I set down my piece of toast. "This is your weekend. I'm sorry about last night, but I'm more prepared now."

"You have nothing to be sorry for. And if you want to talk about it—"

"I don't." I picked Ella up from her carrier and held her to my chest. "Is Mr. Dixon taking Ella while you honeymoon? Where are you going anyway?" Maybe I didn't have the right but I was a little hurt Trish hadn't consulted me about this.

A wistful expression transformed her face. "All I know is somewhere warm."

"Bring me back some sand."

"And a coconut?"

I laughed. "Yeah. A coconut too."

"We talked about it and decided to take Ella with us."

"I get it."

"Andrew doesn't want to be away from her, either."

I kissed the crown of Ella's head. "I'll miss you, but we'll have some girl time when you get back." The realization that Trish and Ella would be away and Mrs. Quinn was busy with Mr. Dixon brought on this feeling of incredible loneliness.

My phone trilled from inside my bag. I juggled Ella as I reached down for it.

"Hello?"

"Is this Baker Holland?"

"Um, yes."

"I'm Juniper Montgomery. I picked up some of your lip gloss from the food truck on Park. I own a boutique down the street and wanted to see how I go about ordering the product for my store."

I looked at Trish with wide eyes and pointed at the phone as I tried not to jump out of my seat.

"That's terrific. I'm so glad you like it." I struggled to contain my excitement and prayed that my voice sounded professional. "What kind of quantity do you need?"

The words came out as a bit of a squeal, and Trish did a fist pump.

"I'm thinking one hundred to start so I can test market. And can we discuss pricing? Is the retail price firm? Because if I'm being perfectly honest, it's too cheap for the quality of the product."

My heart thundered in my ears. Someone thought my product was worth more. It was one thing to hear that from the people I cared about and completely another from a stranger. Pride filled me that I'd created something of value.

"What do you think it should retail for?" I asked carefully.

"In my shop, easily the $8 to $10 range. Maybe more."

I fiddled with the hem of my sweater, even as joy overflowed inside me. "It's important to me that it be affordable."

"I understand, but you shouldn't sell yourself short." A door chime signaled on the other end of the line. "I want to know more about the charity the proceeds go to. Do you have information I can display?"

"Yes," I lied. "That's no problem." I flashed Trish an *oh shit* look.

"What's the turnaround time if I order today?"

I swallowed hard. "We're a little behind because of the demand, but I think I could have fifty to you in a week and the other fifty a week after that."

A noise of dissatisfaction came through the phone. "No sooner?"

"We can try to rush, but I don't want to make promises I can't keep."

"I respect that. Let me give you my details."

"Please. I'll email you the invoice later today." I scrambled for a pen, Trish handed me a paper napkin.

"I've got a feeling about this," she said. "If this sells like I think it will, be ready for me to double my next order."

Next order? Double? Was this real? It was all I could do not to scream I was so excited.

"Thank you so much for reaching out and for the order." My eyes got watery when I realized what this meant. My first order from someone I didn't know. *Wow.* "I can't tell you what it means and how much I look forward to working with you."

I tossed the phone on the table and smacked Trish in the arm.

"What is it?"

"An order for a hundred lip glosses. Because she bought some from your food truck and wants to sell it in her store," I screeched.

Trish whooped. "And you promised her fifty by next week? Are you crazy?"

"Maybe." I bounced Ella to settle my nerves. There was so much to do besides make the glosses. Trish was going to be out of town, so I wouldn't have any help. *Was there enough space at the apartment to start filling orders of this size?*

And I didn't have the money for supplies.

"How much do you need?"

Was she a mind reader?

"I can't do that. You have your own business."

She waved our waiter down and signaled for the bill. "Let's go order what you need so it will be in New York when you get home."

"I'll pay you back."

"I know." She clapped her hands together. "Has Cricket finished the new logo?"

"She's working on it. And this lady wants information on Paths she can display with the product."

"Mrs. Quinn will be able to help with that. She has some incredible flyers. We probably won't have to print any. Oh. What are we going to display the gloss in?"

"What about how you do it? With the tiered cake stand?"

"I'm partial." She winked. "But I think it'll be perfect. I saw an antique shop in town. Maybe they'll have something we can use."

"What about the hike?"

"This is way more important." She stood and hooked Ella's carrier over her arm. "Besides, Andrew wanted to hike, and I couldn't say no."

"Thank God." I shifted Ella to the opposite arm as I picked up my purse. "Have you ever seen me do anything outdoorsy?"

"What about me?" She examined her pale skin with a laugh. "This is perfect. Wedding planner. Order supplies. Shop for cake tiers. Spa. Rehearsal dinner."

"No hike."

We high-fived.

"No hike."

CHAPTER THIRTY-SEVEN

HOLT

I YANKED AT MY TIE.

I'd had it on less than twenty minutes and it was already choking me.

Dad pulled at his, and Mrs. Quinn placed a hand over his to stop his fidgeting.

"Only a couple of hours, right?"

Dad gave me a knowing look. Meanwhile, my brother looked perfectly at home, most comfortable in a suit and tie.

"How was the hike?" Mrs. Quinn sipped her wine.

"It snowed, so we watched baseball instead." I canted my head. "What did you get up to today?"

"A little shopping. And the first massage I've had in about twenty years."

"I beg your pardon." Dad puffed his chest out.

She patted his arm.

"Let's just skip that conversation," I said before she could elaborate.

Andrew flicked his chin toward Patrick. "Any idea if Marlow is going to show up?"

"She said she wouldn't be long." He checked his watch. "That was half an hour ago. Looks like the best man and best woman are free to hang out."

I clenched my fist.

Baker smacked him in the arm. "You wish."

Patrick held his arm where she'd hit him. "Not if you're gonna be like that." He paused, a mischievous grin tilting his lips up. "On second thought . . ."

"We don't have to wait for her," I said, a little too forcefully. "This is your deal. Not hers."

"Let's give her a few more minutes," Trish said.

Patrick slung his arm around Baker's shoulder. She snorted as she wiggled away from him. I picked at the label on my beer and glared. Her dress dipped to reveal a hint of that soft cleavage. She wore her hair swept up in some sort of twist, her smooth neck taunting.

Her eyes met mine. She wrinkled her nose and focused on Patrick, those pouty lips with that gloss I loved to taste twitching with a smile at something he said.

I stared. Because I couldn't not look at her. Once she was out of my life, it would get easier. I'd barely thought of her today. I scrubbed my forehead.

Total truth?

I'd barely thought of anything else.

Mrs. Quinn held up the platter of potato skins. "Better get another before I eat them all."

Absently, I grabbed one and took a bite before dropping it on my plate. All without taking my eyes off Baker. The food was like clay in my mouth as I chewed.

For a second last night, I'd seen how much I hurt her. There wasn't a trace of that now. She made it look easy, like the time we'd spent together meant nothing.

"Not talking to her is a page I *wouldn't* take out of your father's playbook."

I glanced at Mrs. Quinn. "We'd run our course." The words tasted vile as I spoke them in a hushed tone.

Easy's eyes flicked to mine, like she'd heard me. This time, I had to look away.

"Okay." She chewed thoughtfully on an appetizer. "But maybe you want to leave things in a good place. She's your sister-in-law's best friend. You can't avoid her forever."

Wanna bet? I polished off my beer and signaled the server for another.

"I'll think about it."

"I want to thank you."

My brows pinched. "For what?"

"She needed a nudge to get back out there and try the real world again. You gave that to her," she said, keeping her voice low.

"By pretty much daring her to be my roommate? She didn't need me."

"You and I know that. But she doesn't."

Questions swirled in my mind. What had happened to her? We'd promised no talk of the past, but I wanted to know.

"Sorry I'm late." Marlow rushed over to the table, Blake in her arms.

"Everything okay?" Dad stood to help her, taking Blake while she settled in.

"Blake threw up."

"You should have called." Dad smoothed his grandson's hair.

"He grinned at me as soon as it was over. I guess something didn't settle well." She looked across the table at Trish and Andrew. "Sorry I'm not dressed for the occasion. I only brought two. One for tomorrow. The other is ruined."

Trish reached for her hand. Marlow stared in disbelief before reluctantly taking it.

"We're glad you made it. Is Blake okay?"

"Seems to be."

"I saved you and my boy a seat." Dad indicated to the space next to him, and Marlow settled him in.

Her eyes darted to me before she quickly looked away. I wasn't ready for this shit, either. When I looked at my sister, I saw a traitor.

Someone I thought I could depend on when in actuality, she blamed me for the loss of our mother. Had she felt that way for years? Had she always had a resentment toward me and masked it? She'd spent more time with our mother than any of us. Did Marlow now see the truth?

I didn't fault her for her feelings, wasn't even sure I wouldn't have felt the same in her position. But it still hurt, no matter how I didn't want it to.

Blake pointed his chubby finger at me. "How!"

"How, buddy." I reached out my hand, and he clutched my pinky.

"You want Uncle Holt?" Dad nuzzled his hair, and he nodded.

I perched him on my lap. Blake's tiny fists grabbed my tie. "How!" He beamed at me.

"You're feeling pretty good now, aren't you?"

Ella screeched, and Blake echoed her. The back and forth between them went on for a minute, while we all watched. They communicated in some language only they understood.

Trish kissed Andrew on the cheek. "I think we should have a house full of girls."

Andrew's eyes widened. "It'll send me to an early grave."

"At least get married before you die," Patrick said, lifting his whiskey glass. "To Trish and Andrew. May you have a thousand lifetimes of love and happiness."

"Here, here," Dad said, raising his glass.

Patrick lifted his tumbler again. "And to one last night out before you're stuck with each other."

CHAPTER THIRTY-EIGHT

BAKER

"ARE you spending the night with me?"

Trish swayed a little on her barstool. "Nope. I already went the traditional route once. It didn't work out well."

I gaped at her, and she burst out laughing.

"Oh-kay."

Trish never let what happened to her get her down. I admired the way she handled herself, but she rarely spoke so flippantly about it.

She pointed at me. "The look on your face . . . I finally surprised you."

"You surprise me a lot." I hugged her. "I'm happy for you."

She sniffled in my ear. "Big things are going to happen for you."

I shrugged as one of the men I recognized at the bar with Holt last night approached.

"I'm Clark. Well, I'm Judd, but everybody calls me Clark, so . . ."

"Baker. And this is Trish."

"Pleasure." He lifted his beer toward us. "I didn't mean to interrupt, but we didn't get a chance to meet up last night. We've missed that asshole and sort of hogged him." He flicked his chin toward Holt.

"Do you work at the park too?" Trish asked.

"Yeah. Holt and I started around the same time. He's back just in time for me to take my vacation," he said with a grin.

"What do you mean?" I asked before I could stop myself.

"He's back on Monday. I'm going to the hot tub."

"He's staying?" The words fumbled from my mouth.

Clark's brow dipped into a V. "Yeah. That boy isn't city material anymore. He belongs out here." He slung an arm around Holt as he walked past. "Don't you?"

"Don't I what?"

"Belong out here. We knocked the city right out of you."

Holt glanced at me and swallowed hard before playfully punching Clark in the stomach. "You've never knocked anything out of me." He motioned toward the crowd. "Come on. Let's go get my brother a shot before he tries to duck out with his beautiful bride-to-be."

"Hungover or not, he's getting married tomorrow," Trish warned.

"I'm not going to be hungover," Andrew said, sliding an arm around her waist.

"Just the man we're looking for." Holt signaled for the bartender.

"Excuse me." I wedged past and bolted for the bathroom.

I cursed under my breath when I found Marlow in front of the mirror, reapplying . . . my lip gloss?

"I like this stuff." She shrugged and ringed her lips with her pinky. "What's with you? You look like someone hurt your feelings."

"Let's not pretend, okay? You don't like me. I don't like you. And after this weekend, we'll hardly ever see each other."

She turned and propped a hip on the counter. "Things didn't work out with you and my brother?"

"He's none of your business."

She sighed and looked up at the ceiling. "I've said and done a lot of shit I shouldn't have, but contrary to what you might think, I want him to be happy." Her mouth rolled as if what she had to say was painful. "You make him happy."

"You don't know what you're talking about."

She lifted one shoulder. "Maybe. Maybe not." She dropped her lip gloss back in her purse. "But I know he got hurt. Bad enough not to want to try again. You made him forget that."

She shoved past me, the bathroom door closing with a loud thud behind her. The woman said the most obscure things sometimes.

"He didn't forget." I saw with my own eyes exactly how much he remembered when his hands were on *her* hips.

I splashed water on my face, which didn't help. The door opened, and I dried my cheeks.

"What did she say to you?"

I wheeled around, as Holt locked the door.

"What do you care?"

"I won't let her hurt you." He crossed his arms over his chest.

"Oh no? What are you going to do about it when we're back in New York and you're way over here?" I waved my hand around above my head.

"Easy, look—"

"Don't call me that," I screamed as pain lanced through me. "You promised you'd be honest with me. Not about the past, but about now. You never had any intention of staying in New York. Why didn't you just tell me?"

"Listen—"

I stalked over to him and shoved a finger into his chest. "No, you listen. I don't know what kind of sick game you were playing, but it's over. You've got your girl. You've got your life out here. Leave me alone."

I turned the lock, but he didn't budge from where he blocked the door.

"I couldn't tell them I quit."

"I don't want to hear it," I said, tugging on the door handle.

"They were so glad to see me back. I didn't expect that, and I couldn't tell them I was leaving for good."

"Now you don't have to." I pulled again, my hand slipping from the handle. "Give Andrew your forwarding address and I'll pack up the rest of your stuff." I glared at him. "Unless you already did it."

"Baker."

"There's nothing left to say. I've seen and heard it all. Now move." I shoved at his arm.

He stayed rooted in place.

"I'm sorry."

I kept pushing at him and pulling on the door handle. I didn't want to hear his apology.

"I should've told you about the trip. I didn't want any of my family to come."

I whipped my head to him. Did he think I'd believe this crap?

"I wanted to keep here and there separate. Because it's hard for me to be here. It's a reminder of all the shitty decisions I've made."

I softened on the inside as something in his voice got to me. But I kept up the tough façade. I couldn't trust him anymore. Couldn't tell fact from fiction.

"Then maybe coming back here is a way to remember not to make the same mistakes again."

He stepped to the side, and I rushed from the bathroom, though I felt him right behind me.

"I never meant to hurt you."

"You think you have that power?" I wheeled around on him. "No one will ever have that kind of hold on me again. Ever."

"Good. You deserve someone that can be all you need."

"Don't tell me what I deserve." I stormed toward the bar. "And I don't need anyone," I said over my shoulder.

"It's okay to let people in." He reached out, but quickly dropped his arm as if he thought better of touching me.

"For everyone else? Not you, right?"

"I did. And they burned me."

"Now you're the one with the matches?"

"What the hell are you doing here?"

We both turned at the menace in Mr. Dixon's voice. He glared at a woman only a few feet away. One with hair the color of Holt's, eyes like Andrew's, and lips the shape of Marlow's.

Her sinister smile sent a chill through me.

"My son is getting married. What kind of mother would I be to miss that?"

CHAPTER THIRTY-NINE

HOLT

NO FUCKING WAY.

No way was I going to let her ruin my brother's wedding or hurt my father. Marlow stood behind her, face pale.

I pointed at my sister and erased the distance between us. "You. How could you do this?"

"I didn't—"

"I'm supposed to believe that? After what I found?"

"What are you talking about?" Dad's face was a deep crimson, his fists at his sides. Thank God Mrs. Quinn had volunteered to babysit the kids.

Guilt swamped me. Shit. I couldn't lie to him now. I looked to Andrew for help.

He stepped forward. "You need to leave," he said, not bothering to hide his contempt.

"It's a bar, son. You can't force me to go."

"I am not your son."

"The sixteen hours in labor say otherwise." Her artificial smile turned to me. "I've been expecting your call."

Dad's gaze bounced from me to her. He pounded his fist on the bar. "How does she know we're here?"

"You'd better ask your daughter that," I said, wondering how I didn't see exactly who my sister was.

"I—"

"Are you gonna deny it?" I challenged.

"I told her about the wedding," she said, her voice small. "But none of the details."

I exchanged an incredulous look with Andrew and realized I hadn't let go of Baker.

Dad stared at Marlow, imploring her.

"I'm sorry, Daddy."

She hadn't called him that very much since we were kids. He stumbled back a step with the impact of her words.

"I needed a mother," Marlow said, her voice thick.

"I don't begrudge you that," Dad said hoarsely. "But you didn't have to keep it from me."

"I didn't know how to tell you."

"Her fiancé was headed off to war. She was pregnant and alone."

All eyes snapped to the witch who had given us birth.

"Marlow wasn't pregnant until they got married," Dad said with certainty. But Jack's first deployment was when they were engaged. *Holy shit.*

"Before Blake," my mother argued.

"Marlow?" Dad choked out.

"I couldn't tell you." She swiped at the tears coming down her cheeks.

"I'm a modern man," he protested. "Did you think I'd be upset?"

"She miscarried. She needed me."

Marlow needed our never-there mother? What a joke. My sister needed her real family. *How much loss had she been through?*

"And you just happened to be there?" I asked with disgust, hating she'd been around to influence my sister when she was most vulnerable. *Damn.* Marlow had lost my niece or nephew. And then her husband. No wonder she was so angry.

"I've always been there. I told you that."

"I need some air." Dad pushed off the bar and stumbled in a daze toward the exit.

I started after him, but Baker held me. "Give him a minute."

"Stay away from my family." Andrew got up in *her* face. "I don't know what you're up to, but you cannot destroy us."

"Oh, darling. I can do anything I want to."

"You've done enough."

We all jolted in surprise to find Dad standing behind us. I guessed he hadn't said all he'd wanted to.

"I didn't tell her to come." My sister was insistent.

"I don't know if I can trust you, Marlow." The hurt on his face slayed me. "I've got your message loud and clear, Ivette. Now what is it you want?"

She smiled that of an angel. "I told you. To see my son get married." She turned to me. "And introduce my other son to his father."

CHAPTER FORTY

BAKER

THE INSTINCT TO grab Holt around his waist was automatic.

He didn't seem to feel it, his face ashen as he swayed. His mother looked triumphant when a man muscled his way to the front.

I gasped. Mr. Dixon reached for the bar for support. Andrew balled his fists at his sides. Marlow's face twisted in horror.

The striking resemblance was too much to ignore. A tall, muscular build. Caramel hair. Even their olive skin tone was the same.

Holt trembled in my hold as he stared at the man. Everything over the last few days melted away to nothing. Only this bombshell remained, and I felt Holt's pain as if it were my own.

He said nothing. His face blank, devoid of the emotion percolating under the surface.

The man stepped forward and extended his hand. Holt recoiled and looked at that hand as though it were that of the devil himself.

"We probably should have done this before." He refused to drop his hand.

"You're not my father."

Holt lifted his chin and didn't make a move to shake hands.

"Are you that unhappy with your life that you have to screw with ours? You gave this up," Andrew shouted.

His mother appeared pleased with the chaos she'd unleashed.

"I thought I wanted to know you," Holt said, leveling her with his sharp gaze. "But I was wrong. I can't stand the sight of you any longer."

Holt moved with determined steps toward the bar exit, and I followed. Once we were outside next to an old pickup truck, he doubled over and braced his arms on his knees as he struggled for breath.

I rubbed his back as he heaved, at a total loss for words. Based on looks alone, I'd say his mother was telling the truth. I could barely process it myself, let alone begin to imagine what was going through Holt's mind.

It wasn't long before he stood, a vacancy in his eyes. He stabbed a key into the passenger side door lock and yanked the door open. I climbed inside the cab. He jogged around the front and slammed the door behind him.

He dropped the keys twice as he tried to put them in the ignition. I scooted closer and touched his thigh. He stared at my hand a moment before he made another attempt, this time successful.

We peeled out and barreled away from town into the darkness. Tremors wracked his body as he gripped the steering wheel. Helpless, I ran circles over his jeans with my thumb. His knuckles grew whiter the longer we drove.

HE TURNED off the main road down a dirt drive flanked with evergreens. A cabin with a single porch light on came into view.

Without a word, he parked and jumped out of the truck, leaving the door open behind him. I exited on his side and shut it as he unlocked the front door of the house and disappeared inside.

I followed. A spot near the fireplace illuminated by the moon was the only light. The click of the lock echoed in the silence. I wrapped my arms around my middle and shivered. Holt stood in the center of the room, shoulders hunched, keys at his feet.

I moved until I was in front of him. I slid my arms around his waist and rested my head against his chest. His heart thudded in my ear, an erratic pounding.

We stood like that for what felt like an eternity, yet not long enough.

He lifted his arms and enveloped me so tight in them I could barely breathe. He dropped his cheek to the top of my head. Eventually, his rapid breathing slowed.

A phone rang from his front pocket, but neither of us moved. Mine started from across the room where I'd dropped my purse. There was only a beat of silence before they began to ring in tandem.

"We should let them know we're safe," I whispered.

He made no move, so I fished his phone from his pocket and answered.

"Where are you?" Andrew's desperate voice boomed in my ear.

"He's safe," I said.

"Baker?"

"Now isn't a good time."

"I need to talk to him."

Holt didn't move.

"Tomorrow," I said, fisting his shirt in my hand. "Let's all take a breath and regroup tomorrow."

Andrew let out a frustrated sigh. "Okay. Just . . . tell him I love him."

"I will." I gripped the phone. "How's your dad?"

"Not speaking. I—this is such a mess."

"But you'll get through it because you have each other."

"Yeah. Don't forget to tell him what I said."

"I won't."

I ended the call and dropped his phone on the coffee table.

"Andrew said to tell you he loves you."

Holt stopped breathing for a second before he scooped me into his arms. He carried me up to the loft bedroom and gently laid me on the bed.

"I'm going to wash my face. Help yourself to a T-shirt."

He disappeared into the bathroom, but didn't shut the door. I spotted his bag on the floor and grabbed a T-shirt from inside. I breathed in deep, the scent of Holt enveloping me as I changed into it.

The toilet flushed. The faucet ran and stopped.

"I left a clean towel on the sink if you need it," he said when he reappeared.

"Thanks." I quickly washed up and flipped off the light.

I felt my way to the bed and crawled on top of the covers. Holt's scent assaulted me again, minus the hint of motor oil. Longing filled me.

Holt stripped down to his boxer briefs and climbed under the covers. I snuggled against him. His arm went around me, and he tucked my head under his chin.

"This is the first time I've felt right in days."

Me too.

"Holt."

"Don't say it, Easy. I know why you're here. Because you're good." He twirled a strand of hair around his finger. "You'll stay until you think I'm okay, even though you're pissed as hell at me. Which is more than I deserve, considering."

I drew circles on his chest. "Holt—"

He pressed his fingers against my lips. "Shh. It's selfish, but I need this. I need you."

I burrowed deeper into him. *I need you too.*

There wasn't any future for us, especially after seeing him with that other woman, but this hug? I needed it more than anything else at that moment. And I fell asleep . . . peaceful.

I WOKE to an empty bed and a chill in my bones. I pulled the covers up over my mouth. The sound of pots clanged down below.

"Shit." Something banged on the counter—Holt's fist I guessed.

I wandered down the stairs to find Holt yanking on his hair as he stared in the cabinets.

He jolted his head toward me. His eyes roved my bare legs before he returned them to the cupboard.

"No coffee," he grunted.

I leaned against the fridge. "Want me to go get some?"

"I should get you back to the hotel."

He stormed past me and stomped up the stairs. I followed, this need to comfort him overruling everything else.

Holt closed the bathroom door, but I caught it just before it shut. If he noticed, he said nothing, simply shed his underwear and turned on the shower. He stepped inside the small stall without letting the water warm.

I stripped his T-shirt over my head and shimmied out of my panties.

What are you doing, Baker?

I straightened my shoulders.

What I want.

Holt started when I stepped in behind him. I yelped when the ice water hit my feet.

"Get out, Easy, if you don't want anything to happen," he said, voice low.

"Have you been with anyone besides me since you've been back?" I pushed around him so I could see his face. Cold spray hit my back. I hissed, but stood my ground. The image of that woman fought to the front and center of my mind.

I shoved it down.

Lifted my chin.

Waited for him to answer.

"No."

I splayed my hands on his chest. He turned us and backed me against the wall, caging me in.

"Haven't wanted to either."

I swallowed hard. "The way you touched her—"

"I know what it must've looked like, but I was trying to get her away from me. I want nothing to do with her and told her as much."

The steel behind his words made me believe him. I knew as well as anyone how being caught in the wrong moment could make someone look guilty, even when they weren't.

"I believe you."

"That's the past I didn't want you to see. I want to forget it. Forget her."

"Then let's forget," I whispered, cupping his face with my hands.

He stared at me in disbelief. Wiped away a lock of hair matted against my forehead. "Why would you do this for me?"

"I'm doing it for me too." We both deserved to feel good, even if it was only temporary.

His lids drifted closed, and he shuddered. He traced my face with his fingertips, down my neck, shoulders, arms. Memorizing. Because this was it.

The last time.

"So fucking beautiful." He hadn't opened his eyes.

His hands skimmed down my hips to the seam between my legs.

"Holt. Please."

I clawed at his neck as he plunged a finger inside of me. "Me too, Easy. Me too."

Slowly, he pumped, a single digit, stroking until I began to buzz. I fisted his cock and matched his rhythm. A rumble escaped his throat. I dragged his head to mine and fought for his lips. I needed his kiss, the connection that made me complete.

"Stop," he panted into my mouth. "You're gonna make me come. I don't want to yet."

I squeezed the head of his cock, and he hissed. "Are you sure?"

He withdrew his finger and peeled my hand from his shaft. I shivered when he finally graced me with those heated eyes.

"You cold?"

He lifted me, and I crossed my ankles in the small of his back. He turned so I was in the now warm water.

"Put me inside of you."

I teased my clit with the tip. He gritted his teeth as I slid him between my slick heat. His head was swollen, his shaft throbbed in my hand. When I guided him inside, we sagged against each other.

He thrust until he hit home, and we stilled.

"Make me forget," I whispered.

Like a snapped cord, whatever held him back broke loose. Holt slid his hands under my ass, lifting and lowering me onto him like he'd never have the chance again.

I peppered his face with kisses and clawed his shoulders. With every thrust, I saw sparks, until I was flying.

"Easy."

He slowed his pace, and I whimpered, going limp against him. He hooked a finger under my chin. Stared into my eyes. Made love to me, slowly. Sweetly. Until I clamped around him again, this time my release rolling over me in a steady wave.

Holt held me as he came, flooding me with his release. He kissed me long and hard. When our mouths broke apart, we were silent.

I clung to him and committed this moment to memory. *This* was what I would hold onto. *This* would give me comfort when I got lonely.

Because as we washed each other and he tucked a towel around me when we were finished, I knew our time was done.

We'd had our goodbye.

CHAPTER FORTY-ONE

HOLT

BAKER GAVE.

And I took.

Same as it had always been.

I stuffed my wallet in my back pocket. Refused to look at her as she put on the dress she'd worn the night before.

That, what happened in the shower, it felt a whole lot like goodbye. I thought that was what I wanted, what I had to do, until it was staring me in the face.

Now I didn't want it at all.

But she did.

"I'll go get the truck warmed up," I mumbled as she searched the floor, for what I didn't know.

One of her shoes was at the bottom of the staircase, the other dumped over by the coffee table. Just like home.

A pang of longing hit me square in the chest. *Home*. I wanted it so bad, but everything was shot to hell.

I swiped my keys off the hardwood floor and was almost to the door when someone knocked. I detoured to the window, pulled the curtain sheer back, then let it float into place.

"Sorry to come by so early." Rob tugged on the brim of his cowboy hat. "Heard you were in town and wanted to see if I could get that rent check."

"Uh, sure." I stepped out of the doorway to let him inside. "I'm out of coffee." I motioned toward the sofa. "Let me get my checkbook."

I scratched the side of my neck. Where the hell had I put it?

Baker came down the stairs, grabbing a shoe on her way.

"If this is a bad time . . ." He paused halfway to his seat.

"No. No." I waved him off.

"Hello," Baker said as I went upstairs.

I snatched my checkbook off the dresser and bolted back down the stairs. No need to leave the two of them alone longer than necessary. Rob liked to run his mouth.

"That Holt sure is good at making friends wherever he goes," he said as I returned. "You're not from around here. If you were, I'd remember you."

Baker gave him a rigid smile as she stabbed her foot into a shoe. "Nope. Definitely not from around here."

I scrawled out a check and ripped it from the book. "This should cover what I owe."

Rob examined it. "So you aren't moving out?"

Baker refused to look at me.

"I need more time."

"Suits me." He slapped his hands on this thighs and stood. "I better be going."

He disappeared out the front door. I studied Baker from the end of the sofa as she stared at something straight ahead. The silence was oppressive. Even the sound of the heat cutting on did nothing to break the awkwardness.

When she stood and faced me, she'd schooled her features into a polite expression one might give a stranger.

"You've got lots to do." She waved her hand around. "Like get settled back in."

I gave her a tight-lipped smile. "Yeah."

. . .

INSTEAD OF MAKING the turn toward her hotel, I kept straight, away from civilization. If Baker noticed, she didn't say a word. Whatever was out the window was far more interesting than I was.

I navigated to a stretch of open space where a herd of bison were known to roam. They didn't let me down, their chocolate forms dotting the landscape.

I pulled into a dirt drive and parked.

"Do you think animals are happier than we are?" Baker's question floated like she'd spoken it to no one in particular.

"In some respects, yes. Others, no. Living in the wild, it's hard."

"Civilization is too."

I snorted and looked out the windshield. "Yeah. Civilization is too."

"I used to want to run away where no one could find me. Be free like they are."

I understood that sentiment better than I cared to admit. It was partly how I'd ended up in Wyoming.

"You can't run away from the things you want to forget. They follow you."

"I know."

I leaned my head against the back glass. "The older I got, I think I knew Dad might not be my biological father. My mother left right after I was born. For another man. So there had to be a fifty/fifty shot."

"Just because she said that man is your father doesn't make it true."

My instincts were all over the place. I hoped he wasn't, but physically, it was hard to deny. That was how my life had always been in that arena. Beyond cruel.

"For a while, I convinced myself he didn't know. Because if he did, that meant neither of my parents wanted me. It was hard enough knowing one didn't."

I traced the steering wheel.

"It's not really fair to my dad, the one who raised me. I spent so much time focused on my mother. Why didn't she want me? What wasn't good enough? I just wanted a mom, even though I knew deep down I didn't need her. Because Dad, he—" A lump formed in my throat.

"He loves you enough for more than two parents."

I nodded and fought the sting in my eyes.

"All along I wondered why I wasn't enough, but he had to be thinking the same thing. Not only did the woman he love leave him, but he knew we all thought about her. Wanted her to come back. That had to hurt, you know?"

"I'm sure it did." She covered my hand with hers.

"Now? There's the man my mother claims is my father. And I don't want to know that anymore. I hate that I got what I wished for for so long. My mother back in my life. I'm better off—we all were—because she wasn't around."

I slumped down, drained by the whole thing.

"You don't owe any of them anything."

"How could you know you have a child for nearly forty years and do nothing about it? Do both of them think they can just fit into my life like they were always there?" I pounded the steering wheel with my fist.

"I'm not even close to over my sister confirming my worst fears that our mother left because of me and then this happens. I can't go back to New York. I know my dad needs me, but I can't be there. Not knowing my real parents are there."

"They aren't your real parents," she said, her voice quiet.

"Dad showed us unconditional love. He taught us that's what parents do."

"Not all of them." Her face crumpled in pain. "Sometimes there are most definitely conditions."

I had no idea what she'd been through and wished we would've gotten to a place where she was comfortable sharing her past. Even if I couldn't help her, at least she could get it out.

"What happened?" I asked, being selfish again, unloading on her.

"When I was at my lowest, they left me on my own." She clutched the edge of the seat. "I don't blame them. But I needed them, and they weren't there."

She was the kindest, most giving person I'd ever met. Knowing she'd carried so much on her own was a testament to her strength. How could anyone abandon her? Well, you are too, asshole. I wanted to apologize and tell her I was just like her parents, but I hoped she wouldn't see me that way. And even if she did, no doubt she'd get back up on her feet and prosper again.

"You make it look easy."

Her smile was sad as she whimpered, "It's not."

I slid my arm around her shoulders and drew her against me, her head on my shoulder.

"I'm sorry things aren't different, Easy." I kissed her hair. "If they were, I'd give you everything. I wish so bad I could."

"I thought you couldn't stay here?"

I wasn't sure I could, but going back to the city was out of the question. Not when my mother was there. Not when Baker would be so close and I couldn't have her.

"I don't know if I can. I might try to get a transfer to Yosemite or somewhere. I just know I can't go back to New York."

"What about your garage?"

"Maybe I'll lease the building. Sell it. You can still use it if you need to while I decide. I can't think about it now."

Disappointment over letting that dream go slithered through me. It had been so real with Baker. And it wasn't just me losing out. I'd taken it from her too. That was worse than letting my own plans fall by the wayside.

"You're hurting. And you have every right to be. But don't let your dad leave without talking to him. He needs you."

"I won't." I pressed my lips to her hair again. "I'm gonna miss you, Easy."

She gave me a watery smile. "You'll be so busy with your new life, you'll forget all about me."

"Impossible."

CHAPTER FORTY-TWO

BAKER

EVERYTHING HURT.

The feeling only intensified as the day progressed. Trish and Andrew considered putting off the wedding, but decided not to give his mother that kind of power.

Everyone tried to put on a happy front, but the air had somberness to it. They deserved better than that, but in the real world, even the fairy tale became spoiled.

"If you aren't going to get on with the first dance, Baker and I are going to get out there and tear it up." Patrick stood and offered me his hand.

Somehow, he'd managed to make me laugh. I followed him to the small space cleared near the long table we'd dined at. He took me in his arms and dipped me.

"Patrick."

"We've gotta turn this doom and gloom to a party. You in?"

He spun us over toward the band, who was playing a slow tune, and signaled to the singer to pick it up. They immediately transitioned into "She Loves You."

Andrew stood and led Trish to the dance floor as we twirled by.

"I can't believe our first dance is to The Beatles," he said as we passed.

Trish laughed, the first real smile I'd seen from her all day. "It's perfect."

The rest of the party sat almost stoically around the table.

"I think we're about to have to go Dirty Dancing style," Patrick said against my ear.

"What?" I tried to put some distance between us.

"Like how the staff pulled the guests out of their seats to dance at the end." He waggled his brows. "Or we could do what you had in mind."

I slapped at his chest. "You take Mrs. Quinn. I'll take Mr. Dixon."

"Then we'll get them together. Can you handle a spin with Holt?"

"Can you handle Marlow?" I challenged.

"She's putty in my hands."

I cast my gaze to where she sat, sulking. "Looks like it."

"My hands are on you at the moment."

I groaned and grabbed his hand. "Come on."

"Mrs. Quinn, I can't dance with this one any longer. Would you do me the honor? That is, if you don't mind, Mr. Dixon." Patrick bowed gallantly.

Mrs. Quinn cracked a smile. "I'd be thrilled."

"Mr. Dixon, save me please."

He stood and offered me his arm. "My pleasure."

Effortlessly, he led me around the small space.

"I had no idea you were quite the dancer."

Crinkles formed around his eyes. "My children think I sit around at home all day, but I know how to have a good time."

"Bet there are a lot of broken hearts now that you're off the market."

He glanced wistfully over to Mrs. Quinn. "I'm worried I'll mess it all up. *Again*. I seem to excel at driving women away."

"We don't know how capable we are at forgiveness until we try."

"You're a smart young lady." He grinned. "But I already knew that."

I blushed and glanced away.

"What about patience? Are you any good at that?"

"I—" I rubbed my temples. "Honestly, I'm not sure. I think so."

"Can you try to be? With my son? He's—" His eyes got misty as he choked on his words.

"Got a lot to process."

"Not just everything that happened last night." He sighed. "He doesn't talk about it, but he lost his best friend."

"I found the newspaper article about it."

"Did he tell you he was there?"

"Yeah."

"He lost his friend and Celia all at once. He puts up a good front, but it's all compounding."

"What about you? Is it all compounding?" It was deflection at its finest. I couldn't stand to hear anything about the woman Holt might still love.

"May I cut in?"

"Certainly." Mr. Dixon patted Holt's shoulder. "I'd better go save Audrey."

The music was still upbeat, but Holt enveloped me in his arms and gently swayed.

"I don't know what to say to him," he confessed against my hair.

"How about that you love him? That seems like a good place to start."

"Anyone ever tell you how smart you are?"

"I've heard it recently."

Holt tightened his arms around my back. "This dress new?"

"Hayden gave it to me."

"You look beautiful."

I buried my head against his chest and inhaled his forest scent. "I saw you dancing with Marlow."

He stiffened. "I can hardly look at her."

I completely understood. He handled her much better than I would.

"You're trying. For Trish and Andrew."

"She insists she didn't have anything to do with *her* showing up."

"Do you believe her?"

He was quiet a minute. We barely moved little more than a sway.

"I don't know."

"She seemed pretty shaken."

"I can't trust her."

How could he? She'd betrayed them all.

"She's not on my list of favorite people. If she did do this . . ."

"I don't think I can forgive her." The words escaped him in a rush.

"Give it some time."

He jerked back, his eyes searching mine. "Do you think I should?"

"If it's the right thing for you, yes. If not, no. Just don't make a decision now."

"Sounds like you're on her side."

"Definitely not. I'm on yours, but you know that."

He ran a finger down my cheek. "When are you headed back to the city?"

"Sunday."

"Think you'll find a new roommate?" The contrived brightness in his tone clawed at my heart.

"I'm going to leave it open. I can't share a bathroom with just anyone."

"That sorry SOB you lived with before never fixed the bathroom, did he?"

"Nope. The way I look at it, he owes me that."

"I don't think he's gonna get around to it."

Pain from the truth of his word nearly took me down, but I managed to shove it down. Mr. Dixon had asked me if I could forgive his son, and although I still didn't really know what had happened to break him, if he wanted me to forgive him, asked me to wait for him, I knew in my heart I would. Deep down, I loved the man, but until things were cleared, I wouldn't give him those words. That sting of rejection would be hard to recover from. But he needed to know that not only was he wanted, but that his happiness mattered too. That I wanted to be part of that happiness.

I cupped his face. "Take the time you need. You have a lot of things to make up your mind about, including where you want to be. Only you can figure out what's best and stop waffling. When you do, come back to me, Grease Monkey."

His eyes dimmed. "I'm sorry, Easy. But I can't do it. Not even for you."

CHAPTER FORTY-THREE

HOLT

"SON."

Dad caught up to me as I crossed the lobby.

"Good wedding, wasn't it?"

"Have a drink with me?" He gestured toward the bar.

"Sure."

We settled in at a table away from the other patrons and ordered whiskey. Dad toyed with the napkin the server left on the table.

"I'm sorry she did this," I said.

"You're sorry? I can't imagine how you must be feeling. That was a hell of a bomb she dropped on you."

It still made me dizzy with hurt and anger and confusion.

"That's putting it mildly." He opened his mouth to speak, but I cut him off. "I love you, Dad."

His eyes glassed over and he patted my hand. "I don't give a damn what DNA or biology or God or anybody says. You are my son."

I swallowed around the knot in my throat. Everything I'd longed for had been right in front of me all along. "I couldn't have asked for a better father. I still can't grasp the magnitude of raising three kids completely on your own. But you did it without complaint, with infinite patience."

"I wasn't perfect. But I love you all more than anything. I tried to be both parents, though I fell short. When I realized I could only be me, I think I did better."

He did love the three of us more than anything. He'd done nothing but show it over and over.

"You were the best. You wouldn't talk about her, so I never considered how much it hurt you when she walked out. Not until I was older, when I felt my own pain over it."

He cupped his glass, but didn't take a drink. "If I'm being honest, I didn't deal with it well at all. I tried to shield you from that."

"You did."

His shoulders sagged as if I'd lifted a weight off of them.

"It seems like a betrayal to you that all this time I wanted her too," I said. "At first, I thought I just needed an explanation. Then it grew to wanting more. Except in my deluded fantasies, the relationship would be like ours."

Desperation. That's what I'd felt all these years. Maybe I hadn't known how to find her though somehow she'd seemed closed enough to touch, but just out of reach.

"I don't fault you for needing your mother. I'd been a pawn in her manipulations and still had a difficult time seeing her for what she was. And if you want a relationship with her, you have my full support."

I leaned back in my chair and stared at him in disbelief. This man . . . how did I ever get lucky enough to have him as a role model, a best friend, and most important, a father?

"Will you tell me what happened? Back then?"

He took a long sip of his whiskey. "Did you ever get the feeling something was off, but you didn't realize it until you looked back?"

"Yeah. With Celia."

His mouth turned down. "I was blissfully ignorant. Smitten with my wife, two kids, and the baby on the way. We weren't wealthy, but we weren't struggling either. I considered myself the luckiest guy on the planet."

"You've always been like that."

"Because I had the three of you." He cleared his throat. "Five days after you were born, I came home from work. She was waiting for me in the kitchen. Said she couldn't be a mother. Didn't want to be my wife. She was tired of pretending."

He scrubbed his hand behind his neck. "Back then, we knew about pregnancy hormones, but not the effects they can have on women. I thought it was the stress of a newborn, even though you were the best baby out of the three. Slept through the night. Hardly cried."

"You think she had postpartum depression?"

"If I'd known what it was at the time, I'd have probably thought so. Now? No. I don't think that's it at all."

"So that was it? She left?"

It seemed impossible she could just walk out on all of us.

"Yeah. And I was so stunned, I let her go."

I remembered that feeling so well. "It's like a sucker punch with a delayed reaction."

"Yes. That's exactly what it's like." He got a faraway look as if he remembered the feeling as well as he did the day it happened. "I found the divorce papers on my pillow. But I kept thinking she'd come back."

"What?" The more I found out about the woman I'd been so desperate to know, the less I liked her.

"I was on auto-pilot. I worked. I took care of you kids. I didn't even contest the divorce. Everything happened so damn fast."

"Why haven't you ever told us any of this?"

"Because what happened between us didn't have anything to do with you. If the time ever came for you to choose between us, I couldn't have lived with myself if I'd have poisoned your mind with my bitterness."

"Dad—"

He held up his hand. "You're old enough to make your own decisions now."

"How did you find out about the other man?"

He toyed with his glass. "Right after the divorce was final and she'd gotten her half of everything, she told me if I hadn't changed, she wouldn't have been forced into another man's arms."

"She came by?"

"No. I mean literally. We were outside the mediation room, the ink not even dry. The lawyers were still inside socializing."

How could she do that to Dad? He was such a great man and deserved so much better.

"I don't understand how you ever fell in love with someone like that to begin with."

"I haven't ever figured out if she was always this way or she changed. Or maybe she was telling the truth, that I made her leave."

"No. You see what she did. If she gave a shit about me or Andrew or even Marlow, she wouldn't have shown up here."

"That wasn't her final parting shot."

"What else could there be?" Guilt crept up his face. "She told you about me."

"Yeah," he said hoarsely. "Told me you weren't mine, but if I didn't want you, she'd give you away."

My chest seized. She didn't want me. That wasn't news. *Why does is still hurt so much?*

"I didn't believe her. Not that you weren't mine."

I stared at him. "Why didn't you have a test?"

"Because it didn't matter what it said." He swallowed hard. "If you want one now. Or later. Whenever. I'll do whatever you need."

Selfless. Dad was the most selfless person I'd ever known. I prayed one day I could be half the man he was.

"I can't even think about it."

He nodded. "When the dust settles." He pushed his drink away. "You can talk to me about him or them. If you need to. And if you want to pursue a relationship with them, I'm behind you."

"Right now? I don't want anything to do with them."

"You might change your mind."

"Are they still together?" I asked.

"I think so. When she visited me, she said she'd leave him. Had missed me. Regretted our time apart." He ran a hand through his hair.

"It was everything I'd wanted to hear, even after all she'd done. Stupid, right?"

"No." I folded the drink napkin into a triangle, unfolded it, and did it again. "Celia asked me to take her back."

"And?"

"I don't want to. But there's a part of me that remembers what it was like before. How happy we were." I flicked the napkin across the table. "But she'd been cheating on me with Cameron. He'd planned to ask her to marry him, even though he knew she was cheating on me with him. So, no, I wouldn't take her back, especially since I found out Roman's been keeping her bed warm." That wasn't love. That wasn't the sacrificial love I'd had given to me all my life by the man before me.

Had she ever loved me? Even after everything she'd put me through, I wouldn't have considered being with one of her friends, let alone two. Was there something about me that the women I cared for wouldn't stick around?

"I wish you'd never had to experience that. And I know it won't help, but if it hadn't, you wouldn't have Baker."

Mrs. Quinn touched Dad's shoulder. "I'm sorry to interrupt, but I don't have a key to the room."

"Oh." Dad fumbled in his pocket and produced the plastic key card. "I took off without saying anything."

She squeezed. "You didn't need to."

"Would you like to join us?" I indicated to the chair across from me.

"I don't want to intrude—"

"We'd like you to," I said, motioning for the server. "Whiskey okay for you?"

There was a determined set to her jaw when she lifted her chin. "Sure."

WITH A FRESH ROUND OF DRINKS, the mood wasn't quite so heavy.

"We're still scheduled to head out on Sunday, but if you want, we can move it up to tomorrow." Dad looked at me over the rim of his glass.

I shifted in my seat. "I'm not going back."

He clutched his tumbler and cleared his throat. "This time, I'm not leaving you out here on your own. Expect more than one visit a year."

"I look forward to it. Hope you'll come too, Mrs. Quinn." I tipped my glass to her.

"It's not my place to say anything, but I'm going to anyway." Her lips thinned. "Take it from someone who's made the mistake of letting the past dictate her future. Don't do it."

I didn't respond. She had no idea what I'd been through.

"And just so I'm clear, in your case, I'm talking about you walking away from Baker. It's no secret I adore her, but I adore you too. And if you let her go, you will regret it for the rest of your life."

"She might leave me. And I can't take that," I said tightly.

"One day, you'll wake up and wonder how you got this old. Make sure when you open your eyes, there's someone beside you who loves you no matter what." She tossed back her drink. "Stop kidding yourself."

She stood, kissed the top of Dad's head, and then kissed mine. "If I didn't care about you, I'd keep my mouth shut." She kissed me again before leaving Dad and me staring after her.

"She's right."

"I know. But it doesn't matter."

CHAPTER FORTY-FOUR

BAKER

THE ORDER for lip gloss came at the best possible time.

It kept me busy enough that I didn't have time to mope around on the sofa. So I moped and made lip gloss at the same time. *See? Multi-tasking.*

The ache from Holt's absence was my constant companion. I'd even spent the night at the shelter a few times just so I wouldn't have to go home to an empty apartment.

But I'd just delivered the remaining lip gloss to Juniper. Four days early. What was I going to do with all the extra time on my hands?

I wandered from the boutique to Trish's food truck. The line was down the block, so I caught her attention through the window. She unlocked the back door for me.

"Need some help?"

"How'd it go?"

We spoke at the same time and laughed.

"She didn't order more," I said. I shrugged like it was no big deal, but I was disappointed.

"Did you ask?"

"No?"

Was I supposed to?

"Then you can do it tomorrow. Call and make sure everything is okay with the shipment. Then ask if she needs more." Trish was so business savvy. I was lucky to have her.

"Okay," I said, brightening. "Hey, Cricket."

She gave a little wave of acknowledgement from where she boxed up an order.

"The new logo is getting rave reviews," I said.

"That's good," she mumbled without looking up.

I clapped my hands and exchanged a look with Trish. "What can I do?"

"Fill drinks," she said as she went back to the window.

"You got it."

A COUPLE OF HOURS LATER, the three of us walked into Paths. Cricket hadn't said more than a few words the entire time. The girl was an expert at being invisible. But when Trish and I sat down at one of the tables in the dining room, she joined us.

"Have you heard from him?" Trish slid a container of the day's left-over mac and cheese toward me.

I went to grab some silverware from the cart near the wall.

"No," I said as I plopped back down. I pushed around some of the macaroni with my fork. "Has Andrew?"

She put a container of broccoli between us and speared a piece. "Yesterday."

That made four times in a week and a half. I stuffed down the hurt and reminded myself he was in a bad place. He had his family. He didn't need me.

Cricket discreetly stabbed some broccoli.

"Oh. Mr. Dixon wants you to come to Sunday dinner." Trish turned to Cricket. "You too."

She mumbled her excuses, but there was a possibility she might show.

"Did I hear my name?" Mr. Dixon strolled in, Ella in his arms, her diaper bag on his shoulder. "Hey, stranger." He placed a hand on my shoulder. "We missed you Sunday."

"I'll try to make it this weekend," I promised.

"Did you finish making your gloss?"

"Delivered it this afternoon."

He beamed at me. "So proud of you. Let me know if an old man and a little one can be of any help."

"Thanks."

"I can help too." Cricket spoke just loud enough to be heard, but she fidgeted with the sleeves of her flannel shirt.

"I appreciate it."

"Have you been here long?" Mrs. Quinn swept over to the table, a notepad in hand.

"Just got here," Mr. Dixon said.

"There's my sweet girl," she cooed at Ella, who screamed her greeting. "I've missed you too."

"I need to go make a phone call," Cricket muttered as she pushed away from the table.

"Take this with you." Trish offered her a few more containers.

She greedily accepted before she disappeared.

"She okay?" I asked, pointing my chin after her.

A wary expression wound its way across Mrs. Quinn's face. "I don't know. But it's very difficult to help people who don't want to help themselves."

"Did she run off when Officer Wilson came by again?"

"Nope. I still don't know what that was all about."

"I'm glad you came by, Baker. Do you have a minute?"

"Sure."

We moved to the opposite end of the dining room where it was empty.

"Daniel is working on the loose ends to try to keep you protected," she said, her voice hushed.

"How?"

"I didn't ask. I only take him at his word. If he says he's on it, you can trust that."

There were so many people who had reported on the events of that tragic day. They could never all be squelched. It was impossible, but it helped to know Daniel was trying.

I leaned against a dining chair. "Is it wrong to just want to move forward? I don't want to pretend like it never happened—that's not completely true. I want to remember and I want to forget at the same time."

"What happened was tragic. But it's done and if the public finds out your involvement, it could be very difficult on you."

It already was difficult. I lived with this constant need to stay under the radar. This constant regret for what I'd let happen. And I wasn't involved. I'd tried. If I'd known what was going to happen I'd have never gotten in that car, and I would've made sure Kyle didn't either.

"I didn't do enough. They were supposed to stop it. I should have." I dropped my chin to my chest and pinched my eyes shut.

"You did the best you could. It's always easy to look back and focus on what could have been."

She took me in her arms and held me close.

"How do you do it? How do you have unconditional faith and support in every woman here?"

"Sometimes that's all we need to get ourselves off the ground." The lines around her eyes crinkled. "One day I might need yours too."

"You already have it." I hugged her again. "Can you help me make sure the profits from the makeup line get to the victims?"

She canted her head to the side. "Of course."

"I don't want to advertise that. Only the part that will go here."

"You don't have to donate your money here."

"Yeah. I do."

"Whatever you need, all you have to do is ask." She took my hands in hers. "Paths of Purpose is a better place because of your time here."

I blushed. "I don't know about that. Just that you saved my life."

Whether it was fate or pure luck that I'd ended up in Mrs. Quinn's care, I didn't know. That was the one thing that had gone my way after everything else had failed. My own family had once and for all exiled me from their lives, but because of that, I had her. She'd accepted a stranger without question and never made me feel anything less than loved. Without her, I didn't know where I'd be.

Her expression turned soft. "Have you thought about a trip to Wyoming?"

"I'm sorry, Easy. But I can't do it. Not even for you."

His words had been on replay in my head. He couldn't try. Not even for me. I shook my head. "We could have fixed things before. And I know I should go after what I want, but I need him to come after me. That's silly, but I have to know it's not me chasing after another guy. I need to be enough."

"Give him a little more time."

"I'm not going to look for a new relationship, but I'm not going to wait around either. He made his choice. It hurts. More than I want to admit. But . . ."

"You're an incredibly strong woman."

Coming from Mrs. Quinn, that meant a lot. Her faith in me had never ceased, and apart from Trish, she was the only person who'd ever shown that level of support. Well, that wasn't exactly true. Holt had shown he'd believed in me when he'd offered the loft at his garage for my makeup line. But even he didn't want to stick around to be with me. Was that what strength amounted to?

"Being strong isn't what it's cracked up to be."

CHAPTER FORTY-FIVE

HOLT

I SHOVED CLOTHES INTO A BAG.

Then dumped them back out.

"Shit."

I kicked at the mess on the floor. The picture of Celia and me floated on top of a shirt. I snatched it up and studied my face.

I looked happy. Unburdened. Days like that near the lake made me forget about what I'd left behind in New York. It wasn't always like that, but often enough that I could survive.

I pulled out my phone and opened my camera roll. Baker and me on the sofa. Baker and me at Dino's. Me with lips shiny with her gloss. My face buried against her neck before I took off for work.

Every single day with Baker I was happy. Even on the days we fought. Maybe not so much on the ones she wasn't speaking to me. But it didn't take a genius to know what—or who, rather—had turned this hole inside of me to a cavern.

Time and distance was supposed to make this easier, but it hadn't. I missed her like mad.

My decision to stay in Wyoming had made things clearer. It was good to be with the guys again. I enjoyed working at the park, but it wasn't as fulfilling as I remembered.

Or maybe I'd changed.

My reasons for staying didn't seem as pressing as they once had been. I'd run to New York to get away from my problems and found my soul had healed a little while I was there.

I'd spent most of my days thinking about Easy. I couldn't shower without her on my mind. Pizza and beer didn't have the same appeal without sharing it with her.

The nights weren't any better. My bed was cold and empty without her warmth. Her laugh. Her honesty.

I tossed the picture back on the floor and scooped my stuff back into my bag. There was a flight to Chicago in two hours. From there, it should be easy to get back where I belonged. I just needed to make one more stop before the airport.

THE CEMETERY WAS a small plot on the land Cameron's family owned outside of town. He'd always said he'd been born here and he'd die here. I guessed he was right.

The grass was cut and there were fresh flowers on each of the headstones. I hadn't been to this spot since the funeral all those months ago, but I remembered exactly where I was going.

I stood and stared at the granite slab with his name permanently etched in it. Somehow it didn't seem possible he was gone, never to return.

"I was so angry at you, Cameron."

I didn't say anything else for a minute, like I thought he might respond. Somehow releasing those words felt huge. They hung between me and the headstone.

"I was mad at myself too."

While it had been easier to blame him for Celia and the accident, the weight of it sat firmly on my shoulders.

"I couldn't save you," I said hoarsely as my eyes stung. My head was filled with visions of that moment where he slipped from my grasp.

· · ·

"I LOVE CELIA. Was going to ask her to marry me. Will you tell her that? Take care of her?"

Stunned my best friend had been cheating with my girlfriend, I lost my grip. When I realized what I'd done, I tried to catch him. But it was too late.

"I'M SORRY."

I touched the headstone and tried to gain my composure. I'd avoided any thoughts of what had happened on that mountain as best I could. Facing it now wasn't easy.

"It all went down so fast. We had so much training on what to do in an emergency, and I choked when it wasn't a drill." I hung my head.

Survivor's guilt.

I had it in spades and combined with my anger, it was a heavy load.

"I wish you'd told me about you and her."

I meant that. Yeah, I would've been beyond angry. I might not have spoken to either of them for a long time after. Or I might have been more understanding. But I never had the choice.

"You should've told me you loved her. Looking back it's obvious. Maybe you were better together than she and I were." I kicked at the grass. "But I trusted you."

Betrayal. Death. Loss.

They'd all come in a gigantic wave that had knocked me off my feet.

"I miss you, man."

That was what it all came down to. The fresh wounds had faded into this steady hurt. Baker had helped me manage the pain to the point I could be here now, talking to Cameron.

"I don't know if I'm to blame for what happened with the two of you. It doesn't matter now. I just wish you were still around so I could punch you in the mouth." I laughed. How many times had he threatened to do the same thing to me?

I dug in my pocket and pulled out my ranger badge. "I hope wherever you are you're happy." I placed the metal on his headstone. "See you on the other side."

As I walked to my truck, I breathed a little easier. What he'd done was wrong, but it couldn't be fixed. I was the one suffering because I hadn't been able to let it go. And if things hadn't happened the way they did, I'd have missed out on more time with my family. I'd have missed out on playing guinea pig for lip gloss and blush and whatever all that stuff was. Holding on to my anger wasn't worth losing that.

"DIXON. You want to go grab a beer?"

I pressed my phone to my ear. "Roman, I quit."

Silence greeted me before he burst out laughing. "You asshole. For a second, I thought you were serious."

"I am."

"What? You just got back. You can't quit."

"I have to."

"Is it because of Celia?"

"No. No. I'm over it. If you want her, you have my blessing." Something in me had shifted. I hadn't thought it was possible to get over her, but somewhere along the way, I had. Talking to Cameron had helped, but it was Baker who'd shown me what a relationship should be.

"Come over. Let's talk about this."

"I'm at the airport in Chicago, man."

"Damn, you are serious." He let out a long sigh. "Let me add up the vacation you have left. I'll put in your resignation when it runs out. At least that way you'll get paid."

"Thanks." I ran a hand through my hair. "I want a guided tour of the park next time I come into town."

He laughed. "You better, asshole."

"DO YOU KNOW HER ADDRESS?"

"Holt. It's three in the morning," Marlow said, her voice rough.

"Do I sound sleepy?"

The sheets rustled. "I haven't heard from you in a month."

"If I didn't need something from you, I wouldn't be talking to you now."

Silence.

"Do you have it or not?"

"What are you going to do?" She was wide awake now.

"Send flowers. What do you think? I want to talk to her."

She sighed. "I don't think that's a good idea, smart ass."

"Having a relationship with our estranged mother for years behind all of our backs wasn't a good idea." I wasn't sure I'd ever get past her betrayal.

"I've ended it."

"Forgive me if I don't believe you."

"Stay away from her. She'll pack your head with lies."

"Speaking from experience, big sister?"

"Too much."

"Give me the address."

"I don't have it."

"You could have told me that three minutes ago." I ended the call, uncertain if I believed her or not. She'd broken my trust, been the opening through which our dear mother had slithered back into our lives.

I needed closure. To have my say. Part of me thought I should let it go, not give her the satisfaction of a reaction. But I had to do this. I had to find her . . . before I moved on with my life.

THE GARAGE HAD that closed up smell to it when I stepped inside. *Why did I think giving this up was the better option?* Because I'd been blinded by hurt and fear. The time away had made me appreciate New York and everything it represented even more. Being back without the weight of the past had renewed my determination to build a future with the people I cared about.

I wanted to go straight home after a night of flights and layovers, but it was late. Did I think she'd just let me back in? Forgive me when I'd told her I couldn't change, not even for her?

"Take the time you need. You have a lot of things to make up your mind about, including where you want to be. Only you can figure out what's best and stop waffling. When you do, come back to me, Grease Monkey."

Those words gave me hope. But I was delirious with the lack of sleep and smart enough to know I might screw it all up with Baker because of it.

So I'd wait. Get some rest in the leftover office chair. And regroup in the morning.

THE TEXT with an address woke me up a few hours later, quickly followed by another that my sister had called in a favor with a friend.

Yeah, right. I didn't know if she'd always been a liar or if this was a new habit. Either way, I still wasn't ready to even think about forgiving her. She'd shattered our trust and stomped on the pieces.

Damn it. Why hadn't I gone to a hotel? I needed a shower in the worst way.

I checked the clock on my phone. She'd be gone to work by now. I could sneak in, be in and out of the apartment before Baker knew it.

Just go to Dad's.

No, I wanted Easy to be the first to know I was back.

MY HEART POUNDED as I turned the key in the lock. Silence greeted me when I pushed the door open.

Home.

I nearly sagged against the doorframe as relief swept through me. I'd almost given this up, but I wouldn't without a fight now. It hit me what that emptiness I'd felt the last month in Wyoming was.

Homesickness.

Being back in the space that was ours evaporated that.

The kitchen was tidy, but the dining table had more of whatever she used to make her products all over it. There was a string of stickers strewn over the coffee table and tiny boxes stacked on the floor by the windows.

She'd been focusing on her makeup in the last month. *That's my girl.*

I left everything as it was and dropped my bag off in my closet. She hadn't touched a thing. And no one else's shit was in there. I grinned. No new roommate.

I hesitated in the doorway to her room. Honey and all things Easy invaded my nostrils.

I frowned. Her bed was made with a thousand pillows stacked on it. My girl didn't have time for that stuff in the morning, always rushing to get out the door. I glanced back in my room. My side of the bed was disheveled, the sheets back and pillow dented in.

I retraced my steps across the wood floors to my bed, bent, and inhaled deeply. Honey.

"Caught ya, Easy."

I whistled as I sauntered to the shower. Soon I'd make things right. Soon.

CHAPTER FORTY-SIX

HOLT

SHE'S BEEN ... close.

I stared up at the brownstone with my fists clenched at my sides. The location was maybe a fifteen minute walk from Dad's, which in this city was practically next door. In my mind, I'd imagined an Upper East Side address worth tens of millions.

Maybe then I could justify why she'd left.

Sure, this was better than the apartment I'd grown up in, but it wasn't the luxury I'd pictured.

A man gave me a nasty look as he edged around me. I was routed in place in the middle of the sidewalk.

You don't have to do this. She's not worth it.

She most certainly wasn't. I'd gotten a lot of the closure I needed during Andrew's wedding weekend. What I'd seen from the woman who'd given me life was disgusting. She didn't care about any of us.

And I'd let her keep me away from New York and my family for a month. I'd allowed her to steal even more time with the people I loved. It was time to stop running. Time to close the door.

I jogged up the steps and rang the bell.

Please don't let him *answer.*

I wanted nothing to do with the man who might be my biological father.

After an excruciatingly long time, the door creaked open. My pulse accelerated. I shouldn't be nervous. The woman before me didn't matter, yet I lost the words I'd practiced on the way over.

She was as perfectly put together as before. The pale pink starched blouse was a disguise for all that ugly inside. Her pearls around her neck didn't fool me any longer. She wasn't this picture of innocence she tried to portray.

She was the devil in pastels and pearls.

"Hello, son." Her tone was as crisp as her slacks.

"I'm not your son."

It was the same thing my brother had told her, but I needed to say it too.

Her false smile broadened. "They always let you hide in their shadows, didn't they? You never learned to be your own man, have your own thoughts."

I scowled and reminded myself she spewed poison for her own pleasure.

"Stay away from Marlow. Stay away from Dad. Stay away from Andrew and his family. And stay the hell away from me."

I didn't care so much about answers anymore. Why she'd left and if it was my fault no longer mattered. Dad said I wasn't the reason, and that was enough for me. He was the truth. *She* was a web of lies.

And the most important thing was making sure she didn't bother my family anymore.

She laughed, a fake sound that burned my ears. "This is precious. You think you can tell me what to do, *son?*"

I cringed at the word.

"I said I'm not—"

"Why don't you ask me what you really came here to know?"

I hated that she'd cut me off and the certainty in her tone that she held the power.

"Ivette, why are you standing at the—oh, I didn't realize we had a visitor." The man I hadn't wanted to see stood behind her.

I ignored him and focused on my mother. There were more important things I had to do with my time.

"You leaving us was the best thing that ever happened." She opened her mouth to respond, but I didn't let her. "*Stay away from all of us.*"

I spun and trotted back down the steps. This time I wasn't running. I was walking away intentionally.

"I left because of you."

I stumbled. The words were like fire blazing arrows in my back. They were the ones I'd feared most of my life.

She left because of me, son. Don't you ever think otherwise. Ever.

My father's words gave me strength. *He* was the one who'd been there for me through everything. *He* was the one I could trust. And I was finally listening to him.

I kept walking. I'd said what I needed to. *Done.* So very done with her. But if she ignored my warning, I had my family to stand up against her. We had each other. Something she would never get back.

CHAPTER FORTY-SEVEN

BAKER

"I'LL BE THERE IN AN—"

I froze in the doorway and sniffed. *Was that motor oil?* I shook my head to clear it. Obviously, I was hallucinating . . . or losing my mind. Maybe both.

"Baker?" Trish's worried voice came through the phone.

"I'll be there in an hour. You guys go on and eat without me."

"No. Mr. Dixon just started to cook, so you have plenty of time."

"See you soon."

I tossed my keys on the counter and surveyed the room. Everything looked the same. The disappointment was still potent. I'd gotten better, but every day I pictured opening the front door to find Holt standing in the kitchen, coveralls on, beer in hand.

It never happened.

And now I was smelling a garage shop. Lunatic. A delusional lunatic.

"HEY!" A chorus of welcomes greeted me as I came into Mr. Dixon's living room.

Ella screamed the loudest. All was normal.

"Am I late?"

"Right on time," Mrs. Quinn said. "Andrew just set the table."

"He did?"

"I heard that," he called from the dining room.

"Here you are, love." Mr. Dixon passed me a glass of red wine and kissed me on the cheek. "How's the magazine world?"

"Crazy busy?"

"More importantly, how's the cosmetics world?"

What would I do without this family?

I gave him a shy smile. "I have news," I said, loud enough for everyone to hear.

The room stopped. Even Ella was quiet, her attention on me.

"Juniper wants 1000 glosses, 500 blushes, and 500 shadows."

Trish shrieked. "Baker, that's terrific."

"Didn't she just order a couple hundred of the gloss?" Andrew asked.

"Already gone." My chest puffed out a little.

Because of Juniper's interest, I'd moved up the timeline to have everything tested. They were perfectly safe. And Hayden had helped me get my company legally set up . . . with Patrick's and Andrew's help. I was so grateful I had people to look out for me.

Mrs. Quinn hugged me. "So proud of you, my dear."

"When do Ella and I need to report for duty?" Mr. Dixon saluted.

"I'll let you know as soon as the supplies come in." Though I had no idea where I was going to produce all of these things. My setup in the apartment wasn't nearly big enough to handle making larger quantities.

Trish slung an arm around my shoulders. "I hate to add to the pressure, but I'm out too."

I slipped my arm around her waist. "You get preferential treatment. First customer and all."

She winked at me, and I winked back.

"I'll print more labels," Cricket said softly.

"Hey," I said, startled. She was a phantom, appearing and disappearing at will. "That would be great. Oh, and she liked the new packaging you came up with. I showed her a sample this afternoon."

Cricket blushed. "I can get what you need by this weekend."

"Let me know how much and I'll give you the money."

She shrank back into the kitchen without another word.

"Who's hungry?" Mr. Dixon practically glowed, completely in his element with his family around.

"Me." I raised my hand, silly after the spectacular day I'd had.

Funny, the first person I'd wanted to call with the news wasn't in this room. Or this city, for that matter. I'd almost broken down and done it, but I still needed the first move to be his.

AFTER DINNER, we did the dishes and gathered in the living room. The television was on, but muted in the background. Mr. Dixon sat in his chair. Mrs. Quinn took the matching one next to him. Trish and Andrew sank onto the love seat, while Cricket and I settled in on the sofa opposite them.

Andrew's phone buzzed with a text. Lines creased his forehead as his fingers flew across the screen.

"Big client?" Mr. Dixon pointed his chin at the phone.

He slipped it back into his pocket. "I talked to Marlow," he blurted.

"Was that her?"

"No. It was a few days ago." Trish placed a hand on his thigh. "It didn't go well."

His father tightened his fingers around the stem of the wine glass. "It didn't go well when I spoke to her either."

"I thought I was ready. But the second she answered, I realized I'm still so angry with her."

We all were. It was shocking what she'd done.

"Me too. I told her if she needed me, I'm here and I'd like to continue to keep Blake. But I need some time to get over what she did." Mr. Dixon's sadness seeped from every part of him.

"It's not that she was talking to *her*. But inviting *her* to our wedding? That was low." Andrew ran a hand through his hair.

"I can't believe she'd do something like that. If she wanted to try to fix things, that wasn't the place to start," Mr. Dixon said in disbelief.

"She tried to tell me she didn't do it." Andrew didn't sound convinced.

"She told me the same thing. I can't trust her," Mr. Dixon choked out, pain contorting his face.

Mrs. Quinn took his hand into hers.

"If you love her, don't shut her out forever."

All eyes landed on Cricket, who looked down at her lap after she spoke.

"I just need more time," Mr. Dixon said.

"Turn that up." Mrs. Quinn slapped at his arm and pointed toward the TV.

An old DMV photo of my face was plastered on the screen.

"The passenger in the shooting spree in Washington, D.C. three years ago that left twelve people dead and thirty-seven injured has finally been identified."

"Is that true?"

Through blurred vision, the one person I'd never wanted to discover my past stood in the doorway.

Holt.

CHAPTER FORTY-EIGHT

BAKER

Three Years Ago

"WE'RE gonna leave our mark, baby. You and me. Nobody's ever gonna forget us."

Kyle started the ignition to the car, turned up the radio to a deafening volume, and grabbed my hand. He grinned as "Heroes" by Postmodern Jukebox blasted.

I gave him a wary smile. Whenever he played that song, he always got in a weird mood. At that moment, he was giddy to a point I'd never seen. He'd been having these highs and lows a lot more recently.

And they scared me.

So much so that I'd called the police. Told them *something* was happening. They'd never come.

Kyle did illegal things. Things that I chose to overlook because I loved him. Because he treasured me.

But his behavior had become strange, and I feared he'd hurt himself. Or maybe others.

He grabbed the back of my head and smashed his lips to mine. The kiss was bruising. Something beyond passionate. And where I usually settled with his touch, that kiss set me on edge.

When he ripped his lips from mine, he was breathless. "You"—he pointed at me—"are my inspiration."

Those were the kinds of words I'd eaten up from the time we'd started seeing one another. They were the reason I fell so hard and fast.

I touched his cheek, but words failed me. *Tell him you want to go back to school.*

I dropped my hand. Now wasn't the time. Not when he seemed so high. I didn't want to upset him.

He threw the car in reverse and we squealed out of the driveway of our townhome. I gripped the seat as he sped down the street. His hand was tight on mine as he raced around cars and blew through two stop signs.

Another driver slammed on the brakes to avoid crashing into us.

"Kyle. Can we slow down please?"

His answer was to press down harder on the gas.

As we rocketed up the ramp of the I-66 freeway, he sang at the top of his lungs.

Thump. Thump. Thump.

Blood thundered in my ears. My heart pounded so hard my chest hurt.

He released my hand and reached behind us. I turned to see him yank a blanket off the backseat.

Bile rose up my throat.

A pile of guns big enough for a small army lay innocently on the cloth seat.

Kyle grabbed one. He cocked it.

I stared in horror. Frozen.

Is he going to kill me?

He turned up the radio.

4:37 p.m.

Why am I looking at the clock? Why don't I do something?

In slow motion, he smiled at me. Turned his head. Rolled down the window. My hair blew in my face.

He lifted the shot gun. Aimed at the car beside us.

Boom.

CHAPTER FORTY-NINE

HOLT

ONE LOOK at her and I knew the truth.

She was ashen as tears leaked from her eyes.

"I tried to stop it." Desperation clung to her words. "I tried."

Trish bolted across the living room to her side and threw an arm around her.

I blocked out the noise from the TV. I remembered that day well. Most of America did. Some asshole took a joy ride through the capital, shooting innocent people as he went. It wasn't the deadliest killing in our history, but it ranked up near the top of most fucked up.

"Did you—" I couldn't finish the question. Couldn't connect the woman I knew with *that*.

"I was in the car."

Mrs. Quinn cleared her throat. "You'll have more privacy in the kitchen."

I nodded once and went straight for the fridge. Half a beer was down before I felt Easy enter.

A phone rang from the other room, but all I could focus on was Baker. Her arms were folded around her middle like she wanted to make herself small.

I exhaled long and slow. "Tell me your truth. The raw version."

She lifted her eyes to mine. "Why'd you come back? Just give me that before you hear the ugly facts."

"For you."

Her mouth quivered. A few more tears escaped down her cheeks. She lifted her chin.

"I was fifteen when I met Kyle. If there was a god, he was mine."

Immediately, I hated the guy. Not only for what he'd dragged Baker into, but that he'd owned her heart.

She swallowed hard. "He was twenty. I didn't care that he was too old for me. He felt right. In here." She pointed to her chest, and I wrung the neck of my beer bottle.

"He was good to me. Said we were going to do big things. I believed him. He made me believe in him."

She turned away for a moment. I was impatient for the rest of this story, but I'd give her the time she needed.

"It was little things I had to give up at first. They weren't sacrifices at the time. He took care of me, treated me like his queen. So of course I'd rather spend time with him than go to the science club. And my friends, they were nothing compared to him."

"The brainwashing." A light went off, things making more sense.

"I don't know if he even meant to do it. He was that good. I was that stupid." She stared at the floor. I felt her disappointment with herself and could hardly stand it.

"Looking back, it's easy to see everything. But it all comes down to me. I wasn't strong enough." Her voice was bitter. "I was twenty-five when it happened. I didn't have an excuse of being young and naïve anymore."

"You were with him ten years?" The question sounded like it had been shredded with razor blades.

She nodded. "It never occurred to me to get away. Not until he started stockpiling guns," she said hoarsely. "I-I need some water."

I retrieved a bottle out of the fridge and handed it to her. She gulped greedily.

"He dealt in weapons. I was used to his runs in the middle of the night. But he always came home to me. Kept me shielded from it.

Made me feel safe." She got a faraway look. "We lived in a townhouse in Georgetown."

Like she couldn't grasp how one world and the other were one in the same.

"I didn't know what he was going to do. Only something. I went to the police. Told them what I knew. They seemed to take me seriously, but weeks went by and they never came."

The plastic bottle crinkled under her grip.

"I tried again. They said they'd look into it. Nobody did until I managed to wreck the car."

She closed her eyes and sucked in air as if she couldn't get enough.

"You stopped it." I searched through my memories for the footage I'd seen of that day. A mangled car upside down in a ditch surrounded by police cars came to mind. No one should have survived that crash. I remembered thinking that at the time.

"When Kyle started shooting, I didn't really believe it was happening. It was like this bubble. Where I was inside was real. Out past the shimmer was an illusion." Her lids opened to reveal haunted eyes. "Twelve people died and thirty-seven were injured before I tried to do anything."

The sentence crescendoed with self-loathing.

I tried to imagine being in that car. Watching someone you idolized terrorize a city.

"He pulled the trigger over and over while he drove. Even told me he loved me as he reached for another gun. Seven minutes. That's how long it took me to grab the wheel of the car."

"He wasn't killed in the accident." I recalled that now.

"They shot him when he managed to crawl out of the car. I was hanging upside-down by the seatbelt. There was blood. A river of it."

"There was never any mention of you."

"Once the police realized I was telling the truth, that I'd tried and tried to warn them, they kept me out of it. I was in the hospital a few days with a head injury and a broken arm. My parents are pretty high ranking in the federal government. They made sure it stayed buried and disowned me for good. One of the detectives set me up with Mrs. Quinn. Promised me I'd be safe. And I was."

I set down my beer bottle and closed the distance between us. I slipped my fist under her chin, gently forcing her to look at me.

"If you want to forget about the past, we'll never mention it. If you want to talk about it, we can all you like. I love you, either way."

Her lips parted as a V formed between her brows. "What I just told you—"

"Doesn't change a thing." I framed her face with my hands. "I can't even begin to imagine what any of that was like. The last thing I'm going to do is stand here and judge you. Were there things you wish you could have done differently? I can see that in your eyes. If you could go back and change it? You'd give up everything you have to do it. All you can do is respect the people who were hurt while you move forward and live your life."

"It seems so unfair," she whispered. "People died. Were paralyzed. And look at me. I couldn't have dreamt of what I have now."

"You can't pay the penance for his sins."

She studied me, saw those words were as much for me as they were for her.

"I feel like I should try."

"We'll get through it. Together."

She brightened. "Did you say you love me?"

"Came all this way just to tell you."

"Are you here for good?"

"For good." I slid my hands behind her head. "I got back about three this morning, but I had some unfinished business I needed to clear up before I came home."

"What kind of business?"

"I'll tell you when we get home."

She pressed up on her toes and kissed me like she'd been waiting a month to do it. "I love you too."

And right then, the path to this moment had been worth every single thing it took to get me here. I finally felt I was where I belonged.

CHAPTER FIFTY

BAKER

"DANIEL CALLED. Was frantically apologetic about the story."

Mrs. Quinn stood as Holt and I came back into the living room.

"If you talk to him again, please tell him it's not his fault. I'll be sure to tell him too." I looked up at Holt. "Just maybe tomorrow."

Mr. Dixon crowded around us. "Are you home?" He didn't bother to hide the hope in his voice.

"I'm home."

He threw his arms around his son. "I'm so glad. Missed you like crazy."

"I'm glad to be back too." Holt reached for my hand. I clutched his tightly. "If it's okay, I think we're gonna head home."

"You all right?" Trish asked.

"I will be."

"We're behind you. A thousand percent." Mr. Dixon hugged me extra hard.

Everyone else followed suit as we said our goodbyes.

HOLT UNLOCKED the door and held it open for me. I paused in the doorway. "Were you here earlier today?"

The tips of his ears turned pink. "Um . . ."

"I knew it." I pointed at him accusingly.

"Are you mad?"

"I thought I was going crazy when I came by earlier. I smelled the motor oil and for a second, I thought you were home."

"Motor oil?" He cocked a brow.

"I think if we made a cologne, women would buy it in droves." I placed my hands on his sides. "But I kinda want to keep it all to myself."

"You've got me all to yourself." He dipped his head, those lips I craved finding mine. "Missed you. So damn much," he murmured.

I slipped my tongue into his mouth and melted against him. I'd been miserable without him, but hadn't realized just how much until now. He cradled my head with one hand and splayed the other on my back.

This was a welcome home. A promise not to leave. An I can't live without you.

"I'm sorry I was gone so long. I needed the time."

"I understand." I did and I didn't. But he was here now, seemed lighter than when he'd lived here before. That was all that mattered. "What did you do today?"

His mouth flattened. "Tracked down my mother."

I gaped at him. "How'd it go?"

"You sure you want to talk about this tonight? It's been a rough one." Concern rained down on me.

"I'd rather be distracted."

"I can do that." He winked before he brushed his lips against mine. "I know you've been sleeping in my bed."

Oops. I guessed I was bound to get caught someday.

"I kept it warm."

"Not with any other roommates?"

"Just you."

He gave me a satisfied smile. "Good." He kissed my forehead. "Wine? If we have to talk about my mother, I need a beer."

"Long story?"

"No. Long month."

WE SETTLED on opposite ends of the sofa facing one another, our legs tangled up. Holt took a swig of his beer.

"I called Marlow."

"Her phone is ringing off the hook," I said.

"What do you mean?"

"Andrew called her. Your dad did. They didn't elaborate, just said it didn't go well."

"Guess that's a trend too." He picked at his label. "I probably shouldn't have called in the middle of the night, but after what she brought on all of us, she owed me."

"She told you how to find your mother."

"Not on the phone. But a little bit later, she texted me an address. The right one."

"Did you go over there right away?"

He grabbed my foot and massaged. "No. I waited until this afternoon."

"She saw you?"

"Along with the man she claims is my father," he said with disgust. "I didn't even go inside. Said what I needed to say and got out of there."

"You're not going to elaborate?"

He rested his beer on my shin. "I told her leaving us with my father was the best thing she could have ever done. Then I told her to stay away from us."

"What did they say?" I leaned closer as he kneaded my foot.

"Not a damn thing. Both of them looked at me like they'd never seen me before. It was very anti-climactic."

"But you feel better."

"It feels good to finally know what I want from her."

"Which is?"

"Nothing. Absolutely nothing."

I sipped my wine. "What about that man?"

He sighed. "I want nothing to do with him. Even if it turns out he is my biological father."

"Are you going to find out for sure?"

"Do you think I should?"

I fought an inappropriate smile. He cared what I thought. Holt had no idea how much that meant to me.

"This isn't going to help, but that's a decision you need to make."

"What would you do?"

I took a minute to consider. "I think the curious part of me would want to know. That way I could move on. But I'd be worried about what it would do to your dad."

"He said he'd support me no matter what. About the test, I mean."

"Whether you have a DNA test or not, it won't change how you feel about him."

"He says the same. I'm afraid it would, even if we don't mean for it to."

"Think on it then. Talk to him about it. He's pretty wise, and I think it would mean a lot to him if you confided in him."

He nodded. "Okay. Yeah, I'll talk to him. Sounds like you've gotten to know him pretty well."

I smiled. I had. I could now comprehend how fortunate Andrew, Marlow, and Holt had been having Mr. Dixon as their father. Even though his son had ditched me, he'd kept up contact and become a father figure of sorts for me too. And now I got to have both of them. Surreal.

"Yes, I have. He's such a good man. He's been like a father to me, and I hadn't realized what I'd been missing."

"I know exactly what you mean." A shadow crossed his features. "I'm thinking we should get all the shit out of the way now. Sound good?"

It sounded better than good. "Then leave the past where it belongs?"

"The woman you saw me with at the bar, I-I thought she was the one." Pain nearly blinded me, despite I'd already figured that out. "The guy you saw the article about—"

"Cameron?"

"Yeah, Cameron." He stumbled over the name. "We didn't just work together. He was my best friend. The three of us did everything together." He looked down at where he gripped my foot. "I didn't know they were spending so much time together when I wasn't around."

"Holt." I didn't know what else to say.

"She knew about my mom cheating on my dad. He did too. How that was the one thing I couldn't tolerate."

"Please tell me you didn't catch them in the act."

"No. Cameron and I were tagging trees in the woods. It was a pretty vertical hike, cold at that elevation." He shivered. "We were headed back down the trail when he slipped. Somehow he caught himself on a rock. The incline was steep. The angle so awkward. He managed to give me one hand, but I couldn't pull him up."

I covered my mouth with my hand.

"We held onto each other, but he was a big guy. All muscle. It wasn't enough." He looked away and squeezed his eyes shut for a second. "He said to tell Celia he loved her. He was going to ask her to marry him. And he was sorry. Never meant for it to happen, but she was everything to him.

"I was so stunned, my grip on him slipped. I caught him, but couldn't hold on. I wasn't strong enough. He—he fell. I watched him hit a rock below and disappear down the side of the cliff. He screamed her name the whole way down."

I set my glass on the coffee table and did the same with his beer before I vaulted onto him. I hugged him with everything I had.

"I'm so sorry. I know that's not good enough, but—"

"I was such a wreck. I'd failed my best friend and was pissed off at him at the same time."

"You lost everything that day."

"I thought I had." He nuzzled my hair. "It took me moving back to New York to realize maybe I hadn't."

"That's why you said you couldn't trust."

"For you, I'll try." He rubbed the back of his neck. "I'm still angry with him. It's wrong to stay mad at a dead man, but I can't make it stop."

"You didn't have time to work it out. Everything happened at warp speed."

"I went to see him. I'm still mad at him, but I'm in a better place to move past it. You make it not hurt quite as much."

I stroked his cheek. "You're finally facing your feelings instead of ignoring them," I corrected.

"Wouldn't be doing that if it weren't for you."

"I promise I will never betray you."

"I know that." He held me tightly to him. "And I'll never try to control you. All men don't brainwash."

"I'm beginning to believe that," I whispered. "I love you, Holt." He leaned into me and kissed my forehead. And it felt like home having his face so close to mine.

"I love you too, Baker."

WE CLUNG to each other for a long time, our breaths in time with one another.

I straightened. "What about your job at the garage?"

"Not going back."

I frowned. "No more coveralls? Motor oil?"

"There's gonna be plenty of that. Just from our place, not his."

"Our place? Holt, this is your dream—"

"Our place. Our dream. Our future." He was so sexy when he spoke like that.

"Our place." I took a deep breath, giving that more thought. "Can we afford it? To fix up the building and keep up with everyday expenses?" I worried my lip between my teeth.

"It might get a little bit tight, but I've got a decent amount saved. Plus Roman isn't going to make my resignation with the park services

official until all my vacation time is used." He grinned. "Still gettin'
paid."

"Is that offer for the space upstairs still on the table?"

"Always."

"Good. I think I'm going to need it sooner rather than later."

"It's all yours, Easy."

"Welcome home, Grease Monkey. Welcome home."

CHAPTER FIFTY-ONE

BAKER

Three weeks later . . .

"THEY'RE MOVING FAST."

I surveyed the garage. Work was going on everywhere except the apartment.

"How was your day?" Holt slid an arm around my waist and kissed the side of my head.

"I've been nervous."

"Me too," he confessed.

"Is your Dad here yet?"

"On his way." He steered me toward the back office. "All this dust flying, I don't want to get your dress dirty."

I couldn't help but smile. "You got one very dirty at lunch yesterday."

His chest puffed out. "I did, didn't I?"

Two envelopes rested on the desk. Holt picked one up and held it out for me.

"What is it?"

"Open it and see." He nudged my hand with the edge.

I slid my finger under the flap and unfolded the papers inside. My eyes scanned the document.

"You put me on the deed?"

"Yeah."

"But this says Baker Dixon." I pointed to the papers in my now trembling hand.

He shoved his hands in his pockets. "I was hoping you'd want to take my name." His cheeks turned pink.

I looked at him incredulously.

"There's some other stuff in there." He pointed toward the papers with his chin.

I rifled through them. "A marriage license application?"

"I—" He scrubbed the back of his neck. "I don't have a ring. I thought this would show my commitment until we could afford one."

"I don't understand," I whispered. All the pieces were there, but I couldn't believe the picture they made.

"I want to be your husband."

"You do?"

"I really, really do." He gave me a sheepish look. "I guess this wasn't the most romantic way to—"

I jumped him and crashed my lips to his. "I'd love for you to be my husband."

"Whenever you want, Easy. I just, we promised raw and I wanted you to know how I feel."

"I don't need a ring." I waved my hand in the air. "This is so much better than a ring."

"Knock, knock," Mr. Dixon called from the doorway. "Is this a bad time?"

"Perfect timing." Holt's smile was blinding. "Are you gonna tell him?"

I cocked my head. "Mr. Dixon, do you like me?"

He gave me a quizzical look. "You know I do," he said carefully.

"Well enough to have me for a daughter-in-law?"

Realization dawned in his eyes. He clapped his hands. "Definitely well enough for that."

Holt set me on my feet, and I went into Mr. Dixon's waiting arms.

"I'm so happy to be part of your family."

"We wouldn't be the same without you." He kissed the top of my head. "Am I the first to know?"

"Yes."

"Not exactly."

Holt and I spoke at the same time.

"Andrew drew up the papers," he explained. "This is half of Baker Dixon's now."

Mr. Dixon fist bumped his son. "Smooth, son. I taught you well." He winked at me, and I grinned. His expression turned serious. "Ready to do this?"

Holt glanced to the other envelope on the table. He hesitated when his fingers touched it. "Thanks for this, Dad."

Mr. Dixon placed a hand on Holt's arm. "I love you, son. Don't ever forget that."

My eyes stung as I took in the exchange.

Holt looked to me, and I nodded in encouragement. Hastily, he ripped open the envelope, his face blank as he read what was printed on the pages.

He handed it to his father. Mr. Dixon stared at the papers before they fluttered from his grasp. He pulled in Holt and held him tightly.

"I always knew you were mine."

I swallowed hard. Holt's shiny eyes met mine.

"Dad, I didn't doubt. I just needed to know so I could move on."

He patted Holt's shoulder. "No explanation necessary. Like I said, I already knew, but it's good to have concrete proof." The DNA didn't lie. He held out an arm, and I slid into their embrace. "All this good news calls for a celebration."

"Will you save us a table at Dino's? It's not Sunday, but . . ."

Mr. Dixon pointed at Holt. "You've got it. Can I invite everyone?"

"You better," I said. "Tell them it's mandatory."

He saluted me. "Yes, ma'am." He gave me an extra squeeze before he released me. "Ella and I have about two hundred more glosses to put labels on. We should get it done tomorrow."

"Thanks. You've been such a help."

I'd become dependent on him to assist me with fulfilling orders. And I'd had several comments about the charming delivery man.

"Anything for my daughter-in-law." He stroked his chin. "That's got a nice ring to it, don't you think?"

"I prefer wife."

"You won't if you don't fix that bathroom up there." I pointed to the apartment above.

"That's my cue to go. See you in a half hour or so?" Mr. Dixon asked.

"The guys should be wrapped up by then."

Mr. Dixon pulled the door halfway closed as he left.

"One of the girls at Paths is doing an apprenticeship with a plumber. I'm going by to see her tomorrow," I said, folding my arms over my chest.

"You still think I can't do it?"

"We only have one bathroom at the apartment. And we need one here so we don't have to go down the street to the library anymore."

He took me into his arms. "Easy?"

"Yeah?"

His look was a cross between amusement and well—okay, it was mostly amusement.

"Check the bathroom when we get home."

I frowned. "You fixed it?"

He snickered. "It was never broken."

"What?"

"It worked. The whole time."

"But Daniel said—"

"No, I said. He figured me out. Knew exactly what I was up to."

"What were you up to?"

He kissed me. "This."

"You pretended your bathroom didn't work so you could marry me?"

"I didn't exactly plan on getting married, but it's worked out better than I imagined."

I slapped at his chest. "I can't believe you."

"You can't be mad at me," he said, the picture of innocence.

"I sure as hell can." My words lost their fire when one side of my mouth lifted.

He kissed the corner. "I'm not sorry."

"Of course you aren't."

"Are you?"

"No." I sagged in his arms.

"Did I tell you how pretty you look today?" He flashed a crooked grin at me.

I smacked my forehead and tried to scowl, failing miserably. "The Dixon charm."

"As real as the Dixon wink. Don't try to escape." I took a step toward the door. He hooked me by the waist. "I said don't try to escape, woman."

"I'm going to see if this bathroom works." I moved behind the old reception desk.

"No," he said, almost frantic. I eyed him suspiciously. "I'm working on it."

I gave him an *oh really* look.

"The new toilet's coming tomorrow. I thought I'd be able to put it in, but laying tile is a little harder than I thought."

I bit my lip. "Oh yeah?"

"I spent a lot of the last few days on YouTube," he confessed.

The metal door swung open, sunlight flooding the doorway.

I gripped Holt's hand. He mouthed *what the hell?* as he edged closer to me.

Marlow pushed a stroller across the concrete floor until she was on the opposite side of the desk. She looked toward the garage area, an unreadable expression on her face. She took her time surveying the space.

"How!" Blake pumped his fist in the air.

"How, buddy," Holt said, eyes softening.

Marlow was the picture of confidence, but I didn't miss the way her hands gripped the handles of the stroller. "I was wrong."

We both started at the admission. That was as close to an "I'm sorry" as I'd ever heard from her.

"Yeah, you were," Holt said.

She stayed rooted in place. "I didn't mean—" She looked away as if the right words were a struggle to find. Finally, she collected herself. "I love you."

He folded his arms over his chest. "I love you too." But behind that was all the hurt she'd caused him.

"I just needed—" She squeezed her eyes shut. "Never mind." When she looked at him again, there was determination in her gaze. "I'm not speaking to *her* anymore."

He stared at her. "Only time will prove that."

"I swear I didn't tell her about the wedding," she said insistently, but immediately snapped her mouth shut when she realized she'd raised her voice. She cleared her throat. "I know I'm the reason for our problems."

Holt tried to cover the shock on his face, but I didn't miss it. "I said my fair share of awful things too."

With that, there seemed to be some sort of unspoken understanding between them. Maybe it didn't seem like much, but from what I knew of Marlow, those few words were huge.

Holt and Marlow's relationship wasn't perfect. How could it be? But I hoped they could move forward and grow from this point.

If there was anyone who understood how Marlow had been so consumed by her mother's words, it was me.

Maybe she was working on forgiving herself too, because that was the place to start, something I'd worked out in the last few weeks myself through a court-appointed psychologist. I wasn't sure I'd ever let go of the guilt of those victims' lives, but I could understand that I didn't pull the trigger. I had no true concept of what evil could have possessed a man like Kyle to do what he did.

Marlow would eventually forgive herself too. I hoped.

After a moment, she finally spoke.

"Heard you were in the market for a receptionist." She glanced down at Blake. "How about two for the price of one?"

EPILOGUE
HOLT

Later that night . . .

SHE STEPPED FULLY CLOTHED into my old shower and turned the knob. Cold spray hit her in the face. She spluttered and shut off the water.

"Holt!"

I poked my head in the door. "Told you it worked."

ENJOY THIS BOOK?

You can make a huge difference.

Reviews encourage other readers to try out a book. They are critically important to getting your favorite books in the hands of new readers.

We'd appreciate your help in spreading the word. If you could take a quick moment to leave a review on your favorite book site, we would be forever grateful. It can be as short as you like. You can do that on your favorite book retailer, Goodreads, and BookBub.

Email us (grahame@grahameclaire.com) a link to your review so we can be sure to thank you. Together, we can ensure our friends aren't left out.

Thank you so very much.

BONUS SCENE

Want more of Baker and Holt you won't find anywhere else?

By signing up for The List, you'll get this bonus scene, plus be the first to see cover reveals, upcoming excerpts from new releases, exclusive news, and giveaways found nowhere else. You'll find that by going to the link below.

https://www.grahameclaire.com/trust-me-bonus

BOOK STUFF

We had no idea Baker and Holt were going to be a couple until . . .
they met at that Sunday dinner at Dino's in Free Me. There was just
that *something* between them when he called her Miss Easy On The
Eyes. We didn't know either of them all that well at that point, but we
felt their spark.

From there it was natural.

They intrigued us. We found it so interesting they were both anti-
relationship, yet gravitated toward that very thing with one another
despite themselves. That's the fun thing about love, right? It can sneak
up on you and be the very thing you thought you didn't want.

Both of them had *been there, done that, got the postcard, and set it on
fire* when it comes to relationships.

We love that Holt wanted to be roommates with Baker, even
though he'd been burned before. He was curious about her. We don't
think he ever expected to become totally smitten. And it broke our
hearts that he almost gave up his happiness because of his fear. Thank
goodness he found his courage.

What we adore about Baker is her vulnerability. She has confidence to a point, but her insecurities were so relatable. Maybe she
wasn't always open about them with Holt, but she was pretty honest

with herself. She knows her limitations . . . Holt, Trish, Hayden, Mrs. Quinn, and the Dixons helped her see she was capable of so much more.

We don't play favorites when it comes to our books and characters. There are things about each and every one that have special places in our hearts. But we will say that this could be our favorite first chapter.

It's pretty bold for us. It's fun. It's flirty. And it set the tone for writing the rest of this book. We couldn't stop because we had to know what happens next.

We hope you loved Baker and Holt's story as much as we do. These Dixons have taken root in our souls. We're just trying to figure out how to get an invite to Sunday dinner. :)

ACKNOWLEDGMENTS

When a book is released into the world, it seems simple enough. What isn't seen is the struggle when the characters fight back every step of the way. Or when the words won't come. Or when they won't stop. Writing a story is a roller coaster of highs and lows, but there are people with us for every climb and free fall.

We couldn't do this without them.

Our first line of support is our families. They keep us grounded and share our dreams as their own. We love them more than we can say and are so grateful for their support.

The book community is our safe place. Our gratitude for the kindness of the romance world is boundless. We're so lucky to be part of it.

Alessandra Torre, you're always there when we need you. Thank you so much for answering our endless questions. We adore your sweet spirit.

Tia Louise, you are such a light in the book world, and we can't thank you enough for all your kindness.

P. Dangelico, your guidance is invaluable and so much appreciate. Thank you so much for all you do.

Claudia Burgoa, we can't imagine what we'd do without you. Your friendship means more than we can ever say.

Catherine Cowles, this book wouldn't be what it is without your help. Who are we kidding? Neither would we. We're so thankful to have you in our lives.

Emma Renshaw, we love you to pieces. You are an inspiration, and we're so grateful to have you as a friend.

Marion Archer, you took this book and made it something we couldn't have dreamed. Thank you for your insight, your encouragement, and being part of our lives. We adore you.

Karen Lawson and Janet Hitchcock . . . you two . . . you know what you did, and we will *never* forget it. This book needed you (all of them do!) and we adore you both so much. Sorry about the weirdness of the crazy apostrophes. Still trying to figure that one out . . .

Jenn Watson and the Social Butterfly team, working with you has been a dream. Thank you for the answers to endless questions and making this process super stress-free.

SueBee, you have been one of our biggest supporters from before we were even sure we'd publish a book. Thank you for your friendship and love.

The wonderful ladies of Grahame Claire Reader Hangout . . . you are the brightest spot on the internet. Getting to hang out with all of you brings us more joy than you know. And not only will we have ice cream if we ever get to have a big party, but sounds like we need zucchini bread too!

Jessica, Christy, Diane, L. Duarte, Sonia, and Sabrina . . . your never-ending support means everything. Thank you for always being there.

And to you, the most incredible readers in the world . . . your kind messages always make our day. We have to pinch ourselves every day that you love our stories. Thank you so much for being part of our family and taking this ride with us. We're blowing you the biggest kisses!

ALSO BY GRAHAME CLAIRE

PATHS TO LOVE SERIES
It's Not Over
Three Dates
Righting Our Wrongs
Heartbreaker
Dangerous Redemption
Thick As Thieves

———

FREE SERIES
Free Me
Trust Me
Defend Me

ABOUT THE AUTHOR

Grahame Claire is a *USA Today* bestselling author of contemporary romance.

A writer. A blogger. United by our love of stories and all things romance. There was definitely some insta-love. Hello? Books involved. A little courting. A lot of writing. The result . . . Grahame Claire.

Soulmates. Unashamed of our multiple book boyfriends. Especially the ones that rooted in our heads and wouldn't leave us alone. Don't worry. We'll share.

Pleased to meet you.

Our favorite thing about being an author is you, the reader. So please, reach out. If you want to get on the exclusive mailing list (trust us, you do), you can do that at www.grahameclaire.com/newsletter.

Let's chat books on Goodreads. We can gossip about our book boyfriends on Twitter at @grahamewrites, Facebook at www.facebook.com/grahamewrites, our Facebook group Grahame Claire Reader Hangout at www.facebook.com/groups/GrahameClaire-ReaderHangout, Instagram @grahameclaire, or send us an email anytime at grahame@grahameclaire.com.

Follow us on BookBub at www.bookbub.com/authors/grahame-claire

Made in the USA
Columbia, SC
06 September 2020